The Mother-in-Law Cure

Farha Z. Hasan

Copyright © 2013 Farha Hasan

All rights reserved.

ISBN-13: 978-1482634327
ISBN-10: 1482634325

Library of Congress Control Number: 2013906018

DEDICATION

I dedicate my first novel to my first born.

ACKNOWLEDGMENTS

I would like to thank all the friends, family, teachers and mentors that encouraged me along the way. Without you this would not have been possible.

PROLOGUE
Lahore, Pakistan 1970

This is the type of story that should begin with once upon a time. Once upon a time, she breezed into the city like an icy frost on a hot summer's day. She came and went ruthlessly, like a chill that sets deep inside your lungs and leaves you gasping for air. It was August, and the city of Lahore was sweltering with a heat it had not felt in over fifty years. Society had long fallen asleep beneath the suffocating climate and did not so much as raise a curious glance towards the new stranger. In fact, it was only in the evenings, after sunset, when the severity of the sun's fervor had calmed and a mild breeze passed through stale windows, sleepy courtyards and empty bazaars with the promise of redemption, that people slowly made their way out on to the street, and the city finally breathed its first strangled breath. This was the state of the city when she made her appearance.

It would not be correct to say she was a young woman. Some women are never young. It is written in their destiny, though they may not know it at the time. Certainly, it was the last thing on her mind as she crept across this abandoned part of town. Lost and forgotten were its inhabitants. The town's neglect had made them restless. She could feel them stirring. It wasn't a cold night, yet she began to shiver and then laugh at her own anxiety. With all her power, she willed her body from shaking, her teeth from chattering, her blood from running cold, and walked deeper into the cemetery. The voices urged her forward. When she felt something cold grab her ankle, she stopped. Buried between dust and weeds and rubble, it was barely visible, but there was no denying it; this was the grave that had called out to her. She could hear its whispers; she could feel its anger. It was hungry. She took out a small pouch which contained the tiny heart of a new born chick, so fresh it was still warm, a sprig of cinnamon, the dried petals of a rose, all wrapped together with lock of freshly cut human hair. Hair so soft, so rich...and still exhibiting traces of its fragrant shampoo. Redemption at last, thought Humara and she let out a blood-curdling screech, a laugh that would echo for years to come.

❖ ❖ ❖

Perhaps, Naseer Ashruf had heard this echo too, this laughter from the not too distant future whispering in the wind, the laughter of two diverging destinies beckoning him, as he seemed reluctant to leave his residence. He had not intended to go out, but the severity of the day had given way to the softness of the nightfall, and it was under the cover of night that his restlessness gave way and his yearning became too great to bear.

He could feel the weight of the lighter in his pocket...*his fingers began to twitch*. He envisioned the smooth cigarette between his fingers, the excitement of the flame, the anticipation of the first inhale... and then redemption. A good smoke could cure so many ills. It was this and a strong cup of tea that he needed tonight.

Naseer had been worried about the future of his family's business for many months now, but it was not the future he should have been worried about. The future he should have been worried about lay waiting for him like a ripe piece of fruit: its nectar intoxicating; its fragrance kissing the wind.

Standing outside in the open road, Naseer could feel the perspiration trickle down, under his collar and his shirt, yet he had no desire to go inside. He was enjoying the calm of the city in the quiet darkness – *taking deep drags from his cigarette, watching the traffic go by*.

He had arrived at the teahouse early and having a few minutes to spare, he was mulling over the question of his family's estate, its livelihood. It was a question that had plagued him for some time, when he was distracted by a woman's laughter.

It was a voice that beckoned and mocked at the same time. Naseer looked up to see a woman getting out of a rickshaw, laughing carelessly with her girlfriend. To look at, she was a comely girl with smooth skin and hair the color of midnight, but there was something about her gaze that drew him in and held him there. As she passed by, she noticed his stare and bestowed an amused smile upon him. He took a deep breath and smiled—*Jasmine*.

Long after the two women entered the tea house, her scent lingered, distracting him from his thoughts with whispers of untold promises.

Naseer checked his watch and decided to wait for his friend inside. He chose a corner table, keeping the door within his line of vision. He could see that the two women had ordered a drink and were chatting about the color and style of fabric they had left with a local tailor. It was a good twenty minutes later that he heard the ringing of chimes and Ahmed Nawaz walked through the door.

"*Yaar*, you finally made it," said Naseer. "I've been waiting here for an hour."

"Sorry, I was delayed, *yaar*, some family friends dropped by at the last minute and I could not leave," said Ahmed.

"The uncle was an old friend of my father's, and he was practically grilling me like an army sergeant. I suppose he is trying to figure out if I am good enough to marry his niece or daughter or whoever it is he's looking for."

"So what's happening with you? Are you still planning on staying in the city?"

"No, *yaar*. I was planning on checking out the Middle East—the market is booming there—or perhaps Singapore or Indonesia. I haven't decided yet. There is a lot of money in the desert, but I don't think I want to go through the hassle that foreigners, *especially us Pakistanis*, have to face."

"Hmm . . . hmmm." Ahmed nodded. "Well, I'm glad you're open, *yaar*, because there's an opportunity I wanted to talk to you about."

Naseer glanced over at the two women. There were more people in the café now, and he no longer had a clear view. Amidst the chatter of the restaurant, he felt he could still hear the lilt of her voice. If he listened hard enough, he could see the flutter of her hands that moved in unison with her words.

"So what do you think, *yaar*?" said Ahmed, interrupting his thoughts. Naseer realized that he hadn't heard a word Ahmed had said.

"Something distracting you, *yaar*?" said Ahmed with a hint of a smile. "Anyone I know?"

"No . . . no. Nothing like that, *yaar*. I just have a lot on my mind."

"Maybe we should talk again," said Ahmed, getting up to leave.

Naseer checked his watch. It had been over an hour.

"Did you bring your car? I'm parked just outside."
"No, *yaar*. Can you give me a ride?"

Naseer took one final glance back before the two

walked outside. Immediately, they were accosted by the noise and the pollution. They heard a loud thud as a bus backfired. Naseer looked around in the dark, trying to spot his car, when a breeze carried the scent of a woman's perfume. He breathed it in and smiled, recognizing the fragrance. He could see that the two women had come out of the tea house and were looking around for transportation. From their gestures and snippets of their conversation, he gathered that the rickshaw driver had taken off, leaving them stranded and a little frantic. He politely approached the women.

"Is there a problem, miss? Do you need a rickshaw?" asked Naseer, stepping into their line of vision. The two women all of a sudden became very shy, having been approached by a strange man they did not know. It was the mysterious woman with dark hair that finally spoke up, her eyes dark puddles, looking up at Naseer with earnest.

"Sir, we don't know where our rickshaw driver is. He was supposed to be waiting out here for us. It seems he must have taken off, despite our instructions. We thought maybe we would walk."

"Two women should not walk unescorted at night. Let me call a rickshaw for you. My friend will wait with you until I come back," said Naseer, motioning toward Ahmed.

Naseer walked down to the street and hailed a rickshaw within a couple of minutes. As he escorted the two women into the rickshaw, he ventured to ask them about their families and what college they were attending. It was a small town with few women's colleges, and it would be enough information to track her down later.

❖ ❖ ❖

An inquiry with the local women's college was all it took to determine that the full name of the young lady was Humara Khan. She was an orphan who was staying with an uncle who was teaching there. Other than this, very little was known about the girl—or her family. The uncle was quite elderly, remote, and generally kept to himself. *Naseer had to see her again.*

Naseer arranged several visits with a relative who was a chancellor at the college, serendipitously bumping into either Humara or her uncle, Murtaza Khan, while he was on the campus grounds. Eventually, Naseer ran into them so many times that the old uncle had no choice but to invite Naseer over for tea, lest he seem rude. Every time Naseer would visit the Khan household, the few fleeting encounters he had with Humara would leave him craving more. She had what could only be described as a shy coquettishness that Naseer found intensely alluring. It was the way she looked at him through the corner of her eye or the way she passed by him so closely when serving tea. He could almost breathe in the scent of her body and feel a tremor pass through him. Soon his visits to the Khans' household were so frequent, that they became difficult to ignore.

Naseer's mother was the first to become concerned, but her husband barely looked up from his morning paper as she relayed the gossip she had heard.

"So, he visits Professor Khan two or three times a week. The man's an economist. Naseer is probably getting his opinion on business conditions in the Middle East or the Orient, and if someone catches his eye, there is no harm in it. It may even make our job easier."

But Suriya was not convinced that it was as simple as her husband's explanation. She hoped that someone inappropriate had not caught her son's eye, as she had other plans for her him. There were many beautiful girls from prominent families in society—one in particular had caught her eye.

Masooma Ali was the daughter of a diplomat with

strong family connections in government. She was a beautiful girl of marriageable age who had caught the attention of many in their social circle. In Suriya's opinion, she had exactly the type of upbringing and disposition that would make her the ideal wife and daughter-in-law, *and* her father's connections would go a long way to secure their business interests in the city. The last thing Suriya wanted was to see her cherished son leave the country of his birth, and she ached to keep him near her for as long as possible. It had not taken much effort for her to secure an invitation for, tea at Mrs. Ali's house that evening.

❖ ❖ ❖

For the first time in many days, the setting sun brought a cool breeze with it. It was this airy wind that had convinced Tiara Ali that they should have tea in the garden that evening, where they could enjoy the outdoors and take in the gentle fragrance of fresh flowers. She was right. Mrs. Ali could not have hoped for a more pleasant tea with Suriya Ashruf, who now sat directly across from her, sipping a second cup and nibbling on some homemade sweets. Masooma sat in between the two women, dressed in a pale pink *salwar kameez*. Her long chestnut hair fell loosely down to her waist, looking very much like the Madonna her name implied. Mrs. Ali had been courting Suriya Ashruf for some time now, and this was the second time that Mrs. Ashruf had been to their house for a visit, but not much had been said about a union between the two families. Perhaps Mrs. Ashruf was still weighing her options, thought Tiara. She hoped this silence would not last much longer, or she would be forced to consider other families. Mrs. Ali wished to have her daughter married and settled within the next six months.

It was not until much later in the evening, when Masooma had left the room to meet some college friends, that Mrs. Ashruf spoke about how much she liked the girl.

"Of course you have a lovely daughter," said Mrs. Ashruf, "but I can't make any decision until I've talked to my son. He's quite independent."

This statement made Mrs. Ali a little nervous, as she had heard the rumors that had been circulating. Mrs. Ashruf must have noticed her concern, for she quickly responded.

"Of course he's a boy that listens to his mother, too."

So it was agreed that the next time Mrs. Ashruf would come to visit, she would bring her son.

The sighting of the new moon indicated the arrival of Eid-al-Adha or the Eid of the goat—one of the country's biggest celebrations. The coming of Eid brought a momentum with it that temporarily lifted the city out of its slumber and, for a while, the people had a reason to be joyous. Naseer was especially looking forward to Eid so that he could speak seriously to his parents. He planned to approach them about sending a marriage proposal to Humara Khan. She was the girl for him and he was tired of thinking up excuses to see her. He could not stop thinking about her. For this reason, he felt a little irritated that his mother had dragged him over to the Khans' house so soon after Eid prayers. There were many others that he wanted to meet, and he had no interest in any other girl.

Naseer sat with his mother in Tiara and Imran Ali's drawing room, feeling a little impatient. No one seemed to notice his distraction. The two women were caught up in excited chatter about the latest parties, and his father was engaged in a discussion about politics with Mr. Ali that Naseer found only mildly interesting. So far nothing had been mentioned about their daughter, not that he was expecting it this early. Some twenty minutes into the conversation, a young girl carrying a tray of tea approached the group. As she put the tray down on the center table, Naseer's gaze caught her eye, and a look of embarrassment crept across her face.

"*Berta*, please have a seat. Join us," said Suriya.

Masooma shyly took a seat across from her mother. It was perfect because it gave Naseer a discreet view of the girl. He had to admit that she was a lovely girl with beautiful skin and long brown hair—an endless supply of waves that reached almost to her knees. Her smile contained a mixture of warmth and innocence. He could get used to looking at a girl like that, but one thought nagged his mind—what about Humara? The visit did not end before Imran Ali mentioned some useful contacts he had that would benefit Naseer's interests. They were key players that could do much to alleviate his current difficulties. Suriya Ashruf took a glance back at her son. She knew he had been pleased.

It was decided that a week from Friday, marking the beginning of the new moon, would be the most auspicious day for the engagement. The Ashrufs would arrive with an engagement ring, traditional sweets and gifts, and the families would finally make it official.

❖ ❖ ❖

There was no one more excited at the thought of the engagement than Masooma Ali. Despite her family's social standing, she was a simple girl whose ambitions did not reach beyond being a good wife and a good mother and throwing delightful dinner parties and teas for her friends and family. In short, an existence much like the one she already had.

She had known this day would come and had patiently looked forward to it, but now that it was here, on the cusp of her engagement, it all seemed to be happening so fast, like falling down a well that one never noticed was there. Masooma was feeling unusually tired that night, and decided to give in to the dreams of domestic bliss that danced around her mind, sweet visions of children and laughter and *halwa*—all of Masooma's favorite things. It was with these things on her mind that she entered into a seductive sleep that seemed to take her into avenues of delight but, at some point during the night, these fanciful dreams *seemed* to turn. A distressed look crossed her face, as if something darker had crept in. Masooma began to toss and turn, murmuring words that were unrecognizable and sentences that seemed like gibberish. She began to perspire and breathe deeply, almost gasping for air, and just when one thought she might sit up and scream as her discomfort seemed to become unbearable, a serene expression came across her face, and Masooma drifted off into a deep slumber, peaceful and relaxed once more.

When morning came, Masooma felt wide awake and alert. The dark dreams that had plagued her earlier in the night had disappeared without a trace, leaving Masooma with little memory of her night's adventure. She stretched lazily, confident that all was right with the world, and that this day, the day of her engagement, would be engrained in her memory. She sat up in bed, feeling lighter than usual, wondering what she should have for breakfast, hoping there were fresh eggs and milk. A cool breeze seemed to pass through her hair. *She noticed a couple of broken strands on her pillow.*

As she sat up, she noticed that more and more strands of hair had fallen off. Removing the blankets, she saw that the strands had turned into locks, and the locks had turned into clumps. Panic started to set in. She ran to the mirror and let out a piercing scream.

It was her mother who heard her first. Tiara Ali was in the drawing room when her blood turned to ice. She ran to her daughter's room, but when she arrived, a servant was already there, standing in the doorway with a shocked expression on her face. Mrs. Ali entered her daughter's bedroom and saw Masooma standing in front of the mirror, her hair gone. There was nothing left but patches of bald spots exposing her pink skull and locks and locks of beautiful brown hair all around her.

❖ ❖ ❖

The Ashrufs were left dumbfounded when the Alis broke the engagement that very day. When Suriya tried to visit to find out more details, Tiara Ali would not even allow her in the door—letting a servant turn her away. It was an insult.

Soon, and despite his mother's protests, Naseer began seeing Humara again. This time when he approached his parents about sending a proposal or *rishta*, Suriya could not think of any reason to refuse. When they finally announced the engagement between Humara and Naseer, Suriya could not help but notice a look of triumph on the girl's face. It was this look that haunted Suriya.

Not long after the wedding, Naseer decided it would be better for the family business if he were to move his base to a more prosperous region. When Naseer and Humara started packing up their things to ship to the Middle East, Suriya felt all the hard work she had put into keeping her son at home evaporate like mist through her fingers.

On the day, the very day that Naseer and his new bride were set to depart, the heat wave broke and it began to rain. Big, fat, juicy droplets the size of grapes tumbled mercifully from the overcast sky.

ONE

Down Came The Rain
Chicago Illinois, 2010

At first it was nothing more than a shower, a warm trickle of dewdrops, still rich with summer but marking the end of the season, the end of the maniacal heat that had been plaguing the city. Soon the temperature began to drop and the rain became cold... angry. Nothing had been left dry. Before Miriam knew it, it had become a watery world. The relentless rain continued to pound the city, as if it were monsoon season in the subcontinent rather than the sterile suburbs of the Midwest. The pretty summer colors that Miriam enjoyed in late August had all been dulled and washed away, and there was nothing left for her to do but sit by the large bay window overlooking the front yard and watch the torrential flood that had been plaguing the city for weeks, but Miriam accepted the dismal weather, that seemed to drive the residents of this quaint suburb up the wall the way she had always accepted life's showers.

"*It's raining cats and dogs*," Miriam said to herself, despite the fact that she had never liked the phrase or understood exactly what it meant. One of her patients had used it recently, and today Miriam sat mulling over its meaning, having come home early to an empty house, a nice change. *I should look it up*, she thought, *when I have more time…*

She had lived in the house for five years, ever since she married Kashif at the tender age of eighteen and moved to Chicago from the villages of Pakistan. Marriage was a safe haven for girls without kith or kin and Mariam was an orphan. Miriam's mother had always loved the rain. She remembered losing her to tuberculosis when she was ten and her father to a heart attack when she was seventeen, a trajectory that led her into the path of the Ashrufs. She tried not to think about her parents - *it must be the rain bringing back all these memories.*

There was never any shortage of work in the Ashruf household and Miriam was responsible for maintaining it in its entirety. The house itself was massive, which should have made it a struggle. It should have been a task of drudgery had the house not been so alive; filled with rich tapestries, Turkish rugs, Middle Eastern and Islamic art work, a testament to the family's past that took them through Pakistan, the Middle East and even London before settling in the Midwest. It was not just that the house was beautiful but it was the type of place one could never feel alone. It unnerved most people, but Miriam (who was always alone) liked the feeling of being watched and had made friends with the house a long time ago. It was not as though the house *never* scared her. There *were* corridors that seemed to have no end, walls that seemed to whisper and portraits that seem to want to speak… their mouths twitching. *How long could they be silenced?*

Although the house was large enough to accommodate many, only four people currently lived within its realm: Miriam and her husband Kashif, her brother-in-law Adnan, and her mother-in-law, Humara Ashruf. With so few family members, most rooms went unused. When her sister-in-law Sadia had been living with them, her brood of children had run around chasing imaginary friends, chasing

Miriam and one another. In the process, they had knocked over plants and vases and tracked dirt everywhere. Thankfully, they had moved out six months ago, for which even her mother-in-law was grateful. They now lived a couple blocks down in a much smaller house, and Humara had been staying with them for the last couple of weeks, helping Sadia get the place in order. Just thinking about her mother-in-law's absence made Miriam breathe a sigh of relief, glad to be getting a break from the old woman whose calculating gaze seemed to penetrate down to the very depth of her soul. Miriam had felt repelled by her mother-in-law from the first moment she had laid eyes on her. Something in her soul had cringed, as if looking at a creature not quite human - a heavily decorated corpse, something that had lost its soul a long time ago. Although the woman could not have been more than sixty, she looked hundreds of years old, sitting in a wheelchair sipping tea as if it was the most natural thing in the world.

A crash of thunder punctuated the silence.

Miriam shuddered. The rain had all but quarantined them for the last couple of weeks. The remaining members of the household had spent their free time wandering around the house like ghosts, discouraged from going outside by the ghastly weather—but that was fine. Miriam liked ghosts. Since she had been orphaned at a young age, ghosts were a constant in Miriam's life; she saw them everywhere. Everyone that she had become close to was now a ghost. Her husband surely treated her like a ghost, barking instructions at her as if he didn't really see her, as if she wasn't really there. It won't be long, thought Miriam, before I just fade away into one of the dark corridors of the house, where all the other skeletons live. There were many skeletons in this household—*that wasn't their biggest secret*. Whenever Miriam went to the mosque or a community event, she could hear people whispering about them and the strange and sometimes unfortunate occurrences that had become synonymous with the Ashruf household, not the least of which was Afsana - *Kashif's first wife.*

Strangely, she never felt jealous of Afsana, but instead felt a closeness to her, like sisters that had shared a common secret. Kashif had refused to talk about Afsana, and Humara had all but erased her from the family pictures and records, but she still lingered. She lingered in the dark corners of the house where no one but Miriam ventured at night, in the catch of irritation in her mother-in-law's voice when she confused some detail about Miriam with her former daughter-in-law, and in Kashif's touch during the most intimate moments of their relationship, for she knew that such tenderness could never be meant for her. It was in these moments that Miriam would let Afsana's spirit envelope her, consume her . . . take her over, for she, too, could feel Afsana's pain.

Miriam was brought out of her trance by the humming of the garage door. She looked up to see her husband's sleek Mercedes pull into the garage. Funny, Kashif usually wasn't the first to arrive, especially on Mondays. On Mondays he always worked late, seeing patients well into the afternoon and evening. *Oh, well, break over,* thought Miriam, going over the mountain of work she had left to do before her mother-in-law came back and nitpicked over her cleaning. She heard the front door open and Kashif's voice calling from the foyer.

"Miriam, have there been any calls for me?"

His voice reflected a tone he generally used for secretaries and other service people. Miriam often wondered how she felt about him, this husband that wanted nothing to do with her. Kashif was not bad to look at, though his years were starting to take a toll on his appearance. At forty, his dark, thick hair was now laced with gray, and his forehead grew every year as his hairline inched its way back. His weight had started catching up with his height, as an extra twenty pounds encompassed his body. His six-foot frame allowed him to carry the weight well, and his serious eyes, beneath his round spectacles that were a little out of date, gave him a gentle air that helped put patients at ease. Yes, Dr. Ashraf was a well-respected man in the community who never had to answer to anyone—*well, almost anyone.*

"Sadia called."

His body stiffened at the mention of his sister's name.

"She said your mother wants to come home tonight. She wants to see you. There's something she wants to talk to you about . . . and Adnan, too."

As if on cue, an angry crash of thunder emphasized the news. Miriam continued to watch the rain ruthlessly beat down against the gray concrete. Without having to turn around, she could feel his tension; he was worried. She could feel the air become stale just at the mention of the old woman. She did not blame Kashif for being worried. Beneath her mother-in-law's frailty was a will of steel. Fortunately for Miriam, the old woman did not mind her as much as she had Kashif's first wife—*that had been a disaster.*

Miriam was about to say more, but she was taken off guard by a musky odor, perfume. *Claudia's perfume!* She would know it anywhere. It was the first thing she had noticed when she had walked into Kashif's office... heavy and musky and flowery, and then she saw the woman it was coming from sitting at the reception desk.

Claudia was a buxom brunette who wasn't afraid to advertise her attributes. Everything about her was plastic, from her fake eyelashes, to her silicon-infested breasts, to her heavy make-up. Miriam was surprised Kashif had hired her. He always hated it when women dressed too provocatively. He said it made them look cheap. He always made sure Miriam's clothes were plain and drab, even insisting she wear a scarf or veil from time to time. What Miriam wore was considered a reflection on their family.

Claudia's attire on the other hand (and what it might reflect to the community) was, however, *not* a concern. In a thin silk blouse, Claudia oozed of sex in a way that made his traditional *desi* or South Asian patients nervous. They would be sitting in the waiting room with a runny nose, sore throat, and stomachs doing cartwheels. Claudia would pass by and smile in such a way that would leave their heads spinning, unable to remember exactly where they put their health cards, making them perspire as if their fever had just shot up ten degrees. Intoxicated by her perfume, they tried not to look directly at the voluptuous bosom that seemed inches away from freedom.

Miriam had smelled that perfume many times after that, its faint aroma always lingered long after Kashif's day was over, after even Miriam's scent had been washed clean from his body. Miriam was not the only one who noticed it.

"*Someone should tell that girl her husband smells like tramp,*" she had heard a patient remark.

"*Shhh...she'll hear you,*" their friend had replied.

"*Better off leaving well enough alone.*"

The doctor and his tramp, that's how he'll be known, thought Miriam feeling embarrassed. She couldn't help feeling inadequate. She knew that hers wasn't the first husband to meander, but Claudia...Claudia was the polar opposite of Miriam. Claudia was all sin, all lust...all pleasure. In contrast, Afsana had always been his true love, the best part of him, so where did that leave Miriam?

Miriam was a vessel to be filled up anyway he wanted.

As Miriam went to the kitchen to check on dinner, she

could hear her husband on the phone with her sister-in-law, his voice muffled. He spoke with a strained calmness he did not quite feel. Miriam stirred the pot of chicken curry, taking in the aroma and letting it arouse her appetite. The rice was already done, and there were leftovers in the fridge that could be served again. Miriam turned the stove off just in time to hear her brother-in-law coming inside carrying a raincoat, an umbrella, a book bag, and his laptop. He let it all drop with a thud.

"Holy shit," said Adnan, shaking off the rain. "It's like a damn flood out there. What's for dinner? I'm starved."

He walked into the kitchen, peeking into the stovetops, trying to get a whiff of dinner and hoping sheepishly to catch a glance of Miriam.

"Do you need any help?" asked Adnan. But before she could answer, Kashif was on his feet, motioning for him to come into the family room.

"No, no . . . let her do it," said Kashif. "Besides, I need to talk to you."

"About what?" asked Adnan.

"I got a call from Sadia."

"And how is Mom doing?"

"Fine but she wants to come over."

"When?"

"Tonight after dinner."

"Any idea why?" asked Adnan.

"We shall soon see."

Adnan was about to respond, but Kashif cut him off, pulling out some tuition receipts that he wanted to go over.

As Miriam set the table, she stole a glance at Adnan and blushed. It was still pouring outside, and Adnan's T-shirt was moist with perspiration - *it clung to his skin, outlining his hard body.* She hated to admit it, but he was a good-looking guy, with a classic tan and light-brown hair.

At twenty-five years of age, *only a couple years older than Miriam*, he had that Bollywood film-star look that made many a coed and even faculty members swoon. Miriam was willing to bet anything that his rock hard abs were at least partly the reason he was often granted leeway and consideration, despite his shaky academic record.

However, Miriam was the only one that seemed to notice that he had been dropping classes, changing majors, and consulting with his advisor every other week, trying for the last five years to complete a two-year graduate degree with which he was getting nowhere. It appeared that Adnan would research a topic to death only to realize that it was not something he was interested in, or something that seemed inconsequential would balloon into a thesis idea of its own, until some other detail caught his attention and sent him on a completely different tangent. Miriam would tease him sometimes.

"...you know a guy as good looking as you is wasting his time holed up in academics. Shouldn't you be shaking your bootie in a music video...nice tan you got there...get much sunbathing in between classes..."

Adnan would grin, oblivious to the fact that he was being mocked.

"You're not the first person to tell me that, I get it all the time. In fact I think a career in broadcast journalism might be the ticket. Can't you just see me on the evening news, polished suit and, radiating charisma. You gotta admit I have a much sexier voice than Matt Lauer or Anderson Cooper."

His extreme vanity was only made bearable by his ability to not take himself too seriously, *that* and his good nature made him the easiest person to get along with in the Ashruf household. Miriam was glad that he was going to be home today. If anyone could take the edge off the old woman's return home, it was Adnan.

❖ ❖ ❖

"Dinner's on the table," said Miriam cutting into Kashif and Adnan's conversation. Adnan looked relived, anything to get out of discussing school.

TWO

All the King's Horses and All The King's Men Could Not Put Humpty Dumpty Back Together Again

Miriam did not know why Kashif always insisted on eating dinner in the dining room. Miriam would have much rather preferred the coziness of the kitchen. The large ornate dining room could seat up to ten (which made sense when Sadia and her brood were staying with them). There were elaborate mirrors, fancy artwork and family portraits on the wall. It made Miriam feel like they were dining in a museum - the sound of their cutlery permeating the silence, adding to the tension of the meal. Miriam looked up into her mother-in-law's eyes. How they gleamed from inside her portrait. It made Miriam uncomfortable, to eat with a portrait of Humara staring right at her... plotting. That was the word for it. The old woman never stopped plotting.

Miriam forced herself to look away. In between mouthfuls of chicken curry, she watched Kashif pick at his food and Adnan eat voraciously, even taking seconds. The tension in the room did not seem to affect him. He stretched out his long legs, pulled out his iPod and began shuffling through his music until he appeared to find a beat that he liked and gently bopped his head to the music, as if in a trance. No doubt he was focusing on his plans for later that evening. Miriam did not mind, but it annoyed the hell out of Kashif.

"Will you put that away," he growled. "Sometimes you remind me of a child."

That was it, wasn't it? Adnan was an over gown child. He seemed to be enjoying the childhood Kashif and even Miriam had been denied - *a regular Peter Pan*. Adnan was seldom home, flying from one adventure to another. Miriam could go days without seeing him. It did not seem to be a concern to anyone and was barely noticed by Kashif or her mother-in-law. Everyone knew Kashif was the old woman's favorite. Her attention more often than not focused on her first born and now and then it focused on her daughter, Sadia, whom the old woman seemed to view as an afterthought.

Adnan, on the other hand, always seemed to be viewed as harmless, benign, and totally inconsequential by just about everyone. Kashif, who was more like a father to him than anyone else, simply doled out money and left him alone.

The hurt look on Adnan's face, when he was told to put away his toy made Miriam think of taking candy from a baby. She tried to catch Adnan's gaze to give him a reassuring smile, but he was too absorbed in his thoughts to notice. Miriam wasn't sure, but it looked like he was gazing at himself in the mirror, smiling…giving himself a wink…*Mirror, Mirror on the wall, who's the fairest of them all?*

Miriam inadvertently let out a chuckle but, before she could say anything, she noticed Kashif looking at her with a raised eyebrow. Miriam quickly adjusted her expression and looked back down at her food.

"*The chicken seems to be a little dry,*" he said, and Miriam made a note add more gravy from now on.

Miriam looked up again at Kashif, but his thoughts seemed to be elsewhere. He looked visibly worried and picked at his food, eating slowly as if it were his last meal. No doubt that whatever the old woman wanted, it would involve a favor from him—last time it had meant Sadia, her husband, and their brood of three staying with them for six months while Sadia's husband Kamran was unemployed. Finally, it was Kashif himself who used his connections to get him an offer at a mid-sized consulting firm, where one of his patients was a partner. The old woman could have just given Sadia the money and waited for an offer to come around, but she knew Kashif would work his connections faster to restore peace and quiet to his orderly home. Kashif was not a man who appreciated chaos, while Adnan, his polar opposite, thrived on it. Adnan was the only who did not look tense at the table.

❖ ❖ ❖

Humara sat lazily on the recliner, her legs comfortably stretched out, sipping a cup of tea with satisfaction. There was nothing that made her feel better at the end of the day than a hot cup of tea. Absorbed in the rich flavor of the beverage, it gave her the opportunity to clear her head and mentally plan her next move. Humara had always felt that life had to be planned coolly and carefully, without getting too attached to sentiment—something her late husband and her sons had never learned. It was the downside of being born into privilege, a consequence from which Humara herself had never suffered. Privilege and comfort had made them soft. She had always found that to be a mixed blessing.

Humara looked up from her tea to notice her family looking a little agitated. It was true she was taking her time to reveal the news, but as Humara had learned at a very early age, timing was everything. Kashif looked visibly uncomfortable, but there was nothing she could do about it. One had to make tough decisions to ensure survival. She knew they wouldn't be happy, but eventually, they would learn to adjust. After all, she only had their best interests at heart.

"May I get you another cup of tea?" asked Miriam.

"Yes, maybe one more," said Humara, "but make sure it's hot and not too much sugar. You always make it so sweet."

Humara continued to shrewdly assess her two sons. Adnan should have been more worried; instead, he was seated on the sofa across from Kashif, casually flipping through a *GQ* magazine, wondering if he could pull off the same look as the model on the cover. *Those Armani sunglasses would look so hot on me*, he seemed to be thinking. Every now and then Adnan would look up casually to assess if his mother was anywhere close to getting to the point as she chatted endlessly about family gossip.

Humara had come with news; that much was evident, but she was taking her time disclosing it. Both Kashif and Adnan had learned from past experience that whatever was going to happen could not be good. The two brothers sat on the sofa going through the motions of pleasant conversation as a muted episode of *Law and Order* played in the background. Adnan felt bad for his brother already. It was for this reason that Adnan looked up in astonishment as the old woman began to address him directly.

Humara gazed up at her younger son intently for almost a minute before she actually spoke, and when she did, her words were careful and deliberate. She could not help but notice the surprise and then relief in her elder son's eyes.

"*Berta*, how are your studies going?"
Adnan looked up, a little startled, and bit his lip before he answered.

"They are going fine, *Ammah*."
"Fine," she said. *Did he think she was stupid?*

The old woman had had her eye on him for some time. What to do about this careless little boy who'd lose his head if it weren't attached to his body? She had been way too lax. At this rate, he would still be in grad school when he was her age. It was time to wake from this dream, to shatter this illusion. Even before she started, she knew this would cost her a couple more of her thinning gray hair and add of few more wrinkles in her already weathered face. When Humara continued, her voice took on a sharper tone.

"Fine? You just dropped another class, and you changed your major for the fifth time. You call that *fine?*"

"It's taken some time to figure out what to do. I'm meeting with my advisor again..."

Now the old woman's voice took on a softer tone, almost seductive.

"*Berta*, did you ever think that academics might not be right for you? Perhaps you need to take a break from this and do something else," she cooed.

"Like what?" asked Adnan, his voice trembling slightly.

"*Berta*, now what about getting married? I've been thinking about you a lot, about your future, and I've found a nice girl for you."

Adnan gasped. His expression was a mixture of shock, terror, and outrage. *This could not be happening to him. This was not the way his life went!*

Humara continued, barely missing a beat, viewing her son's reaction as an unexpected inconvenience.

"A nice girl from a nice family," she went on. "Her father is a developer in Dubai."

"But Ma, you didn't! I'm not ready to get married. Besides, I'm still a student. How would I even support her?"

"No need to worry about that. The family has connections in all kinds of places. Now, Mr. and Mrs.

Lakahni will be visiting in two weeks. You will be gracious."

From the corner of her eye, Miriam thought she saw Kashif smirk.

THREE

What Are Little Boys Made of?
Frogs and Snails and Puppy-dogs' Tails,

The house was quiet. Everyone had retired to their respective rooms, except Adnan. He wasn't home yet and Miriam wasn't expecting him anytime soon. On her way upstairs she passed Kashif's study, the door was closed but the light was on. She could hear him whispering on the phone. He was using his "husky" voice - *the one he thought made him sound sexy*. Perhaps, if it was the soft murmur of tenderness Miriam would not have felt so bad but, instead, it was the crass guttural sound of unharnessed, animalistic sex. There was no doubt to whom he was speaking. If this was what they were like on the phone Miriam couldn't imagine what they were like together. For a moment Miriam considered bursting in, catching him red handed and demanding an explanation. She listened for a while feeling like a thief in her own home, embarrassed at their level of intimacy. She never thought that her husband was the type of man that would enjoy phone sex but lately he seemed to have ventured into all sorts of arenas.

Claudia had no inhibitions. *That* was apparent. A few

days ago, she had tried to check her email, only the browser had opened up Kashif's email instead. Unknowingly, she had clicked on a message. At first she had thought it was spam…an X-rated porn site, but the woman looking back at her seemed a little amateurish. It was then that recognition hit and she realized that it was Claudia on the screen.

Claudia with her wanton eyes and her pillowy breasts… Claudia bending over in a checkered miniskirt, no panties (the naughty school girl and the headmaster)…Claudia in a see through teddy…

And there were other images. Images that made Miriam shudder. The murmurs on the other side of the door had increased in intensity. She knew where this was leading. It made Miriam want to vomit. No, she realized, with a sinking feeling in her stomach, nothing she could do would change anything. As Miriam hurried back to her room she noticed another light on. Humara had not yet retired for the night. She wondered what the old woman was doing up so late.

❖ ❖ ❖

Humara carefully pulled the pins out of her hair; snowy grey locks fell to her shoulders. The color and luster had long drained out of her profile. Only her eyes and her thick dark lashes seemed to gleam, as if absorbing all that had faded from her youth. The flutter of her lashes, the expression in her eyes could sometimes be delicate, like a gentle old woman and sometime perilous like a carnivorous flower (one that could both mesmerize you and puncture your soul). It was these eyes that had always unnerved Kashif from the time he was an awkward and gangly youth to well into his adult years. Was Kashif ever as naïve and doe eyed as his younger brother? Yes. She remembers it as if it were yesterday.

Kashif also doesn't like to refer to this phase in his life; he keeps it buried in the recesses of his mind. It's a little of where his stiffness comes from, and it makes him appear sterner than he actually is. It started when he received his acceptance letter to medical school. Humara was elated, but soon he could feel the old woman's invisible eyes on him, plotting his future, carefully eyeing the daughter of one family or another, pestering him with pictures of one girl or the other. Kashif in his youth was too tall, too thin, and all elbows and knees. He barely knew how to talk to his own mother, much less some strange girl sitting across from him in a buffet of finger food: *onion fritters, samosas, curried chickpeas, and an assortment of cakes and pastries too numerous to mention.*

An overdressed auntie would casually chat with Humara, as if Kashif were not in the room. His name would come up from time to time, and Kashif would not be sure of what to say. Was he supposed to interject? He was never comfortable with so many women looking at *him* as if *he*, the man, were on display. Where were the men in the household . . . the father. . . the brother . . . anyone?

Time and time again he had found himself in that position without exactly knowing how he got there. After Kashif had been thoroughly emasculated, there would be the long drive home, with Humara's cheerfulness at the success of the afternoon permeating through the car.

He knew that he could not go on like this much longer. Yet he dreaded the dark expression that crossed her face, the way her color drained into paleness, making her eyes appear even darker—*an expression that his father had not known enough to fear.* It was with much reluctance and with his back against the wall (having completely been cornered into it) that he told her that there was someone else. At first, her face went blank, as if she couldn't fathom what he had said to her. She had never expected to be surprised by Kashif. As Kashif confessed all the intricate little details, the hows and the whereofs, her expression began to soften. When everything had spilled out, there was silence. Kashif was not sure if she was angry or not, and for this reason her silence could be most terrible. Much to his dismay, she seemed almost amenable. For a brief fleeting moment, Kashif was happy, but that was a long time ago.

Kashif never regretted marrying Afsana. That much she had not been able to take from him, even after it turned ugly... even after Afsana left him and threatened to never come back. Kashif never thought to blame the old woman. How could he? Ammah always meant well. *It was an accident... a terrible accident,* was what he kept telling himself over... and over again...until the voice he heard was no longer his own but that of Humara's... and the face in his mind not of Afsana but the old woman, those dark eyes, those endless pools hypnotizing him, lulling him to sleep.

❖ ❖ ❖

Humara sat in front of her bedroom mirror and finished combing her hair (dark pools that held every secret of her soul looked back at her). She always knew when *he* was asleep - *a mother always knows*.

Miriam had long turned in for the night and even the cat was snoring. There was one more person she was waiting for...ah, there it was. She heard the click of a key turn in the front door and Adnan swear as he bumped into a chair or a table. Now she could go to bed.

❖ ❖ ❖

Adnan stumbled in through the doorway. He had been mommy's little lamb for so many years but tonight after twenty-five years (just like in his favorite fairy tale), he had found out what big teeth mommy had and no amount of booze could wash that away. Adnan would have a nasty hangover in the morning, but right now he was too inebriated to put one foot in front of the other. It was two in the morning, and his friends had dropped him off in front of his house and watched as he wobbled up the driveway and fumbled with the keys. It was a miracle he remembered that he had keys and did not started banging on the doors until Miriam, who was a light sleeper, came down to let him in. Unfortunately, she did not always hear him, and on more than one occasion she had found him snoring soundly on the front porch when she collected the daily paper at six in the morning—the whack of the paper hitting the front porch making no impression on him at all nor the paper boy looking him over wearily as he went along to the next house on his route.

Tonight was one of those nights that he had made it into the house. No matter how many drinks he had consumed, it had not been enough to knock last night's chilling news out of him. That little bit of sobriety followed him around all night, like an annoying kid sister threatening to tattle. Adnan sat in the cushy La-Z-Boy, the one usually reserved for the old woman, closed his eyes, and reviewed the evening. They had started out at a bar. Saif had been with him, and they had had a couple beers before heading to a club. The music had been loud, he had done a couple of shots, he danced with a girl...two girls...several girls, he couldn't remember. After a few drinks, they all began to look alike. He just wanted to keep on moving. Had Adnan been in a fight or a brawl that night? Probably not, pretty boys are not generally thuggish and Adnan was as pretty as they got. Adnan couldn't remember what time they left the club, just that they seemed to be driving around for the longest time. How much had Saif had that night? He hadn't been paying attention.

There was a girl in the backseat with him. She had a joint in her hand, and he couldn't remember if he had taken a puff (he probably had). A bad decision—the joint could have been laced with something. He had had a couple of near misses in the past and had woken up with chills. This time, he felt his body shake as if he was going into convulsions. He held himself tight in the fetal position and waited for it to pass. When it did, he drank a glass of water and slowly wobbled up the staircase and into his bedroom, dropping into bed without taking off his clothes.

Tomorrow . . . tomorrow his head would spin and his mouth would feel parched and dry, but right now, the warm bed against the cold rain was the most attractive invitation he had had all night.

FOUR

That's the Way the Money Goes...

Adnan woke up in a haze around noon. The torrential rains had left the world in perpetual darkness, causing him to sleep a good two hours more than he had intended. Adnan had hit the snooze button at least a half dozen times before he realized that it was already midday. There was no chance of him making his morning classes now. Adnan let out one final yawn before he began to get his bearings. He was at home in his bed; that much was certain. There was a dull ache in his temple with which he was not unfamiliar. He had been at a party last night. He had not intended to get this wasted, but so was life. Did he have his car? No. It was Saif who had driven him home, although Saif had been pretty high himself. He tried to recall the events of the party. Did he have fun? He thought so, anything important that he should remember? Oh, yeah…it was coming back to him. He had broken up with his girlfriend—*Shari or Carrie*, whatever her name was. Or she had broken up with him. She had seen him making out with her friend Anne, the one she had brought to set up with Saif. She had been so pissed off! Now it was coming back to him . . . but where was Anne? He felt inside the pockets of his denims. There it was—a scrap of paper with Anne's phone number on it stuffed casually into his jeans. He would call her tonight. Shari was out, Anne was in; it was all good. Adnan was happy as he muddled out of bed and headed for the bathroom, stifling another big yawn and lazily scratching his behind. He felt a twinge at the back of his mind. There was something else he should remember . . .

Oh, well, thought Adnan. If it's important, it will come back to me. He stepped into the shower and let the warm water caress his body, slowly bringing him back to earth. A hot shower, a couple extra, extra-strength Tylenols, and some ginger ale was all it would take to bring Adnan back. By the time Adnan had dressed, styled his hair, and spent sufficient time admiring himself in the mirror, he almost had his appetite back. Adnan went down to breakfast almost humming. Of course, Kashif was long gone. Humara sat in the dining room knitting while Miriam, who had the day off, pondered what to make for dinner that night.

"You seem to be in a good mood," said Humara, eying her son.

"Of course, *Ammah*. I'm always in a good mood," he said.

"That's good, *Berta*. It's nice to see you're coming around."

Adnan finally began to feel an inkling of recognition. Reality started setting in with a tingling in his spine and a dull ache in the pit of his stomach. The old woman continued, clearly pleased by her younger son's attitude.

"You know, *Berta*, in time you'll appreciate what a good decision this is and how much more stable your life will be. I can't wait for you to meet the Lakhanis. They were once close friends of your father's, but that was before your time. Now, I can see from the window that my ride is here. I'll be at a women's lecture series at the mosque, but when I get back, we can speak some more. Miriam . . . Miriam are you ready?" she called.

"Coming," said Miriam grabbing an umbrella.

Awkwardly, Miriam held the umbrella over the old woman as she wheeled her towards the mini-van. Carefully, Miriam put down the umbrella and helped Humara from the seat of the wheel chair into the seat of the car. It was funny to see the old woman so vulnerable. She was as light as a feather, her bones felt frail and delicate within Miriam's grip, as if they would snap like twigs, if only Miriam applied the right amount of pressure. It almost inspired a wave of tenderness within her...*almost* as Miriam only had to look in Humara's dark domineering eyes to feel the weight of her personality.

As Humara entered the vehicle, the chattering of the other women seemed to die down. The four women looked at Humara a little apprehensively. They had been laughing and gossiping throughout most of the ride and now looked like they weren't quite sure what to say. For a little while, there was a nervous silence. There was one more to pick-up before heading out to the mosque.

The local mosque hosted a variety of scholars and this lecture series, geared towards women, had proved to be extremely popular. Although most of the Ashruf family's participation in religious activities had become fragmented and infrequent, the old woman's presence at the mosque had increased, and Humara had become more involved, taking an interest in women's programs, raising money for charitable causes, and generally offering her two cents on every problem, policy, or issue, whether asked for or not. Although this was not unusual with the elders of the community, society itself had a peculiar relationship with the old woman, and it would not be wrong to say their feelings were a curious mix of fear and pity.

Even though religious thought did not allow for it, for years the community had suspected her of being a witch. Humara, as a young girl and as an old woman, had been at the center of too many odd coincidences. This unnerved them along with her decrepit appearance. Over the last fifteen years, she had seemed to age exponentially, her skin becoming old and shriveled, her luscious hair falling off, and her legs giving out allowing her to take no more than a few steps at a time. The only thing that appeared not to be dying was her eyes; they seemed more sharp and alive than ever, as if her whole life force was focused on that one part of the body. In that state, she seemed more daunting than ever, her power growing… even as her body declined. This was something that most people's sensibilities would not let themselves admit, and in their daily lives they had found ways to work around it, treating it like a dormant volcano, for they had more pressing problems to think about, no matter how petty or mundane they may seem in the greater scheme of things.

Finally, one of the younger women, *a new comer* broke the silence that Humara's presence had instigated. She looked admiringly at the Ashruf property, in awe of their majestic residence. The house stood on top of a hill and looked like a castle with green vines curving up and down its walls. It jutted proudly from its beautifully landscaped lawn.

"*Mashallah*, you have a beautiful home Auntie," she said innocently. The other women held their breath. Even after so many years, it was a sore point with the community. The Ashruf residence had been one of the most coveted properties in the neighborhood back then. No one knew how she had done it, but Humara Ashruf had snatched that house right out from underneath the real estate market.

"Thank you *Berta*," she said sweetly. "I acquired it years ago when I still had a head for business."

She wanted to say another life time ago, but that would have been an understatement, thought Humara. The grand residence where the Ashruf's now lived had cost Humara. It was where she had gotten the tremor in her hand, wisps of gray had begun to snake through her hair almost overnight, and the laugh lines around her eyes had begun to turn into wrinkles. At the time, she had thought it well worth the investment.

The posh suburb was still being established when the previous owner (an investor) had put the house on the market. It had been a foreclosure and, as the neighborhood was gaining in prestige, he had expectations of high returns. Humara was recently widowed with three children and though not young anymore, she was still mesmerizing. The owner, Vijay Banergee, had all but laughed her off. The offer she made was well below the asking price. *He was not in the business of charity, even for beautiful widows*. Humara still re-called his smugness, the way he would smile contemptuously at her, as if she were a little slow. That was when his problems started... He had bought and sold many houses, but this mansion (which should have been a cinch) he confessed to his broker, had become quite a challenge - *not to mention that damned widow kept calling every other day wanting to know if he had considered her offer.*

He had repaired the wiring, put in a new kitchen, redone the hardwood floors, and installed a state-of-the-art heating system. Yet he could not get rid of the occasional draft. Often, he would wake up freezing in the middle of the night. He would check the thermostat only to find it had been set to cool instead of heat. It was a minor glitch for the amount of money a house like that could bring in this neighborhood. The house had been a foreclosure, and he intended to double his money—*his best investment yet!*

He had already begun getting offers. He would even see Humara Ashruf's dark blue Mercedes drive by in the afternoons. *Good*, he thought. *Maybe she'll increase her offer.* He was willing to bet that she could afford more than she was letting on. *Maybe he could start a bidding war. Wouldn't that be nice?* But whenever he waved, signaling for her to come inside and have a cup of tea, the car would drive off without any response.

No matter, a smart American couple had put in a generous bid and the way they eyed the large backyard and the oversized kitchen, he knew he could get a little more out of them. *He would show Humara Ashruf...*

It was for that reason that he was more than a little perplexed when the negotiation fizzled out and the couple made an offer on the house across the street. The seller was asking for ten percent more, and the house was in need of renovations. When Vijay approached the couple again, they began to get awkward and fidgety. An embarrassed look crossed their face as they explained that the house gave them a *bad feeling*—not in the beginning, but as they spent more and more time in it, well, it just did not feel right. It did not feel like *their* house. Vijay did not know what to say to them. He had never expected such foolishness from a young modern couple in this day and age, *but I guess looks can be deceiving,* he thought. *I need to do business with more rational people.*

This was Vijay's last thought as he drifted off into a deep rhythmic sleep, his large belly rising and falling with each breath, until at one point, his breath stopped. Vijay woke up suddenly, gasping for air, and that's when he heard it—*the crash*. For a second, Vijay wondered if it was a burglar, but then he heard the telltale jingle of Billu's collar. It was freezing. No doubt the thermostat was on the fritz again. Vijay swung his legs around the bed and walked into the hall. It was only when he got halfway down the stairs that he remembered he had forgotten his glasses. As he went downstairs, it got colder and colder, yet instead of shivering, he began to perspire, sweat blurring his vision... his undershirt sticking to his body. First, he went into the living room.

"Here kitty, kitty. Here, kitty."

"Hey, Billu. Ay, Billu" But no kitty. Then he went into the dining room.

"Here, Billu. Here, Billu . . ." he whispered. But no kitty.

Finally, he went into the kitchen. It was colder there than in any other room. He was about to call for Billu again, when his voice got stuck in his throat. Then he heard it, a faint *meow*. Billu had knocked over a pitcher of juice and was greedily licking it up. There was glass everywhere. Only then did he realize that he was barefoot. That was going to be quite a mess to clean up in the middle of the night; he would need his glasses and some slippers. He was about to turn on the light so that he could see the extent of the damage, when he felt someone tap him on the shoulder—*fingers like ice*. He could feel the presence of someone standing behind him, the faint smell of a woman's perfume. She had been waiting patiently for him all this time... all these nights.

Vijay wet himself. Then, without turning around, he ran upstairs, locked the bedroom door, and climbed into bed like a child that has just seen the boogey man. He woke up in his soiled pajamas and bed sheets, the sun shining brightly through the window. Still, he lay there shuddering for an hour before he crept downstairs, went into the kitchen, and cleaned up the mess. Billu gave him a knowing meow. His white coat stained with juice. He would need a bath.

He accepted Humara Ashruf's offer the very next day.

FIVE

*Here Come the Sweet Potatoes and
Here's the Sunday Meat,
I Guess We Must be Ready Now to Eat, Eat, Eat.*

Miriam walked briskly back into the house tightly gripping the flimsy umbrella. The rain had increased in intensity. The old woman had been packed off to the women's lecture series, and Miriam was looking forward to spending time with one of her oldest friends…solitude; when she noticed that she had a missed call on her cell phone. *It was Sonia.* She was back in town. Miriam's heart skipped a beat! Sonia was Miriam's oldest (and perhaps only) friend and she had been gone for months on a work assignment. Sonia' voice message sounded urgent. There was a nervousness in her tone that was usually *never* there. Sonia was one of the most level headed people Miriam knew. Miriam wondered what was wrong. She was about to call Sonia back, but as she entered the family room, she saw Adnan hunched over the table with his head in his hands. *Maybe this can wait*, she thought.

"Are you OK?" said Miriam. "You look pretty sick."
Adnan carefully raised his head and looked around… *the*

house was empty.

"My life is over," he said. "I can't get married…"

"Can't you just tell her?" said Miriam.

"No one can tell *Ammah* anything."

"What about Kashif? Maybe he can say something."

"*Especially not Kashif!* Don't you know he's Mom's lap dog? If *Ammah* said bark, he would ask how loud?"

"Well, that's true," said Miriam, smiling in spite of herself.

"What's so funny?" said Adnan, looking up at Miriam.

"Nothing," said Miriam, all of a sudden becoming shy.

"No, you were laughing at me. You were laughing at me and my pathetic life," said Adnan with a big grin. "Admit it."

Miriam began to raise her voice. "*You have a pathetic life?*" she said. "You live in a mansion, you do what you want, and you're probably going to marry an heiress . . ."

"You forgot my *movie-star* good looks."

"Shut up," said Miriam, throwing a dishrag at his face. "I, on the other hand, have to spend my day off cooking and cleaning."

"That sucks. Hey why don't you let me take you out to lunch? You can slave away after we get back."

"Don't you have class?"

"Psshh. Class can wait."

"All right, then. I'll grab my purse."

It took them almost an hour to find the place that Adnan claimed had the best Indian food in the city. The journey took them into one of the city's sketchier neighborhoods. The block was packed with ethnic businesses, laundromats, immigration lawyers, and pawnshops, all a stone's throw from subsidized housing. When they finally found the restaurant, there was barely any parking. Although Adnan felt completely at ease,

Miriam felt more than a little anxious leaving Adnan's new car exposed in the neighborhood. Kashif, not to mention the old woman, would have a fit if the car got stolen.

When they went inside, there was barely a wall separating the kitchen and the rickety table and chair that was the eating area—clearly this was a place meant for takeout. In the corner of the room, there was a grungy red pail sitting on the floor, collecting the drippings of the leaky roof. Adnan grabbed a stray newspaper and dusted a chair for Miriam to sit on while he went to the cashier to place an order. Miriam looked at the chair for a good two minutes before she decided to sit down. Soon after, a bus boy came and wiped down the table. After five minutes, Adnan returned and casually sat down across from Miriam.

"They don't seem to have anything written down. I asked him what they had on the menu. They've got five or six entrees cooking today, so I asked for a single serving of all of them. I hope you don't mind."

"I guess not," said Miriam, "but are you sure it's safe to eat here?"

"Yeah. Saif says he eats here all the time. Besides, if the food's crap, we'll grab a few burgers and I'll owe you a rain-check."

But no sooner had Adnan uttered these words than the waiter arrived at the table with a plate of fresh *chaat papri* and hot *samosas*. It was then that Miriam realized how hungry she was, the tight feeling in her stomach getting the best of her. The two eyed the plates as if they were gold and started helping themselves. The food was good—better, much better than Miriam had anticipated. Once they began eating, more and more entrees magically appeared on their table. Miriam and Adnan barely looked up before they sampled the kabobs, the tandoori chicken, the biryani, and the aloo muttar (potato & peas) curry. By then, they barely noticed the room or the neighborhood that they were in.

It was clear that Miriam and Adnan shared the same

taste in greasy Indian food, fighting over the last piece of chicken or naan. When they finished, two hours had passed, and they were holding their stomachs, unbuttoning their trousers, and generally imparting their blessings on the cook, who was a small sinewy man who had his eye on three pots at the same time.

"Ohhh . . . it hurts so good," groaned Adnan.

"I don't think I can get out of this chair," said Miriam.

"What time is it?" asked Adnan.

"Holy shit," said Miriam. "It's four o'clock. I've got to get home and make dinner."

"Don't worry about it," said Adnan. "We'll get a couple entrees to go. Besides, you must have some leftovers in the fridge."

❖ ❖ ❖

When Humara returned, she found the house cold and empty. There was no bustling in the kitchen, there was no aroma of dinner being prepared, and there was no chatter of Adnan on the phone. The temperature had dropped, and no one had bothered to turn the heat on. Humara wheeled herself into her bedroom. It was just as she had left it. The oak dresser with its large mirror rested in the center, and a gleam of finely crafted perfume bottles lined its edge. Collecting different scents and perfumes had long been an interest of Humara's and she had accumulated a large collection. She picked up one or two bottles, looked at them closely, smelled them, and held them up to the light—*not today*, she thought.

She moved past the dresser and toward the wardrobe. What she was looking for was way in the back. Humara pulled out an ornate wood chest with an intricate carving on the lid. Slowly, she opened the locked box and shuffled through its contents: there was a lock of a woman's hair, a locket with a picture of a young man smiling, a burnt-out old candle. Humara continued rifling through the box when she heard a racket downstairs and then voices. Miriam and Adnan had returned.

❖ ❖ ❖

Miriam stood in the foyer, dripping wet from head to toe, her T-shirt drenched and plastered to her thin body.

"I can't believe you forgot to bring an umbrella," she said.

"I thought I had one in the car," replied Adnan.

"Obviously not," said Miriam, giving her loose hair a good shake and spraying Adnan with a bout of rainwater.

"Hey, will you watch where you do that? This is a nice sweater."

"Argh . . . I'll nice sweater you," said Miriam, and she was about to continue when her mouth dropped. There was Humara, sitting in her wheelchair at the entrance of the family room with a sour expression on her face, glaring at the two of them through her deeply lined face—each wrinkle a testament to her bad mood.

"*Ammah* . . . you're back," said Miriam. "How was your lecture?"

"It went well. What have *you* been up to? I do hope you made it to class today, Adnan. There is that annoying little matter of a degree before you start your career as a world-class journalist," she said sarcastically.

Adnan looked at Humara and stammered something about an instructor being sick, which was half the truth, as it only applied to one class and not for today but the day before.

"You're a mess Miriam. You have mascara dripping down your face. I hope the neighbors did not see you in those tattered clothes, and what about dinner?" continued Humara. "Kashif will be home in a couple hours."

Miriam turned red. Every now and then a neighbor

would see Miriam scrubbing the outside steps or moving the lawn and mistake her for the help. It had become a little embarrassing for the old woman when people started asking her how much she paid their maid.

"No problem *Ammah*. I got dinner," said Adnan, holding a wet bag of takeout from the Indian restaurant they had been lunching at only hours before.

"We found this greasy spoon near campus. They make the best Indian food. It's really spicy, so brace yourself," said Adnan.

Humara looked at the clock and scowled.

"Well, it's too late to make something now. Miriam, warm up some of the leftovers from yesterday along with the food you've brought home. I will try your greasy spoon…"

SIX

When the Cat's Away...

That night, the sound of toilet bowls flushing in unison echoed throughout the house. As she passed through the halls, the old woman could hear her family making offerings to the old porcelain god with great gusto, temporarily distracting her from the rain. Everyone had been to the toilet at least once that night—Kashif three times, each time accompanied by a great deal of retching. Adnan had been twice, and he could be heard murmuring, "*Oh man . . . oh, maann . . .*" Miriam had been once, her stomach a little stronger, having come from a third world country— though she still felt queasy.

    Humara felt quite confident as she sat in her bedroom sipping ginger ale that this would be the last time they would get takeout from *that* greasy spoon. Her heartburn was much better, and comparatively, she had gotten off quite easy after that overly spicy meal (she generally did). She couldn't help it, adding a little dab of a dried spice while Miriam warmed up the entrees. *Tasteless, odorless, but the results were undeniable.* She could feel the food in her stomach churning for quite some time. Funny how over the years she had developed a tolerance for things most people could not stomach—including her late husband Naseer, though he was more than happy to reap the benefits that followed.

On Humara's night table was a silver lighter. It had belonged to Naseer, smooth and cold to the touch, it still shone like new. She had found it in her chest in the back of the closet. It wasn't what she was looking for, but it would do. She picked it up and caressed it slowly like something very precious. If she looked closely, she could still see the innocuous little message engraved in the bottom. That message turned out to be anything but innocuous. When she held it the first time, she almost missed the inscription: *Best Wishes – SH*. She had been a lot younger then and busy with three children. Naseer's business was growing and he was home late almost every single night. She had not thought anything of it. She had been foolish. Holding the smooth lighter in her hand, she realized how foolish she had been, such tiny letters etched in metal... so easy to miss.

Who was SH? She had wondered. No one she could think of. She held the lighter up to her nose, closed her eyes, and inhaled. What she got was a vision of flowers in spring, fresh and young and ready to bloom. The lighter had been her first clue; later there were others, and gradually the clues began to add up.

She had asked Naseer about the lighter one day. He had never been inclined to the gaudiness of shiny objects. If Humara had picked out a lighter for him, it would have been a cool, dark color that he could slip discreetly into his breast pocket—not one that shone like a flashlight. Naseer had told her that it had been a gift from a colleague, stammering a little and changing the subject too quickly. When she asked which colleague, he became irritable, and Humara knew not to pursue it. She had what she needed. She had never found Naseer difficult to read. His thoughts and emotions were always on the surface, though he thought he hid them very well. It would pass, she thought. He would become bored with this woman and return to his family—but he didn't.

It wasn't until she was doing some routine banking that she realized how far it had gone. She discovered that Naseer had been transferring money out of their accounts—*sums too large to ignore.*

Humara felt a deep freeze from the pit of her stomach to her heart. She was ice. His study—the answer would lie in Naseer's study. Not knowing exactly what she was looking for, she picked the lock to his desk, the one in his private den, and went through all his paperwork. And there it was, staring her in the face. That's when she knew—he was leaving her. It *almost* scared her.

She could have forgiven him his indiscretions—God knows she had had a few herself, but after all these years and all the sacrifices she had made. She couldn't let it end that way. As she went through his calendar, it became apparent where he had been spending his long lunches and late-night meetings. She tried not to picture the two of them together. It made her furious—*not good.* Better to let that fire cool into a stinging ice.

That night she waited up for him and even made him a cup of tea. He was always partial to apple-cinnamon tea with honey before he went to bed. It always made him sleep so well.

"This is very good," he said, sitting in his armchair, his face a little weathered, his hair laced with gray, giving him a seasoned but distinguished look. As Humara watched him drink his tea, all she could think of was *her*—SH, the woman who had given him the lighter, and the affair that had been going on for several months. She watched him closely that night, his expression, his gestures. She noticed the tight control he had over his voice as he spoke of a routine day at the office, asked her how the children were doing. Humara responded just as pleasantly, just as controlled as she had always been, but there was an edge to her voice. Something lurked beneath the surface of their conversation, an electricity that threatened to rise up and consume them both.

Naseer drank his tea slowly, often looking up at his wife between sips and seeing her again for the first time, only now he saw a stranger looking back at him. She was still beautiful to him, still alluring, but he could not live with this woman anymore—*he could not trust her.* There was an unsettled feeling at the pit of his stomach that felt a lot like fear, and it was this fear that had propelled him into the arms of someone safe.

It had not been raining that night, but perhaps it should have been. It was the type of night one would expect a storm, but instead the weather was unusually calm, and the only thunder was the sound of voices as they hurled accusations at one another. Naseer didn't even try to deny the affair but stood resolutely against Humara's fury, and when the storm cleared, she knew she had lost him. He left that night, left her, left the children, never to return. She *almost* didn't expect that phone call in the middle of the night—the one from the police that said her husband had fallen asleep at the wheel, swerved into the opposing lane, and collided with another car. That's the story that everyone else got: the children, the family, the community.

Tasteless, odorless . . . it always made him sleep so well.

SEVEN

A Midsummer Night's Dream
Middle East, 1980s

There are times when there is a stirring deep within and the quiet harmony of everyday life no longer brings the same comfort and then no matter... no matter what the outcome, the beast must be let out. Humara had watched *him* for a while. It was something that would seem unthinkable to him, sleeping with a married woman—but he would come around.

His name was Adeel Lakhani but they called him Adeel *Lakho wallah*, for his determination and good luck in turning one dollar into three. Adeel had committed his share of sins, many of them legal, but just as underhanded as any vice ranging from violating contractual obligations to betraying confidences to profiting from privileged information. But these were the everyday sins of business as usual and Adeel was learning his lessons well. Yet he was quite the novice when it came to women, single or otherwise. That was good... that was very good. Humara liked innocence and was drawn to it like a bee to nectar.

The Ashrufs' home was one befitting their status, and

they entertained quite frequently. Humara had become quite the socialite. She did exceptionally well in the nouveau riche circles of the Middle East. She was not beautiful, but alluring. She was poised, gracious and fashionable, but her fashion consisted of an understated elegance, one that impressed without threatening or competing. The couples they entertained were all of some prominence in the community, and Adeel had either heard of the Ashrufs by name or seen them in various circles of the upper crust. It was only a matter of time before their paths crossed.

And so it happened one late evening after a grueling day of negotiating and nitpicking over the finer points of a contract. A colleague of Adeel's, (Kevan Osmany) was finally leaving the office, rushing slightly so as not to be late for his next engagement, when he saw Adeel hunched over his desk, poring over some paperwork—*the lone worker in a sea of empty desks*.

"*Yaar*, don't sit here by yourself. You're making me feel guilty . . . as a junior in the firm you should leave well before I do. At least take a break and eat something. What are you doing for dinner?"

"*Um, well, I don't know. I was thinking . . .*"

"You're coming with me as my guest for dinner at Naseer Ashruf's."

"Naseer Ashruf?"

"*Yaar*, are you telling me you have not heard of Naseer Ashruf yet? He's someone that's definitely worth your while to meet."

There were three other couples at the dinner party. Adeel and Kevan were the only singles, and only because Kevan's wife was visiting relatives in London.

The dinner conversation was purposely kept lighthearted and humorous. Naseer Ashruf was a friendly man, prone to telling stories and giving anecdotes. Naseer, seeing Adeel as a young duckling, took an interest in his background and even turned out to be acquainted with one of his uncles. The women, seeing Adeel as a shy young man, took pleasure in chiding him on his single status, urging him to hurry up and get married. Before the evening was out, Adeel had secured a couple more dinner invitations from sympathetic wives. Out of all the women, the one who offered him the least attention was Humara Ashruf. At one point, he was even worried that he may have inadvertently offended her—but it was not so.

After dinner, the men retired to the study for billiards and brandy while the women took tea and dessert on the patio. It was in Naseer's private study that the old boys' club finally came to order and they began to discuss all the topics that were purposely kept off the dinner table. Amongst the hottest items up for debate was the latest cricket match. Adeel found Naseer to be quite an engaging man, whether he was describing his latest venture or an unfair penalty imposed on his favorite football team. Naseer, in turn, found Adeel to be a hardworking and intelligent young man and one who was not afraid to take risks. Naseer had long been looking for an assistant, a protégé, someone he could turn into a junior partner… someone who he could trust with his interests. He was seriously inclined to recruit Adeel Lakahani.

When the topic of economic progress came up, everyone had an opinion, and when the debate had hit an insurmountable wall, it was Kevan that brought to everyone's attention an article in the *London Times* regarding international exports. Realizing that he had given his copy to Adeel that morning, he asked if Adeel still had the paper on hand.

"Oh, yes, the paper is in my briefcase," said Adeel, looking around for the brown-leather case that had been a graduation present from his uncle, purchased in London during a trip abroad and saved for his graduation three months later. The briefcase was of fine quality and accompanied him most of the time. At present, it was nowhere in sight. Adeel looked around and, realizing that he had left his briefcase in the dining room, retreated to the last place he had carried it. Adeel picked up his briefcase and was on his way back when he saw the women rushing back inside, carrying plates full of dessert. It had started to rain. It was the type of rain that started out gently like a summer shower but gradually increased its fury to an angry storm before it died out as abruptly as it came.

When everyone else had come inside, still standing alone on the patio amidst this unseasonable rain was Humara Ashruf. She was standing absolutely still. Adeel stepped outside, feeling the warm droplets of rain on his face and in his clothes. As he approached, he noticed that her eyes were closed. Standing alone in the rain, she had become quite wet—soaked, in fact. Beads of rain trickled down her face to her throat, past her breastbone, and into her blouse, where they seemed to quench a deeper thirst. He let his eyes linger there for a moment. He had never really thought about women her age before, and it occurred to him that Humara Ashruf was quite handsome.

He was about to speak and ask her why she was out in the rain, if there was something he could get for her, when she abruptly opened her eyes, her gaze landing on his. Adeel realized that she was now conscious of his presence...*of him staring at her.* He felt his face flush and his throat began to constrict.

"*Bhabi* . . . I was just wondering why you're standing out in the rain. I mean, is there something I can get for you?" he stammered.

"No. I'm sorry if I embarrassed you. I was just enjoying the breeze. It's usually so hot here that I have to wonder what water angel brought down this blessing." She had a rich voice, one he could see himself listening to for many hours. Suddenly, he started feeling very uncomfortable.

"Well, I'm sorry I disturbed you. I just wanted to

retrieve my briefcase," he said, realizing that he had left the briefcase in the dining room.

Humara took a few steps forward, unaware of the rain that had soaked through her clothes, plastering them to her body like a second skin, now merely inches away from him. Paralyzed, Adeel could feel his heart thud against his chest. She looked up into his face and smiled, lightly touching his chest, brushing away a stray leaf.

"You're the young man Kevan brought," she said, as if seeing him for the first time. "I can tell Naseer thinks well of you. Do enjoy the rest of your evening. I see that you're soaked. I won't keep you any longer," she said and walked back into the house, leaving Adeel in the summer storm to cool his blood.

That's how it all had started. Adeel Lakhani swore to himself that he would never sleep with her. He really wasn't that kind of man—until one chance afternoon.

Years later, Adeel would wonder if his encounters with Humara had been as serendipitous as they had seemed. Having ingratiated himself with Naseer Ashruf and been recruited to work on a couple of side ventures, Adeel found himself at the house quite frequently, either as a visitor or as an associate, and at all hours of the day and night, for Naseer never stopped working.

Several times, Adeel would find himself dropping off documents, either before his workday or on his way home, only to find Naseer summoning him after dinner to discuss some detail. It was one such night when Adeel came to the house. Having been let in by a servant, he entered the study only to realize that Naseer had already left, and whatever had seemed so important at the time would have to wait until tomorrow. On his way out, he caught a glimpse of Humara entering the parlor. The scent of jasmine followed her, and it was that scent that first caught Adeel's attention. She was dressed in a pale green that he wouldn't have expected to be becoming on a woman of her complexion; having put her young children to bed, she was ready for a cup of tea and the evening paper. Adeel could not help standing at the doorway staring at her for a few moments before he announced himself.

To this day, he's not quite certain how it happened—just that she had invited him to join her for tea, and Adeel, left with some unexpected time on his hands, had decided to accept. Adeel remembered the feel of sweat trickling down his body, the futility of the fan above. Thinking back, he had to question if it was really the heat or if it was something else that had made him feel unusually warm and uncomfortable that day.

When it first happened, it was like an intoxicating dream. One moment they were sipping tea, chuckling over a joke. He loved the sound of her laughter, the way she teased him—and the next moment, he felt a wave sweeping over him. He looked into her eyes, and he could tell she felt it, too. She dropped her cup, but before she could pick it up, he grabbed her hand and took her into his arms. He could feel her tremble at his touch. He still remembered the scent of her skin, the warmth of her breath, her soft cries.

Afterward, he felt confused and angry. He left abruptly. He knew she was hurt, and he wasn't sure why he had acted that way or with whom he was angry—himself? Naseer? Humara?

Surely he was the one who had wanted this . . .

It was not long before he returned. He tried not to, but he thought about her constantly. During the day, he would go over the viability of different ventures with Naseer, carefully keeping his voice level, trying to keep the vision of Naseer's naked wife off his mind. Later, when that vision became a reality, he would bite into her just to satisfy that hunger, to hear her cry out. He wanted to own that cry, the whimper she made when he bore down into her, but every time he tried to possess it, he would lose a little of himself in the attempt. Now when Adeel visited Humara, there was little pretext as to why he was there. They met at all hours. She need only send the signal. He had been working so closely with Naseer over the last couple of weeks that it did not arouse any suspicion.

The affair went on successfully for several months, during which Adeel had shed the last notions of guilt that plagued him about his actions. He visited Humara with more frequency and took what he needed from her without reserve. During one such time, when he was taking her especially brutally, he could feel her trembling body and her cries becoming more and more urgent, but he could not—*would not* make himself stop. He hoped that he was not hurting her too much, and then, as if suddenly coming back to Earth, he noticed an expression of horror on her voice as she cried, "Naseer . . . no . . . *oh, my God, Naseer . . .*"

It was then that he stopped in time to see Naseer standing in the doorway, his face contorted with rage. It finally hit him—the enormity of what he had done. Swiftly, Adeel got out of bed, hiding his nakedness with a blanket. Naseer yelled threats at both of them, promising to ruin Adeel. Adeel tried to speak, but he could not utter a single word. Naseer roared on. "You bastard . . . *haramzada*! I trusted you. I took you under my wing. This is how you repay me! I'll kill you. I'll ruin you. You will live to regret this day," he threatened, assuming a combative position toward Adeel.

Humara, seeing this, cried out. "No . . . no! Naseer, don't hurt him."

This angered him all the more. He turned toward Humara.

"You shut up, you slut. I should have never married you, you conniving whore." He slapped her hard across the face. Humara stumbled backward and fell to the ground. Naseer was about to strike her again when Adeel stepped forward to restrain him, but before Adeel could get his arms around him, Naseer began to clutch his chest, stumble forward, and fall to the ground.

Humara screamed, "Adeel, call an ambulance!"

Several hours later, Naseer was resting comfortably in the intensive-care unit of a hospital, recovering from a mild heart attack. Humara was sitting by his bed, weary and exhausted, and Adeel was outside, pacing in the waiting room along with other friends and relations that had arrived. The doctor came in and addressed Humara.

"Mrs. Ashruf," said the doctor, a middle-aged man with an Indian accent. "May I speak with you for a moment?"

Humara stepped out into the hallway. As the doctor spoke to her, Humara's face was visibly tense, but as the conversation progressed, Humara began to look relieved. She then went into the waiting room to address their friends.

"It looks like Naseer is going to be OK," she said. One of the women in the waiting room gave her a hug. Adeel was about to leave when Kevan patted him on the shoulder.

"You're such a loyal friend to come here like this. Naseer is lucky to have you."

Adeel grunted an awkward response and walked away.

❖ ❖ ❖

Adeel assumes that after this, he will be dismissed and his relations with the Ashrufs will come to an end. It is for this reason that he is surprised several weeks later when he is summoned for a meeting with Naseer Ashruf.

When Adeel comes to the house, he is let in by a servant and cheerfully greeted by Humara, who asks him how he's been. Since the house is still filled with servants and well-wishers, he hardly knows how to answer.

"I'm well," he says, "but worried about Naseer, of course."

"Oh, how sweet you are," she coos. "Go right on up. He's expecting you. He's been asking for you for a while now, but I wanted him to wait until he got his strength up."

Adeel looks at her as if she's crazy. He's feels like he's walked into an absurd dream. He looks at Humara quizzically, but Humara only smiles as if she has no idea what he's talking about.

When Adeel enters Naseer's room, he finds him propped up on a pillow, his half eaten breakfast remains on a tray, and he is seriously looking over the business section of a London newspaper. When he sees Adeel, he motions for him to come in.

"Come in. Come in. I'm glad you're here," says Naseer cheerfully.

Adeel walks in apprehensively, wondering what Naseer has in store for him. He suspects that since the house is full of people and Naseer has just gone through a heart attack, he may not wish to make a scene and over-exert himself.

"Please sit down," Naseer continues. "As you know, for the last several months, we've been putting together the framework for many successful ventures to which I've been immensely committed. In my enthusiasm, I have been blinded to my failing health. This near-fatal episode serves to remind me that I have others to think about besides myself—namely my lovely wife and children, and so it is for their benefit as well as my own that I have decided to settle my accounts, pass on my business interests and responsibilities to an associate of mine, Ibrahim Zaidi, and join a relative of mine in business in America. He has been writing to me for several months, and I have been putting it off, but I now realize that a less strenuous lifestyle and more family time is what I need. I truly regret having to tell you so abruptly, but I do assure you that Mr. Zaidi is an excellent partner to work with, and you will be in good hands. I wish you much success in the future." And with that, Naseer holds out his hand.

Adeel looks at him, dumbfounded, before shaking his hand awkwardly.

"Isn't there anything else you would like to say to me?" he asks, but Naseer just stares at him blankly.

"Don't worry," he says, as if speaking to a faltering child, "you'll do just fine on your own."

Adeel wishes Naseer well and starts to leave several times. He wants to approach Humara to ask her what in God's name is going on, but there are too many people around, including Humara's children. As he heads out the door, he looks back once more and catches Humara's gaze. Their eyes lock, and she gives him a knowing glance…

EIGHT

Here We Go Round the Mulberry Bush

Life is strange, thought Miriam, flipping through some still shots on her screen.

It had been a chaotic morning at Markville Dental. The new temp that covered Miriam's days off had double booked. Consequently, the office was packed, and Miriam spent most of the morning rescheduling appointments, trying to fit everyone in as close as possible to their original time slots. On top of this, two patients had called unexpectedly in an enormous amount of pain, asking if there was any way she could fit them in. Miriam grimaced in sympathy, knowing that Dr. Geller was juggling three root canals that morning and the hygienist would be coming in late. Still, she was glad to be busy, glad to be working through her lunch, especially given the delicate state of her stomach. Miriam wondered if losing her taste for spicy food perhaps made her a little "Americanized." She hoped not.

As Miriam sat processing the last of the insurance forms and looking over tomorrow's schedule, she realized that the room was strangely quiet, and the day that had started with a roar was ending with a whimper. Generally, the office was a lively practice. Strategically located where the city met the suburbs, the dental office attracted a mixed bag of patients, from students to housewives to professionals. In fact, many from Miriam's Pakistani community lived in the neighboring suburbs and were on the roaster of patients. It put community members and newer immigrants at ease to have Miriam, who could speak their language and knew their family background, at the reception desk. Though they were outwardly nice and appreciated Miriam's help, there was an invisible wall that kept them from getting too close. They approached Miriam with a mixture of caution and morbid curiosity. If asked, all would admit that they liked Miriam and thought of her as a lovely girl, but there was an old superstition that the community never quite got over—*bad luck was contagious*.

The Ashrufs' background was full of strange events ranging from the absurd to the tragic, but there was no one more tragic in that family than young Miriam, whose mother-in-law's impatience and husband's disdain were obvious to everyone. It was this overwhelming sense of pity that kept people from developing any kind of real friendship with her.

Miriam was far from ignorant regarding the rumors that circulated about her and about the Ashrufs. They created an impenetrable wall around her, as sturdy and as isolating as any prison. Miriam found these rumors as unpleasant as a bad bout of gas. She had heard people whisper about her, and although Miriam tried to feel a sort of a kinship to them, she could see that behind their smiles of gratitude lay pity, curiosity, and sometimes suspicion. They all wondered how she could have married Kashif (at the tender age of eighteen), but worst of all, they still talked about his last wife.

Miriam sighed, coming out of her trance. The gentle

hum of the drill had almost put her to sleep, and it was at these moments, halfway between sleep and wakefulness, between this world and the next, that she would allow her mind to wander. Fortunately, no one had noticed. Miriam looked up to find a lone patient poring over the *Daily Globe*, his eyebrows furrowed in an expression of either concentration or pain (she could never be sure in a dental office), not noticing the soft hum of the drill coming from the back. Miriam found the sound rather relaxing and soothing. It put her at ease. Unfortunately, she could not say the same for many of their patients.

Miriam often used this time to look at her still shots. She had uploaded a bunch of black-and-white photographs with the intentions of going through them during her down time. It was Miriam's goal to select five or six of her best ones and send them to Sonia. As Miriam stared at her subjects, they stared back at her. They were not pretty, but they were compelling. Many were aged and feeble—close to dying, but it was that frailty that made them beautiful. Often they were victims of Alzheimer's, strokes, or cancer, things that made most people, especially young teenagers, uneasy. It was no wonder that the seniors' home had not been the most coveted assignment in Miriam's high-school photography class.

Miriam's first few years in America had seemed completely overwhelming. The people were bigger, louder, bolder. It was like experiencing a world in neon. It made her eyes hurt. She felt herself wilt in comparison. Perhaps it was for that reason that she preferred the stillness and the solitude of black-and-white photography.

As expected, when the class assignment was announced, subjects like the zoo, the school play, and the local sporting events all went first. By the time Miriam got to the sign-up sheet, there were only a couple of choices lefts. Perhaps she stood staring at it a little too long because Mrs. Kerpopple, the photography teacher, came up behind her and took the sheet from her hand. She looked at Miriam for a couple of minutes through her huge glasses, the glasses that kept falling down her button nose and reminded Miriam of goggles. It was the first time Miriam really stared at Mrs. Kerpopple's face, and Miriam began to wonder if her wild hair, always threatening to break out of her bun, was silver or a pale blonde. Usually Miriam was too distracted by the bright colors of her attire to pay attention to such details. Today, she wore a purple dress with white polka dots and lime-green tights. Miriam could only imagine how she put those colors together. On her feet, Mrs. Kerpopple wore a pair of boring brown Oxfords. For some reason, it was the shoes that bothered Miriam the most.

Today, Miriam was forced to look at Mrs. Kerpopple head-on, and her pale, yellowish eyes had a twinkle of excitement in them that reminded Miriam of a fairy godmother right before she turns your rags into a beautiful gown or a pumpkin into a spectacular carriage.

"How about the Rosedale Seniors' Home? Yes, I think that would be a good fit," she said.

It did not occur to Miriam to disagree. When Miriam went to the home, she found it to be old and dingy. There were a couple of residents sitting in wheelchairs with vacant expressions on their faces. The TV was on, but no one was paying attention to it. It was *Wheel of Fortune*. Miriam had always liked that show, but now it felt tainted and left a bad taste in her mouth. Mrs. Kerpopple had arranged for her to photograph a resident's birthday celebration, but Miriam was so overcome with the bleakness of the building that for a second she considered leaving, but then the receptionist returned to her desk. She greeted Miriam cheerfully, as if the home might have been a four-star hotel. Seeing the camera around Miriam's neck, she directed Miriam to the party room, where an elderly woman had just turned the ripe old age of one hundred. In addition to the hospital staff, her family surrounded her.

There were a couple of young grandchildren who were more preoccupied with hiding under the table then they were with Grandma. A frustrated young mother tried to coax them out, but they would not budge—and then a cake arrived.

It was a plain sheet cake with thick blue-and-yellow frosting. Miriam had arrived just in time for the big moment, and she began to get her camera ready. Once Miriam began clicking, she could not stop. Soon, she began to feel an intimacy between her and her subjects. Miriam did not stop clicking until the party was long over. Three hours later, Miriam sat by herself, eating a large slice of cake that the kitchen had saved for her, when she felt someone tug at her elbow. It was the birthday resident. She patted Miriam on the hand and pinched her cheek, murmuring something in a language Miriam deduced was either Italian or Portuguese.

"She likes you," said the head nurse. "You've done a terrific job. We would love it if you came back. We don't have much of a budget, but maybe we could arrange for some extra credit with Mrs. Kerpopple."

So Miriam returned week after week, where she caught the warmth and the strength that lay buried in the stark shadows of black and white within these residents. She snapped candids of parties, daily activities, and family visits. It was evident that many of the residents had not had an easy life, but it was those demons that made them seem otherworldly—*much like Miriam*.

Eventually, they became more like family to her than her own community, and as they began to fade, they became even more alive to Miriam than ever, and Miriam began to photograph not their presence but their absence—the unfinished business we all leave behind.

Yes, life is strange, thought Miriam, glancing back at the pictures on her computer. She had learned a lot from that photography class, from Mrs. Kerpopple. She could still hear Mrs. Kerpopple's voice in her head encouraging her to be less shy.

"Speak up Dear, I can barely hear you." She would say.

It was something Miriam still needed to work on. When dealing with people her natural instinct was to retreat, rather than to go forward and although Miriam could talk quite loudly in her head when she actually had to confront someone Miriam would feel her thoughts become dry and her voice come out like a squawk. For the first year of her marriage, Kashif barely understood when she was talking to him and the *old woman*, having never heard her speak, was concerned she might be dumb. Miriam's aunt, worried that they might send her back, had assured them that this was not the case and that Miriam was fully functioning.

"You must be a little smarter B*erta*, you're a married woman now," she had said.

Miriam's stomach began to growl. It was late in the afternoon, and Miriam had skipped breakfast and lunch. Her stomach had still felt a little woozy that morning after a night of diarrhea, and it was finally starting to settle. She would have to grab a quick bite. The place across the street made the best sandwiches. Miriam's mouth watered thinking of grilled portabella mushrooms and goat cheese on sun-dried tomato bread.

Miriam attached all her favorite shots and pressed the "send" button. In a few short seconds, Sonia would receive them: Sonia, who had perfect teeth and no cavities. Always conscious of her appearance, Miriam could tell that Sonia spent a lot of time bleaching her teeth and had recently gotten them capped.

Miriam smiled to herself, her mood picking up. It was good to have Sonia back. Sonia had been in Honk Kong nine long months, but it might has well have been the moon. Miriam had missed her like crazy and when Sonia had finally come back, it was from an amazing adventure -

and with a handsome new husband no less. It made Miriam realizes how much she valued Sonia's friendship.

Sonia was one of the few people who had looked at little homespun Miriam, and in between dentist's appointments and community events, something resembling a friendship had started to bloom. Sonia was always very kind to Miriam and Miriam liked to believe that Sonia's interest in her was more than just pity. One day on an impulse, Miriam had showed Sonia a couple of her pictures.

"These are really amazing. Have you shown them to anyone?" Sonia asked. "The look in this man's eyes just breaks your heart, but it's beautiful; it really is. I mean, he could be my grandfather," said Sonia, amazed.

Sonia had always suspected that Miriam was articulate and braver than most gave her credit for. It was clear that someone who was bold, someone who could look unwaveringly at aspects of life that made others turn away, had taken these images.

"Keep your fingers crossed," said Sonia, giving Miriam a wink. "These are better than I thought, and I think my friend will love them. Send a few more. I'd like him to see a whole range."

Miriam had smiled back, trying not to be too hopeful. Hope had always been a fickle friend to Miriam. She hoped for many things she dare not say out loud. Although her job was not the ideal career choice for Miriam, she was lucky to have it. Kashif had never been too keen on her having a job, and her mother-in-law naturally assumed that she would be too busy raising her many grandchildren to work. There was something about Miriam having her own money, as paltry as it was, and her own bank account that made Humara nervous. As a result, every month Miriam signed her paycheck over to her mother-in-law, who would give her a weekly allowance for personal items, claiming that the remainder was being deposited in a savings account. The sum she got every week barely covered lunch and bus fare, and Miriam would often go without meals so that she could splurge on luxuries such as makeup or a nice article of clothing; *it was preferable to asking the old woman for a cent.* Often, Sonia who would pass along a spare lipstick or eyeliner, saying, "This color does not suit me at all, but it would be perfect on you" or "I have some jewelry that would really bring out that outfit. You're welcome to borrow it anytime."

It was in moments such as these that Miriam was torn between gratitude and shame. Miriam would politely decline Sonia's gifts, trying to put up a pretense of a somewhat normal family situation. It wasn't just Miriam who relied on the old woman for money. All the property was in Humara's name, including the house they lived in, old Mr. Ashruf's business (in which Humara was still a silent partner and received regular checks), and his retirement portfolio. In fact, Humara had inherited the entire estate since her husband's passing. The old woman had used the money to pay for Kashif's medical school, his elaborate wedding, and the setup of his practice, for which he was still paying her back - *with interest!*

Although Humara herself had never held a job in her life, every time Kashif would buy a new car or take a fancy vacation or fly first class, the old woman would comment on the virtues of austerity and knowing the value of the dollar that his late father had worked so hard to earn. The only one in the family who spent money without a care was Adnan—free-spirited, uncontrollable Adnan.

Miriam wondered what kind of husband Adnan would be—*definitely a frightened one*, she thought, unable to keep a smile from her lips. She could just see him now, like a small animal caught in the light of a large oncoming train—*crash*. Still, she knew that whomever the girl was and wherever she came from, she would be getting the better end of the deal. Although she knew that Adnan could be superficial, he was also charming and sensitive and kind—even the old woman had a soft spot for him. Adnan's engagement prospect must really be something, thought Miriam. She imagined the perfect partner for Adnan would be beautiful, modern, and fashionable . . . captivating and chic. Miriam had never had a sister; maybe she might find one in a sister-in-law. *An ally—that would be nice*, thought Miriam. Someone to go shopping with, someone to confide in, and Miriam, in turn, would help her deal with the old woman. The two of them would laugh at the old woman's antics, as if she were an unruly child. Together, they would diffuse the spell she had cast over the household. Miriam hoped that this marriage would last and that the new daughter-in-law did not get on the old woman's wrong side. Miriam could never think about Afsana without getting a chill, and to lose another family member would be devastating.

The sound of Dr. Geller approaching brought Miriam back to her senses. Dr. Geller walked into the reception area and dropped a file on Miriam's desk. He smiled a greeting to the patient in the waiting area and motioned for him to come inside. This had been an urgent case. The patient was a stout man in his forties with a persona that already embraced middle age, the type of person you would expect to live alone. He had fallen face first while coming out of the shower and knocked out a couple of teeth. He was in a lot of pain and was going to need X-rays. Dr. Geller led him out of the waiting area while glancing at Miriam, who was already busy with the paperwork.

NINE

I Saw A Ship Sailing

Mr. Lakahni glanced in the mirror and adjusted the tie on his wiry frame, then took it off. It was only dinner—no need to be so formal. Now an older, more weathered man, Adeel Lakahni still hated ties and rarely thought about the past. It was for that reason that he felt a little cautious and maybe even a little reluctant about opening this once-closed door, but he was running out of options. He was having dinner one night with an associate when *she* called...

It had been a late dinner, and he had been trying to concentrate on the details of a technology venture with an entrepreneur he had worked with in the past. The associate was a large man who chewed unabashedly with his mouth open. Adeel had barely touched his food. For such an expensive meal, the chicken was a little dry, he had thought, and he'd wondered if the lamb tasted any better. The phone had begun to ring. The shrill ring tone annoyed the hell out of him, and he had answered the phone with irritation. He expected it to be Rosina. She had called twice already, and he had told her they would discuss London when he got back, but it was not his wife.

"Hello," he had said, a little gruffly.

"Adeel," she had said, and just like that, he was taken back to his youth . . . the smell of her skin, the deep lilt of her voice . . . she had not changed after all this time. For a split second, he had forgotten that he was an established businessman, happily married, and he had panicked. And then reason had set in. From then on, the meeting was over. He barely listened. He had closed his eyes and taken several deep breaths. He swore he could smell the rain exactly as it had been all those years ago. It had been a long time since he had felt young. When the Ashrufs suddenly packed up and left all those years ago, he had suddenly aged overnight. He became quieter. He spoke even less frequently than before, and his face began to take on the grave expression that he still wore. He never knew whether to feel angry or relieved that things had worked out the way they had. She had ruined him, ruined him for all other women. Night after night, it was her he craved, and for that reason alone he detested her. There was nothing else to do but bury himself in his job, and it had worked. He had lived up to the Lakahni name and ended up a rich man and, in doing so, he had caught the attention of many influential families with eligible daughters. They were all the same to him—the pretty ones, the plain ones, the charming ones, the dull ones. In fact, it was the pretty ones who annoyed him the most, as their fair skin and features seemed so garish in comparison to Humara's dark complexion and natural grace.

His opposition to marriage frustrated his family to no end; his mother crying that she would never live to see a grandchild. Adeel did not know what to do in the face of such drama, so he continued with business as usual, becoming all the more ruthless in pursuing his interests. He was close to becoming a confirmed bachelor when one of his few friends brought to his attention a girl whose family had much-needed contacts in London. Adeel observed the girl from a distance. She was skinny with strong features, not quite plain, but not quite pretty, either. There was something about her gait that reminded him of an exotic bird. Her clothes and her jewelry were the most colorful he had ever seen. She was somewhat younger than he preferred, but that was not considered a disadvantage back them. No one could have guessed that Adeel would have had a preference for this beaky little bird, and so the news was received with much astonishment and joy. First, an engagement, and then an elaborate wedding followed. Adeel never took the time to get to know her until after the nuptials, and then he proceeded to settle into married life, spending more time with his family and his in-laws. Everyone agreed that marriage became him, and Adeel *Lahko Wallah* (as his friends and family still teased him for obtaining his fortune at such a young age), forgot his episode with the Ashrufs.

Now, as he drove back home, he stole glances of himself in the rearview mirror. His hair was thinning, his skin was loose, and he had accumulated a spare tire or two around the middle. It was with much disappointment that he realized he had let himself go over the last thirty years. Even his clothes seemed a little stuffy and dated, like the clothes of an old man who doesn't realize that the styles have changed. They would be meeting under very different circumstances now; little could be done to renew the past. Humara was a widow, and he was a married man. This meeting would not be about them; it would be about their children. Still, Adeel had enough vanity left to resolve to skip dessert for the next several weeks, take a long walk every night, and get his wife to pick out a more fashionable wardrobe for him, something she had been insisting on for some time.

Although Adeel *Lakho Wallah*'s initial response was to turn down Humara's proposal, he began to reconsider on the drive home, to understand the advantages of the union to both parties. America would be a good place for them. Dubai was starting to feel small, and London well; London was a place where they were a little too well known. Starting over in a new city would be good for Rosina and for their daughter. When he returned home that evening, instead of discussing London with his wife, he made arrangements to go to the U.S. London would have to wait. This seemed like a far better deal.

TEN

The Spider and the Fly

It took a mere two weeks to pack up and arrange for a trip to the Midwest. Although the Lakahnis would have preferred a more exciting destination like New York or L.A., they resigned themselves to a quaint Midwestern suburb. As Humara had recommended, they rented a suite for a couple of months, but Adeel was prepared to extend the stay if need be. The suite was spacious without being ostentatious and was closer to the city than to the suburbs, so the family could amuse themselves in their spare time. The only information that Adeel had about the prospective bridegroom was a picture and a sketchy resume. For now, that would have to do. It was with much anticipation that Adeel looked forward to the meeting, wondering for the umpteenth time if he had made the right decision—but then again, he was not in a position to be picky.

Rosina was in the bedroom, already dressed and absorbed in picking out something appropriate for their daughter to wear that would make her look pretty— though Adeel was not sure what that might be. Getting one's daughter married off was not easy under normal circumstances, but it was especially difficult with Baby. She rejected most of the suitors that found her acceptable. She was his only child, and he was determined to do whatever was necessary to keep her happy. It was with much care that he finally accepted Humara's suggestion to visit them in America. Humara had assured him that Adnan was a nice boy—just one that needed a little direction. That he could live with. If Baby was happy, Adeel wouldn't have to worry—he had plenty of experience giving people direction.

It was not a long drive to the Ashrufs' home, but there was a lot of traffic, and the rain delayed them considerably. After a couple of hours on the freeway, they were more than an hour late for dinner. The Ashrufs would no doubt accuse them of arriving at *desi* standard time, even though Adeel had tried his best to be punctual. Adeel Lakhni turned into the Ashrufs' driveway. It was quite a large lot. Naseer's new business must have progressed well after all, and he must have left Humara a sizable estate. Adeel was glad that he wouldn't have to face him tonight. He was in no mood for those types of memories.

Adeel glanced over at Rosina, who had dozed off for a while. Neither his wife nor his daughter was good at handling jet lag. He took another look at the house. It seemed to look back at him. He could hear Baby's loud snoring in the backseat. He hoped this match would work out. Gently, he woke them up.

❖ ❖ ❖

It was Miriam, a little frustrated and a little disheveled, who answered the doorbell. All day, the old woman had been driving her crazy. Never had she been so particular about how the meal should be prepared, asking Miriam to do things over two or three times. She was sweaty and tired and had just managed to take a shower

The Mother-in-Law Cure

and throw on a nice *salwar kameez* before putting the finishing touches on a dessert and hearing the doorbell ring. Adnan and Kashif were watching the game on TV, and Miriam could hear them yelling at the television. Miriam suspected that Humara was probably taking a nap before dinner.

"Everyone, they're here," said Miriam through the intercom before she headed to the foyer and opened the main door.

"Please come in, Uncle . . . Auntie. Let me take your coats. We've been waiting for you. I hope you found our directions were acceptable."

"Of course, of course, *Berta*, perfectly clear. We would have been here an hour earlier if it wasn't for all that traffic on the expressway," said Adeel Lakahni, taking in Humara's daughter-in-law.

Miriam looked like a waif with her round face and dark wispy hair, thought Adeel. *She's practically a girl herself.* And then he remembered this must be the young new daughter-in-law he had heard about.

"*Ammi* and Kashif will be down to greet you in a minute," said Miriam. "And where is your lovely daughter?"

As Baby entered the room, Miriam stifled a soft gasp, and her smile froze. Miriam was left speechless for two or three seconds. Regaining her composure, Miriam led the family to the good living room where everyone was waiting. As they entered, Kashif and Adnan stood up to greet them. During the first few minutes, Humara did not even see Baby. Her eyes were locked on Adeel. The young boy Humara had known so long ago had changed into a distinguished man. She looked up at him and searched his face. She recognized bits and pieces of him. The eyes were the same, but now a pool of wrinkles surrounded his eyes. He was the same height but looked frailer than before. His thick black hair had receded and was laced with gray, and his normally clean-shaven face now had a beard. But when he smiled that slightly awkward smile that Humara had always found so appealing, he was still that young boy whose appetites and desires she had awakened for the first time. She would have gotten up and walked over to him if it weren't for that damn chair . . . and then she saw Baby.

Whatever the old woman thought of Adeel and Rosina Lakahni's prodigy, she kept it to herself, but Miriam could tell from the look on Adnan's face that Baby was not the type of girl he went for *at all*. Baby was hardly the thin, fashionable debutante Miriam was expecting. *In fact, Baby was the size of a baby elephant*; dressed in a hot-pink salwar kameez. Her voluptuousness oozed out of the net sleeves like hot caramel, reminding Miriam of a decadent sundae. Miriam's stomach began to growl, another reminder that she hadn't eaten all day.

Although her features were pleasant and her complexion was fair, Baby's makeup was bright almost to the point of being garish, and her brown hair was streaked with copper highlights. There was something about her that reminded Miriam of a hula doll she had seen as a child (a mechanical toy depicting a plump woman in a grass skirt that would smile and shake her large belly when you wound her up). In comparison, Adnan looked more the movie star than ever, wearing a blazer on top of a casual shirt. He looked tall and broad-shouldered, and with the house lights on full blast, you could even see the flecks of green in his brown eyes.

Miriam looked over at Kashif for his reaction, but Kashif kept his usual poker face, and Miriam had a hard time deciphering his thoughts. Adnan's face was also stone blank, but Miriam figured that was more out of shock than anything else. For the first time, Miriam wondered how much leeway Adnan had to reject the match. The person that showed the most emotion at the meeting was Baby. She looked as if she was in a state of euphoria; her face carried an expression akin to love at first sight. Her overblushed face became even redder, and her richly glossed lips puckered a little as she began to salivate. She looked at Adnan with such naked desire that Miriam had to turn away. *There's no way she's going to let him go*, thought Miriam.

During dinner, Adnan looked visibly distressed sitting across the table from the Lakahnis. Mr. Lakahni, with his long, thin face and moustache, sat nibbling at the delicate appetizers. Miriam watched his mouth twitch as he chewed on the delicate morsels of food. As he ate, his narrow eyes astutely took in all the elements of the dinner, the size of the house, and the décor. His gaze rested on a vase that had been a wedding present. The capitalist in him was shrewdly making calculations on all visible assets, and when he looked at Adnan, the numbers began to roll.

"Adnan...*Berta*," he said. "I hear you're in grad school, what are you taking?"

"Well...um...I was studying communications but now I think I'm switching to journalism."

"Hun...I see very good, very good," replied Mr. Lakahni looking skeptical.

"Miriam, are you studying as well?" asked Rosina Lakahni.

"Our Baby just finished a course in interior design."

"Well, I was thinking one day I'd like to study..." started Miriam when Humara abruptly interjected.

"*Miriam...No, she's never been bookish.*"

Humara continued in a softening her tone, "She has a camera that she tinkers with but I don't think she really knows how it works."

"That's right *Ammah*, I'm all thumbs," said Miriam.

"Well don't worry *Berta*," said Mrs. Lakahni. "I also find gadgets very confusing. We women were not built for such things. Creating a loving home and a family that's our place," she said looking at Baby.

The dinner conversation teetered from polite to

awkward. Almost everyone was too nervous to eat. Mrs. Lakahni, a petite woman, sat pecking at her food without ever really putting anything in her mouth. She had a slightly vacant expression on her face, as if concentrating on any one thing required too much effort and she would rather leave most of the heavy thinking to her husband. Only Baby seemed to be digging in without pause, thoroughly immersed in the act of dining. No doubt she was one of those people who ate when they were nervous.

The whole affair might have been quite amusing had Adnan not looked as if he was in so much obvious terror, like an animal that was caught in a trap and was unsure whether to gnaw its paw off to escape or accept a slow death. He had become incredibly twitchy, and from time to time he would sneak horrified glances at Baby. Kashif kept looking at him with apprehension, as if he expected Adnan to get up and bolt, while his mother's cold gaze kept him nailed to his seat. The Lakahnis, however, did not seem to notice, and Mrs. Lakahni would give Adnan a sugary smile every so often as she complimented him.

"*My, Baby, isn't he a handsome boy*," Mrs. Lakhni would say to her daughter, who would let out a shy giggle. She looked at Adnan as if he were a lamb chop she couldn't wait to devour.

Kashif was the one that primarily carried the dinner conversation, discussing with Mr. Lakahni the economy, international trade, and politics. Mrs. Lakahni and the old woman talked about how the Middle East had changed since the Ashrufs had left and what an adorable couple the two children made. Adnan looked on in horror, but nothing could prepare him for what was about to come next. Near the end of the meal, Miriam heard a strange hissing sound that reminded her of a kettle just before it was about to blow. Then a strange aroma started to creep into the room. At first, Miriam was irritated. She thought that the neighborhood kids had released a stink bomb on their property, but then she remembered that between the intermittent rain and thunder, the children had not been out in weeks. A blush crept over Miriam as she began to realize what it was.

Baby, seemingly unfazed, let out a giggle. Very quickly, the whole family would come to realize that Baby had the tendency to get gas and quite often. At the end of dinner, Baby let out a satisfied belch indicating that she had been satisfied. She followed it with a coquettish, "Excuse me" in her sugary voice. Her advances toward Adnan became bolder. She would stare at him unabashedly. During dessert, she cornered him on the couch. Adnan was squeezed between Baby and the sofa's arm, and when Baby put her hand on his knee, Adnan looked as if he was going to wet his pants.

It was Kashif that saved him by calling him over and suggesting that he tell Mr. Lakhani more about his graduate work. Adnan nearly leapt off the sofa, and Miriam ended up taking his place next to Baby. Although Miriam found herself with more room than Adnan (Baby did not feel inclined to snuggle up next to her), the strength of Baby's perfume was enough to make Miriam feel dizzy. Within minutes, Miriam had a pulsating headache. It was much to everyone's relief (especially Adnan's) that the evening finally came to an end.

The old woman considered the meeting to be a profound success.

"We must do this again," she said. "Perhaps these two should get together on their own sometime without the families getting in the way."

Both Adnan and Kashif looked aghast.

"You are absolutely right. I couldn't agree more," said Mr. Lakahani. As Miriam brought everyone their coats, she couldn't help but give Adnan a sympathetic smile. He smiled back giving her his, "*Look at me; I'm in deep shit*" grin, and Miriam giggled, but not before she caught Baby looking at her with something resembling suspicion. Miriam felt her cheeks flush as if she had been caught doing something she shouldn't and she stepped into the background, hoping she didn't look too guilty.

❖ ❖ ❖

"You can't be serious," said Adnan after dinner. The Lakahni were long gone, and Miriam was clearing the table.

"I'm not going out with her. She's a monster!"

"Listen to me, *Berta*. You are not getting any younger, and I'm not putting up with your behavior any longer. For too long, I have been lenient." Humara's eyes sparkled as she said this, the way they always did when she was executing a plan. Her voice was steel. When she continued, her tone was warm and sugary.

"Now, Adnan, be a good boy and do what Mama tells you. You are going to make this work, or I'm cutting you off. Don't push me. You may think you're tough, but you would not last two days without your Starbucks coffee in the morning, much less the luxury you've become used to."

There was a strange flush to the old woman's face, indicating that she was excited and that was it. The transformation was complete. The old woman had turned from mother to man-eater.

Humara's sense of elation always peeked just before a goal was successfully accomplished... like a hunger satisfied *but to whom this appetite belonged she was not always certain.* It was later that she would feel the weariness in her bones.

Adnan was about to protest but Kashif, having recognized the look in his mother's eyes, put a fatherly hand on his shoulder.

"Wait a couple days. Now's not the time," he whispered.

ELEVEN

Rain, Rain, Go Away;
Come Again Another Day

The little clock radio crackled with static, paralleling the gruesome weather outside. From deep within, the smooth, silky voice of the announcer reflected a calm that wasn't in the atmosphere.

"It's NRG 108.5 FM, and Chicago, we're going through our third week of rain, and wow, it's still coming down out there! More weather after these messages . . ."

Miriam looked out the bedroom window into a world that was blurry and distorted, as if it was spiraling down a cosmic drain. The streaks of water pouring down the windowpane made Miriam think of living under the sea. She stared at it for quite some time, hypnotized by the downpour. Somehow, the more she looked outside, the more it prevented her from looking inside—inside herself, inside her life, and most importantly, inside the brochures she held in her lap—the bright shiny brochures that were such a contrast to the dreary weather outside.

Miriam quickly folded the brochures and put them back in the drawer. The happy glossy lives of the people on the cover seemed too bright, too unattainable. Looking at them for too long hurt her eyes. She had been hungry for them only a month ago. She had inhaled them the way a starving child devours a piece of candy, chewing on course descriptions, faculty biographies, even highlighting the ones she liked the most. But the Hamilton School of Photography was a two-year program, and it was not cheap.

She quickly put the brochures away after looking at the price. Her part-time income would not cover it, especially since the money she received went straight into Humara's account. From the meager funds Kashif and sometimes Humara gave her, she was able to put away a little bit each month, but her savings weren't nearly enough to afford this. She would need some kind of financial aid, but financial aid was not her biggest concern . . .

She had never asked Kashif for a favor before, and she would never dream of asking Humara for anything. It would be too humiliating . . . too dreadful. She knew all too well that neither one of them was capable of an ounce of generosity. She did not want to persuade, beg, or cajole. The old woman would look at her as if she had suggested buying the Taj Mahal. She would look up, arch her eyebrow, and give her an once-over, making her feel naked and exposed—as if she was feeding off every flaw, every blemish, and every insecurity, drawing strength like a bottom dweller. Her voice would be smooth and even a little sugary, the way it got when she gave bad news. But her eyes would say, *you foolish, foolish girl. Did you really think you could fly away so easily?*

Miriam knew fully why she was brought into this family. If Afsana was sunshine—strong, vibrant, and opinionated, Miriam was the rain—submissive, quiet, and withdrawn, as if she had already accepted life's defeat. Everyone knew that Miriam's true purpose was to serve the old woman and to provide her with another brood of grandchildren. Well, Miriam was young and healthy, but after five years of marriage, it was becoming more and more certain that no offspring were going to come from this union. It was just as well; Kashif never did care much for fatherhood. Perhaps, Adnan would do better *and Miriam...?*

Kashif had always insinuated that Miriam had received the better end of the deal—an opportunity to move to a wealthier country, a nice home, and some position in the community. *What else could an orphan of questionable birth expect?* Humara had always pointed that out to her and, until now, Miriam had always believed her. In the end, perhaps it was a better fate than that of Afsana, who had died so tragically.

So the brochures had remained in the drawer for several weeks, sleeping until Miriam decided to wake them. Sonia had finally gotten back to her the other day. Miriam was just about to leave work and had almost stepped out the door when she heard the phone ringing—*probably an emergency or a cancellation*, she thought, but it was Sonia. She sounded upbeat, as if she was bringing good news—and she almost was. She said that her friend loved the concepts, but he was looking for a more polished eye. He wanted to know where she had gone to school. "Ridgefield Community College," said Miriam.

"No, photography school. He wants to know where you studied photography," Sonia said.

"Nowhere," said Miriam.

"That's what I thought. I told him I didn't think you had any formal training. He recommended this school on Newton Avenue."

"I know the place," said Miriam, thinking back to the brochures. "It's the Hamilton School of Photography. I pass by there sometimes on my way to work or the mall."

"Good," said Sonia. "Check it out. Drop in sometime and let me know what you think."

"OK," said Miriam, knowing that it wasn't what she thought that counted the most. Sonia had forced her to go back to a place she hadn't wanted to think about. Would she dare approach the subject? Would Kashif agree? What would the old woman say?

Miriam sat staring out the window with a vacant expression on her face, her photographs still in her hand. For the first time, she was contemplating a real future. Yes, perhaps it was time to broach the subject again. Since the engagement, the old woman's mood had lightened, which meant that she might not be stressing Kashif out as much. In fact, Kashif almost looked as if he was in a good mood these days. He was more relaxed and less irritable despite the long hours he had been working. Miriam noticed that he was a little preoccupied, but still, it was an improvement, and Miriam was willing to take what she could get. Perhaps now with another daughter-in-law coming into the family, it might take some of the pressure off her.

As Miriam put the brochures back in the drawer, she caught Adnan staring over her shoulder. How long had he been standing there?

"Not a bad idea," he said. "You should try it."

"Well, I don't know what Kashif would say about that," said Miriam.

"True. Kashif's a cheap bastard, but you've earned it, and your stuff is good."

"You think so?" she said, testing the waters a little. But Adnan did not reply, the blaring of his cell phone interrupted their conversation, and he quickly made his way downstairs. Miriam knew that Kashif had a late meeting that day. She would approach him before he left for work.

❖ ❖ ❖

Miriam started her day feeling almost optimistic. By the time Miriam fought her way through the crowded public transport system to get to work, she was feeling anything

The Mother-in-Law Cure

but cheerful. She had actually gotten to the office early. In fact she had rushed out after talking to Kashif, plowing through the mass of early-morning commuters like a bulldozer on speed.

It wasn't that Kashif had said no; it was the way he had said it—slowly, as if speaking to a child that was slightly retarded. He sipped his tea as he looked at her portfolio (like many *desis*, he preferred tea to coffee). He lay each picture down on the table, spreading it before him like a fan, though Miriam wondered if he really saw them and if he really saw her. He looked bored, maybe even detached.

"Sonia has a friend in photography. He really liked them. He really went for my approach, says I have a lot of talent. He thinks some more formal training might be good for me," said Miriam taking a deep breath and controlling her voice the just way she had practiced in the mirror.

"Sonia...yes. That half-Pakistani girl you hang out with? She's a real feminist type, isn't she?" he said with distaste.

"What does that have to do with anything? She's smart, and she's well connected. What do you think? Do you like them?" said Miriam beginning to lose her cool, her voice trembling slightly. It was one of the few times Miriam found it difficult to guard her true emotions but Miriam swallowed what lay on the tip of her tongue for the hundredth time. Some things were better left unsaid, for now anyway...

"Dear," Kashif added. "I'm perfectly supportive of your hobbies, and if you want to fool around with a camera now and then, well, that's all well and good . . . but Sonia's friend didn't say he liked them well enough to use them now, *did he?*"

"Well no," said Miriam, her eyes welling up, but Kashif pretended not to notice.

"Look. You have a very handy skill—but turning this into a career, enrolling in a full time program—where is the sense in that? It's only money thrown down the drain."

"If you're worried about the cost, there's always financial aid, and . . ."

"Now, Miriam," he said, cutting her off, "a girl like you would never survive in that arena. So why don't you stick to what you're good at?"

Adnan saw the look on Miriam's face, a cross between humiliation and indignation, and began to interject.

"Aren't you being a little harsh?" he said.

"I'm only telling her like it is, sparing her embarrassment and disappointment later on. If someone had told you that you weren't cracked up to be a model or a professional playboy, you might not be in the position that you're in right now. I hardly think the prince of delusions is qualified to advise anyone of anything," said Kashif.

"You're a real prick," said Adnan, as he grabbed his car keys and headed out the door.

TWELVE

Prince Charming

Adnan was gone and Miriam did not know when he'd be back. Kashif was on the phone with his whore. Funny, how she could always tell now. Miriam sat very still, looking back at the photographs in her hand thinking about how embarrassed she would be to tell Sonia that Kashif just wouldn't let her take more classes. The more she thought of Sonia, the more Miriam was reminded of their first encounter. It seemed prophetic. In fact, the two women had met when Miriam married Kashif and since it was at their wedding, you couldn't really call it a meeting so much as an introduction. Miriam remembered, the whole wedding had been rushed, from the moment she said yes, it was only a couple weeks later that she was married. The whole production seemed like an afterthought, from the borrowed clothes, to the last minute invitations, to the mediocre catering. Miriam's wedding had been in the middle of the week because that was when the Mosque had space (the weekends had been booked a long time ago). What was missing was also evident. There was no reception, no music, and no dancing followed the ceremony. The Ashrufs were never known to be *that* religious.

Miriam had sat demurely like the child bride that she was, an exotic doll, her head bowed, her eyes glazed, the slightest tremor in her bottom lip. Beside her, there was a weathered looking mother-in-law on one side and a jovial looking aunt on the other side. Somewhere nearby was the matchmaker. One by one, the guests would come in, congratulate the women of both families, and take a look at the bride as if inspecting a rare find. When Miriam's neck began to feel crimped from looking down, she directed her gaze upwards amidst a sea of people wearing colorful looking outfits. She did not know whom to focus on and that's when her eyes locked with Sonia's.

As the evening progressed, many guests came to offer her their congratulations. Eventually, Miriam was able to see Sonia up close. She was an attractive girl with a sun kissed complexion, hair as deep as chocolate and eyes that were slightly lighter than the average Pakistani's. Miriam noticed some of the aunties eying Sonia quizzically. At the time, Miriam wasn't sure why. It was much later that she understood that Sonia was someone who came from mixed parentage.

Men and women had been segregated and Miriam remembered looking at the big-screen TVs, where the men's side was reflected onto the women's section. There were two Imams (clad in white robes), one representing the bride's interests and the other representing the groom's. Kashif and Adnan sat side by side, Adnan looking more like the young debonair groom than his older brother. Miriam suddenly had an irrational thought, *what if it could be a double wedding...what if Adnan were marrying Sonia?* Then she would have a sister and she wouldn't feel so alone. Miriam had clung to that thought for the rest of the evening.

❖ ❖ ❖

As time progressed, Miriam ran into Sonia on numerous occasions. Once Miriam was there when Sonia stopped by Kashif's office to pick up a prescription for her grandmother. The receptionist had to leave early that day and Miriam was covering the last couple hours of her shift. Usually, Kashif would have left prescriptions at reception with her. Miriam remembered a woman with a baby and an elderly gentleman were seated in the waiting area when Sonia arrived. She was about to page Kashif about the prescription, when he came out wearing a white coat and stethoscope. He greeted Sonia like an old acquaintance, even though she knew they barely knew each other (even giving Sonia a kiss on the cheek). Miriam could tell it made Sonia uncomfortable.

Kashif asked some routine questions about her grandmother's health and what medications she was on. He then wrote the prescription, which he held in his hand a little too long. There was an awkward silence as Dr. Ashruf's gaze rested on Sonia in a way that made Miriam blush. Finally, he gave her the prescription along with his business card, in which he handwrote his cell number *in case anything should come up;* and guided her out of the office with his hand carefully placed on the small of her back.

Miriam felt heat rise up her back and cheeks. She looked up at the patients in the waiting area but neither the young mother nor the elderly man gave any indication that they had noticed the exchange.

Thinking about that afternoon still made Miriam's skin crawl. Even after they became friends, she never talked to Sonia about it...ever.

When Sonia and Miriam eventually became friends, it was after Miriam started working at Markham Dental. Outside of the household, some of Miriam's shyness fell away. She would smile more often and, every now and then, even crack a joke. Her clothes and hairstyle were still pitiful, but her attitude was anything but. In the beginning,

Sonia genuinely seemed surprised by Miriam's composure, and friendliness. Later on, especially, after seeing Miriam's photography, Sonia began to get a glimpse of the depth of Miriam's soul. One might even go so far as to say second sight, for Miriam picked up on things that others routinely missed. Inevitably, a rapport and perhaps even a bond developed between the two women. It was this connection that helped both women get through their respective hurdles and Sonia found herself confessing more to Miriam than she intended. It was Miriam's uncanny knack on picking up on when something was bothering Sonia, even when she was being her most cheerful. That being said, the diamond ring on Sonia's finger was hard to miss.

"Congratulations, you should be thrilled." But Sonia's happy news was clouded by complications.

"It had begun in Hong Kong," Sonia explained. Within a couple months of starting as an associate at a prominent law firm, Sonia had accepted a transfer to Hong Kong. At first, Sonia was thrilled, but excitement quickly dissipated into loneliness. That's when she met Michael Blaine. Michael was a senior associate at the firm when their friendship began to bloom. He had proved to be an invaluable mentor and one of Sonia's closest friends until the line between their friendship had become so blurred, that she did not know where he began and she ended, and now things were more serious than she had ever dreamed. Sonia looked at the diamond on her finger and a shiver went up her spine.

Not being able to think of anything to say, Miriam put her hand on top of Sonia's covering up the cold hard stone.

"You'll know what to do when the time comes. Sometimes you just need to settle your soul."

THIRTEEN

Hansel and Gretel
Chicago, Illinois, 1989

It always seems so innocent in the beginning: people's intentions, the house made up of gingerbread, the kindly old woman. Although nobody could call Humara old, she was still only middle aged. In the prime of her life some would say, but as Humara approached middle age, a curious thing happened. She became a little plumper, the sharp angles of her body rounding into a matronly curve, the features in her face softening. It gave her a benign unassuming quality - *a sheep in wolves' clothing.*

The house was, indeed, sugarcoated. Humara was an excellent cook. Her baking filled the air with the sweet scent of apples and cinnamon and brown sugar, of brownies and icing and sweet breads, of peppermint and vanilla... and aromas so sweet one felt they could die and go to gingerbread heaven. Like Hansel and Gretel, Kashif and Afsana entered the old woman's house with the most voracious of appetites.

There are certain things that Afsana would always remember about her mother-in-law. In spite of her motherly exterior, she was younger than Afsana had expected, more modern and much more fashionable than Afsana's own mother. Afsana had been wary of meeting her after hearing about her initial reaction to the engagement, but Kashif had assured her that his mother had come around and supported the marriage wholeheartedly. When they finally did meet, Afsana saw a woman dressed in beiges and creams, a crinkle in her eye, her hair knotted in a bun and a rope of pearls around her neck, looking like part aunt and part older sister – *all of Afsana's initial nervousness melted like warm gooey chocolate inside your tongue.*

Since Afsana was Kashif's betrothed, Humara showered her with gifts from clothes to jewelry, even including some chic spa certificates. Humara was also more than accommodating during the wedding preparations—asking Afsana's opinion on every detail and complimenting her on her sense of style and her good judgment. Afsana accepted the attention gratefully but with some unease. For despite the friendly gestures and Humara's kindly appearance, Afsana could never decipher what her mother-in-law was thinking, and when she spoke, Afsana could feel the weight of Humara's gaze. So focused was her concentration, that it often made Afsana feel paralyzed, embarrassed, and exposed all at once, as if someone had shone a spotlight over her. In Afsana's rational mind, those were no reasons to dislike the woman who meant so much to the man she loved. Still, it was with the utmost reluctance and against her better judgment that Afsana agreed to live with her in-laws. It was not until later that she began regret her decision, for her mother-in-law had a subtle way of extracting control that was not always obvious—at least not right away.

Desi men can seldom foresee the problems of living in an extended-family situation and consider having their wives and their mothers in the same home the best of both worlds. Kashif was no exception. He assured Afsana that they would have their privacy, and that there was plenty of

The Mother-in-Law Cure

space, and that Afsana would not have to worry about cooking, cleaning, or supervising the help. Humara would take care of it. Since Kashif's father passed away, Humara had become more dependent upon her son. "And it would make it easier for me to check in on Humara and little Adnan should anything happen, and wouldn't it be nice to have a home-cooked meal every evening when we get home from work?" he added—and in the beginning, it was.

Humara was a phenomenal cook. She prepared fresh curries that included a vegetable dish, a meat dish, homemade chapattis, and basmati rice every evening. Never had Afsana been taken care of so well. At night, they would come home to a hot meal and a clean house, for Humara supervised the help meticulously. Life in the gingerbread house went incredibly well. It took a little while for the sugarhouse to start to melt. When the rain finally came down, it started with the smallest of annoyances.

Afsana began to find it difficult to locate things. She understood where everything was supposed to be but could never find something when she was looking for it. She attributed it to the fact that she was home so infrequently. She knew where all the linen closets were and where the pantry was and the type of items that were kept in the basement or the garage, but often when she was looking for something specific—a beach towel that she had bought a couple months ago, a specific style of pillowcase, bed sheets she wanted to use—she was not able to find it. Afsana would look all over, carefully emptying the linen closet and putting it all back, checking the guest rooms, and finally thinking to herself *I don't have all day* and giving up only to come across the item several weeks later underneath some old bedding. Things were never where she expected them to be.

It was a lazy Saturday afternoon when Afsana woke

up from a nap craving ice cream. She had slept soundly, as if drugged into unconsciousness under a thick comforter, and she had awoken drenched in sweat, her tank top clinging to her body and her throat dry. Greedily, her mind went to the pint of ice cream in the freezer; caramel mocha was her favorite. She had just bought it a couple of days ago. Not bothering to put on slippers, liking the feel of her bare feet on the cool marble, she plodded into the kitchen and opened the refrigerator door—but it wasn't there. *Someone must have put it in the large freezer in the pantry*, she thought. When she looked, she found Kashif's favorite, maple walnut, Adnan's popsicles, and the kulfi Humara always liked to eat. Disappointed, she grabbed a grape popsicle, thinking that someone else had eaten her ice cream or that they had served it to guests. No more than a week later, Kashif was putting away groceries. He took out a box of caramel-mocha ice cream to make room for the frozen vegetables.

"Are you ever going to eat this or are you just going to let it sit here?" he asked.

Afsana looked at the box in bewilderment and grabbed a couple of bowls from the shelf.

"You know, I was just looking for that a couple days ago. Things in this house have a tendency to disappear on me. It must be a testament to how hard I'm working. I must be losing my mind."

Kashif had laughed and called her dramatic.

"Really, it's not funny. Not only that, but I've started to misplace stuff."

"Like what?"

"Oh, I don't know. An old bracelet of mine, one of my earrings, a hair clip . . ."

"I'll look around our room for them. Perhaps the cleaning service is stealing," he'd suggested.

"I don't think so. A couple of trinkets are hardly worth stealing."

"Still, I'll ask *Ammah* to keep an eye on the service

and move our valuables out of sight," said Kashif, kissing her on the forehead. Afsana felt strangely reassured and comforted.

That reassuring feeling would not last. Afsana would sleep less and less at night. She would wake up tired and irritable in the mornings. Dark shadows began to appear under her eyes. Kashif's schedule became busier, and he was home less often and at times when Afsana was scheduled to work. Isolated from her family and friends, Afsana became edgy and paranoid as the loneliness and the grueling schedule began to take their toll. Humara expressed concern, urging her not to work so hard and to eat more and rest more, but her mater-of-fact tone only caused Afsana to doubt her concern. When Kashif was home, he barely noticed his wife, spending much of his time on research. The only thing he seemed to relish or even notice was his food. He always ate as if he was someone who had not eaten for many days and was not sure when he'd eat again. Afsana, in contrast, barely touched her food, for she felt strangely suspicious of the meals before her. Later, she would compare it to being offered a poisoned apple that dripped with sweetness and provided a false sense of security.

Afsana's paranoia continued to grow. She accused Kashif of flirting with a waitress, of excluding her from his friends, and of having an affair with a colleague.

"Don't be silly. She's married and has three kids," he said.

Finally, Afsana had an idea. She would make dinner on her day off. It was the only way she could think of to get the affection she was craving, even if it was only for her casserole.

"I don't know why you insist on doing this," Kashif had said, looking perplexed. "*Ammah* is perfectly fine cooking for us."

"I just wanted to give her a break. I want to cook something different."

"I don't know if *Ammah* is used to American food."
"One night won't kill anyone," said Afsana.
"Hmmm," said Kashif.

Afsana, on a mission, cheerfully went to the halal meat store to pick up boneless chicken breasts and then to the supermarket to pick up ingredients for the stuffing: *spinach, mushrooms, bread crumbs, mozzarella cheese*. When she got home, she carefully put away her items. She wanted to make sure she could find the ingredients when she needed them. There was something about her system of organization that was directly at odds with Humara's. It frustrated Afsana to no end. At times she would be left in tears when she could not find a utensil she was looking for, and Kashif would try to comfort her as if she was a child.

"There, there," he would say. "I'm sure it's there. You just missed it."

It was on a Sunday afternoon that Afsana began preparing dinner. The first thing she needed to do, was defrost the chicken breasts. She looked for them in the freezer, but they weren't there.

"OK, they've got to be here somewhere," she said. Slowly, she moved around all the items of the freezer, thinking they might be hidden by something, but she did not see them. Then, one by one, she took each item out of the freezer. When the freezer was empty, she began to freak out.

"Kashif, my chicken breasts are gone. Do you know what happened to them?"

"Dear, I'm sure they're there. Where could they have walked off? It's not as if they have wings," said Kashif, smiling at his own joke.

"Don't patronize me, Kashif. They're not there."

"What do you think—that someone stole them? You're not sounding rational. Maybe *Ammah* can help you find them." Kashif walked over to his mother, who sat knitting on the chaise.

"*Ammah,* do you have any idea where Afsana's chicken could have gone? It seems to have flown the coup."

Humara raised an eyebrow but did not look up. "Oh. Now that I think about it, I did see some chicken pieces in the freezer a couple of days ago. They were sitting there for so long. I didn't know if you were ever going to make them, so I put them in the large freezer in the pantry until you were ready for them."

"Ha! Mystery solved," said Kashif, not noticing Afsana fuming.

Afsana went to the pantry and took out her chicken breasts. Then, when she could not find the can of soup and some other items she was looking for, she sweetly asked Humara if she knew where they might be.

"Perhaps you could show me," Afsana asked, and sure enough, Humara had re-shelved all of the items. She had forgotten to tell Afsana and was very sorry for the inconvenience. Afsana cooked so infrequently that it hadn't occurred to her that she might want to use them.

Finally, Afsana assembled the ingredients and defrosted the chicken breasts, stuffed them, glazed them, and preheated the oven. She put the chicken in. It should have been done in thirty minutes, but when she checked the oven, the pieces still looked raw. She let them sit for twenty minutes more. There was still no change, so she turned the oven up. *That should do it,* she thought, and she went into the living room to watch TV. Fifteen minutes later, a smoky aroma drifted into the room. The hairs on Afsana's neck stood up. She ran to the kitchen. The chicken had turned a deep brown, all the liquid in the baking pan had dried up, and the edges of the pan were encrusted in black. Quickly, Afsana turned off the oven and grabbed the chicken, putting it on the cool surface of the stove. It sat bubbling. Tears blurred her vision.

"Dinner's ready," she called out.

Afsana could only remember how red she felt, how she felt her face and the back of her neck burning up during dinner when everyone sat picking at their chicken. It was way too dry. The cheese had fizzled and burnt out. Only five-year-old Adnan seemed to be unaware of the awkwardness.

"It's very tasty," said Kashif, taking a mouthful and washing it down with a glass of water. "Can't wait to see what's for dessert."

"I like the cheese," said Adnan.

"These are very interesting spices. However did you make this, dear?" said Humara.

"I just marinated it, stuffed it, *and burnt it*, in the oven" said Afsana.

"Burnt it! Oh, *Berta* you must only use the stovetops. You can't bake anything in that oven. It's so unpredictable."

Upon hearing this, Afsana gave Kashif one of her *"see what I mean?"* looks. After half an hour of everyone picking at their food, Afsana cleared the plates, feeling like a total and miserable failure. Dessert was a store bought cake.

❖ ❖ ❖

That night, Afsana and Kashif had one of their biggest fights.

"Your mother is insufferable."

"Your cooking is not her fault. I don't understand how you can blame her for this."

"I don't understand how you cannot. I'm tired of this, Kashif. I want to move out. I don't understand why we have to live here with your family."

"Oh, no. Not this again," said Kashif. The quarrel continued well into the night until a frustrated Afsana threw Kashif's pillow and blanket out the bedroom door and Kashif spent the night in the study.

Humara re-organized the kitchen that night, as she did every night, humming a wistful tune before the night was done, she'd re-arrange the linen closets…

FOURTEEN

When the Bough Breaks, the Cradle Will Fall
Chicago, Illinois, 1990

It was a warm morning, making the smell of the streets that much more pungent as vendors lined up their wares for sale. Humara briskly walked past all of them, knowing that they did not have what she was looking for. While most of the city slept, Chinatown was starting to awaken with quiet activity. Shop owners, street vendors, and restaurateurs started preparing for the day at hand. It was only at the outer fringe of the market that she found the place she sought—a small shop in an even smaller alley. The owner had a reputation for selling hard-to-find items and ingredients that Humara could not do without, including small "pets" when they came into season: hamsters, squirrels, turtles, and chickens. It all depended on when the next shipment arrived. It was there that Humara had come to purchase a live chicken, but the best they could do that day was rabbit. Humara looked at the scrawny, slightly malnourished animal. *Did it have to be white?* she thought.

"Just one left," said the owner. "Gone by tomorrow.

The Mother-in-Law Cure

Take it or leave it."

The price he was charging was exorbitant, but the animal was alive and frisky. *It will have to do,* she thought. She had already left little Adnan by himself for way too long. She would make it work. At least she would be back home that morning instead of in the middle of the day, where nosy neighbors might notice her unusual purchase hopping around in the backyard. She did not like the attention they had been getting lately. Kashif and Afsana had progressed from fighting at home to fighting in public, turning their marriage into a peep show for the entire community. Amidst the separation, people were watching them all with much more scrutiny. It had been a quiet year, and this was the most delicious piece of gossip to come up in a while…but that was where it would end, thought Humara. She had risen when it was still black outside and taken two taxis and the train so that she could be at the market early and back home again before Adnan left for school—before he really knew she was gone.

When Humara arrived home, it was eight thirty in the morning. Adnan was almost out the door.

"Where were you?" he said, panicked. "I came down, and you were gone. You didn't leave a note or anything."

"Remember, I told you that I might have to go out for a little while in the morning. I told you that you might have to fix your own breakfast," she said. Humara had not intended for Adnan to see the rabbit, but he spotted it before she had a chance to put it in the garage.

"Wow, what's that?" he said, seeing the cage in her hand.

"This…this is a pet. I'm just holding it for an auntie," she said. "I'll have to give it back soon."

"Can I pet it?"

But before Humara had a chance to say, "No, you'll be late for school," Adnan had already unfastened the cage and was holding the rabbit in his hands and stroking its fur. He held it up to his face.

"What's your name, little guy? I think I'll call you 'Tasmanian Devil' or maybe 'Bugs the Second.'"

"Adnan, you'll be late for school. Besides, the rabbit is not for you. It's for Auntie. She'll be coming by for it tomorrow."

"I know," he said, feeling a little dejected.

Adnan had never had a pet. Humara thought he was too irresponsible to take care of an animal, and she herself had no interest in cleaning and taking care of one. Kashif had always promised him that they would get a dog together. They had even gone to the pet store and decided that they both really liked a Lab, but then Kashif had gone away to med school, and when he finally came home, he was engaged to Afsana. So Adnan was again left to find his own friends.

"They're not going to eat the rabbit, are they?" asked Adnan, concerned.

"No sweetheart. It's a pet for Auntie's daughter."

"Good," said Adnan, relieved. He grabbed his book bag and headed out the door, glad to be leaving the empty house. At one point, it had felt as if they were a real family, when Afsana and Kashif were happy. The house was full of people and noise, but then Afsana had left and Kashif had started working more and more. Now there was silence, and *Ammah* acted as if she barely noticed.

He wished that he could keep the rabbit or get a dog. Then he could play catch and teach the dog tricks, take it to the park, and walk it after school. His friend Jamaal had a dog, but his would be bigger and better. His dog would kick Jamaal's dog's hairy ass. He didn't need a rabbit; he was going to have a great big dog one day . . .

When Adnan came home from school, he went into the garage to check on the rabbit. He wondered what rabbits ate. Perhaps he should feed it or give it some water. Adnan checked the cage, but it was empty; the rabbit was gone...He went out into the yard. He could hear a rustling.

The rabbit was watching him.

"Here bunny...bunny...bunny," he began to call out but the rabbit eluded him and then all of a sudden, he got very scared. He thought he saw dark red eyes looking at him from the shadows. Adnan got back on his bike and headed to Jamaal's house—maybe they could hang out.

When Adnan was long gone and the street had become silent, Humara emerged from behind a large tree in the garden. She still had the bunny in her hand.

❖ ❖ ❖

Despite Humara's attempt at discretion, the community loved a scandal, and an eligible doctor going through a divorce was always susceptible to speculation. They all wondered what had happened to break up such a perfect couple.

Perhaps he was having an affair...
Perhaps she was too frigid. Doctors always worked long hours—it was just a matter of time before it started to affect the relationship...
Then again, maybe it was the mother-in-law...everyone knew she had never liked the girl...

When Afsana moved out, some speculated that Humara had asked her to leave. Others said that Kashif had begged her to stay. All agreed that a change had occurred in the energy of the house from that day. Passersby could sense its remoteness, like a house waiting to be haunted.

It wasn't the type of day that would make you raise an eyebrow. In fact, there was nothing unusual about it except for the chirping of birds. The winter snow had begun to melt, bringing with it the promise of an early spring, lulling everyone into a false sense of security. Only those who paid attention might notice that the air was a little too still and the call of the birds a little too hollow, not really announcing the new season but warning of the storm at hand.

It was on a morning such as this that Afsana did not arrive for work. First, she was five minutes late, then fifteen, and then twenty-five, and then two hours... Several messages were left at her home and on her cell. She had been paged half a dozen times. It was the first time in years that Afsana had missed a day of work. Soon she had not only missed a day of work but a meeting with her lawyer, her day in court, and her sister's birthday. No one answered the knocks on her door until her lawyer convinced the super to let him in. They found her on the floor of her bedroom, barely breathing, her body worn out after going through several convulsions and lying in a pool of blood, soaked from the waist down.

"Call 911," said her lawyer. "I think she's had a miscarriage."

Even as the paramedics rushed her to the hospital, the life seeped out of her body in small whispers. Eventually, there was nothing they could do to resuscitate her. Afsana Ashruf was pronounced dead at two a.m. that morning.

❖ ❖ ❖

Culturally, funerals are considered a religious event, one that everyone will attend regardless of whether they knew the deceased or not. Afsana's was no exception. The entire community attended, and her parents and siblings flew in from out of state along with close childhood friends and colleagues, as many had known both Afsana and Kashif. There was some speculation as to whether the Ashrufs would attend the funeral, but the whole family came. They said that Kashif cried when he saw the coffin and that Humara stood stoically, ignoring the suspicious and sometimes accusatory glances of those who loved Afsana. Adnan, who was a beautiful child even then, stood silent and withdrawn, not saying much and not showing any emotion, as if going through an elaborate ritual. Yet, when the funeral was over and everyone went back to daily life, it was Adnan who had trouble sleeping for several months afterward. But no one noticed that. What everyone did notice was how quickly Humara had aged—*almost overnight.*

Her posture had become stooped; her hair gray, her eyes had sunk into their sockets, and fine lines began to appear around her eyes and the corners of her mouth. It wasn't long before people began to mistake her for an old woman.

After the funeral, whether the Ashrufs realized it or not, they were not living in the house alone. Afsana's spirit was drawn to the house the way one is drawn to a familiar scent. She wandered through the grounds until she found what she was looking for, buried deep within the soft earth beneath Humara's rosebushes, whose soft pink blossoms would never betray the innocence of the decaying rabbit that lay underneath, with its eyes removed and its genitals stitched together. It was here that the restless soul hovered and here that it remained, marking the house and marking the people in the house. From then on, neighbors would look at the house with suspicion; children would make up stories about the family that lived there, daring one another to knock on the door when a ball accidentally fell into the backyard; and pedestrians would inadvertently quicken their pace as they walked by, not knowing why they felt such apprehension.

FIFTEEN

The Ants Go Marching One By One

Saturday was as good a day as any for an outing. The torrential rains had subsided to a manageable shower, and even the temperature had improved. Clad in raincoats and umbrellas, carrying purses, allergy medication, bottled water, and snacks, the two clans ventured into the precarious streets of Little India, where the hustle and bustle had died down to a mild buzz as a result of the rain. The weather had hindered customers, and retailers were ready to bargain. With thoughts of fabulous deals running through their heads, the Lakahnis and the Ashrufs rushed from store to store with Kashif or Mr. Lahakani pushing Humara's formidable wheelchair.

It wasn't the type of courtship one would expect for anyone with modern values, but Adnan *was* the Brat Prince and Baby was *not* his Cinderella. It became obvious to the old woman early on that Adnan was not going to call or email Baby, much less take her out on a date. The old woman, therefore, had to devise some other way to bring the two families together. It had been Kashif's idea to take the Lakahnis on a tour of Devan Street, otherwise known as Little India.

One could always sense the district before arriving from the aroma of the street vendors selling everything from samosas to *chaat papri* and *pani poori*. The scents drifted from Devan Street to its neighboring blocks. It was one of Miriam's favorite places and reminded her of life in the old country, of a place Miriam had not lived since her childhood and would never again visit. There, the ghosts of her childhood waited for her—memories of her parents, her friends, and her cousins. It was because of them that she had developed a taste for spicy food. Food at the Ashruf household was often a bland, watered-down version of the real thing.

"Makes your stomach growl, doesn't it?" whispered Adnan softly.

"I never touch the stuff," said Kashif. "You never know how they prepare it, and it always gives me heartburn."

Adnan just rolled his eyes.

Humara, who directed Kashif to the stores she wanted to see, led the Ashruf-Lakahni caravan. Everyone else followed, with Rosina Lakahni keeping pace with Humara and chatting endlessly about nothing in particular and Adnan walking a tightrope in between Baby and Miriam. If Adnan thought a family setting would cocoon him against Baby's flagrant advances, he was mistaken. Every time Baby brushed up next to him, she nearly knocked him over, forcing Adnan to grab hold of Miriam to steady himself. At times she would attempt to grab his hand or whisper in his ear; at one point Adnan let out a yelp as Baby pinched his bottom. Miriam stifled a chuckle, but Adnan turned as red as a beet. Baby only smiled indulgently and giggled as if dealing with a naughty puppy. *Run if you must, but soon you will be mine*, she seemed to say.

In little more than two hours, they had visited two jewelry shops and one boutique, but Humara had seemed unimpressed. When stores did not have a wheelchair ramp (and most did not), Kashif and Adnan had to carry Humara's wheelchair up the stairs and into the boutiques while a member of the family held the door open. After doing this two or three times, Kashif looked so out of breath and sweaty that Miriam thought it might cause a premature heart attack, but Humara did not seem fazed. She was on a mission, and she had just spotted what she was looking for the way a sailor spots land after several months at sea. An expression of naked triumph passed over her as she said, "Oh, there's that new boutique I've been hearing so much about *Dulan*, up ahead. Kashif, I want to go there."

"Yes, *Ammah*," said Kashif, trudging along like a dutiful son.

Just above the store hung the face of a beautiful bride dressed in turquoise and gold, her eyes cast downward shyly. The store window contained mannequins dressed in opulent wedding attire, looking both elegant and stylish, like an ad out of *Asian Bride*.

"Oh, no," moaned Adnan, but Baby's expression after seeing the billboard was nearly orgasmic. Humara marched right in—or did what might constitute marching for an old woman in a wheelchair. In military fashion, they all traipsed in behind her and began to appraise the stock. Mrs. Lakahni went towards the saris, Miriam started looking at the spring wear, and Kashif looked at all the prices, wondering how much the store was going to set him back. Only Adnan hung back and seemed disinterested until Baby grabbed his arm and dragged him to the back of the store to look at formal and bridal wear.

It had been a slow day. Ram Virk was about to go on break and grab a cup of chai when he looked across the counter to see a jubilant obese girl clutching a terrified-looking young man like a prize she had just won at the local fair.

"Excuse me... Yes, I would like to see some of those suits over there," she said pointing to a sheer gold suit, a bright turquoise number, and a shocking pink *langa* (skirt). The clerk took the outfits out in large and extra-large sizes, but even those looked dainty in comparison to the girl who stood before him. Humara and Mrs. Lakahni, being close by, heard the request and made their way to the back of the store. Miriam followed soon after. The outfits Baby had chosen were all shiny, glittery, or clubby in bright, over-the-top colors. Many of them had low-cut or sheer elements, plunging necklines, short sleeves or no sleeves, or blouses designed to expose the midriff—the type of fashion that Baby loved and Baby went right to work ploughing through them comparing this one with that, holding the various colors next to her skin, *hmm...which suit would bring out her complexion the best?*

While everyone else was attending to Baby, Miriam decided to walk around the store. She looked at the various mannequins ornately dressed. There were some simple cotton suits in the back, there was also a glass case filled with jewelry. Most of it was gold but there was some crystal mixed in, and if you didn't want to spend quite that much, there also a ton of faux jewelry. It looked remarkably real. It was kept up front in velvet boxes. Even though the gems were fake she knew each set would still cost hundreds of dollars - almost as much as the outfits themselves. Many women in the community were willing to pay an outrageous amount in the blink of an eye to have a set that matched their outfit. Every time Miriam saw Sonia at a formal event, her clothes and jewelry were always stunning.

Miriam inadvertently let out a sigh. She could hear Baby's incessant chattering in the background. She saw Kashif walk out the door with Adeel Lakahni. They were talking to a street vendor then headed towards a coffee shop across the street. *Guess they're ditching Adnan,* she thought. She couldn't blame them. Adnan was caught in the middle as three women surrounded him with outfits of different shapes and colors. This was definitely going to take a while. Miriam plopped herself down in front of a glass counter and started brooding. Miriam was lost in her own thoughts when she heard the sales clerk say,

"We have that outfit."

"*What?*"

That's when Miriam noticed the magazine, *Desi Bride*, on the counter flipped open to a page with model wearing a dusty pink *langha* (skirt) decorated with pearls and a cropped sleeveless blouse exposing the midriff. A shear stole hung from her shoulder, adding to the allure of the gown.

"We have this in stock, it would look great on you…"

"*Umm…I don't know*," said Miriam.

"Just try it on," she said pulling the outfit out from a shelf.

"If it doesn't work we'll try something else… *but I think it will.*" she added with a wink."

Miriam reluctantly followed her into the change room.

❖ ❖ ❖

Baby had gone through twenty outfits. Nothing was exactly right. The sales clerk a man of modest size was now glistening with perspiration, his armpits wet with moisture from all the heavy lifting. Each outfit was large (especially in Baby's size) ornate and moving several of them up and down the shelves was enough to make Ram's heart beat fast. Finally, the ladies had narrowed it down to three.

"Three very sexy outfits for a beautiful woman," said the clerk, knowing where his bread was buttered and winking at Adnan.

"Let me take a couple more out that I think you would like," he said, taking out a red-and-yellow tie-dyed *salwar kameez* with silver embroidery. Baby looked at the outfits, carefully holding them up against her.

"They're all very beautiful," said Mrs. Lakahni. Everyone else looked skeptically at the clothes and then back at Baby. *Would anyone dare suggest something more conservative?* There was an awkward silence, and then they all did a double take as Humara said to Baby, "*Berta*, why don't you try them on? You might find a good engagement outfit."

"Wonderful idea," said the clerk, seizing the opportunity to make his commission.

Baby chose a gold sequined outfit that made Miriam's eyes hurt. It had a wide neck that was covered in gauzy fabric, making certain that "the girls" got lots of exposure. Baby came out of the changing room looking like the sun on steroids.

The image of Baby looking as if she had just stepped out of a Bollywood movie from the '70s made Adnan relieved that disco was long dead. Baby, catering to a different opinion, admired herself in the mirror, pleased with the outfit's effect. She turned to Adnan coquettishly and ran her hands over her hips like a Hollywood vixen. "Do you like it, love bug? I think it really brings out my figure."

"*Wah*, I've never seen this outfit look so good on anyone," said the clerk. "Shall I ring it up?"

"What do you think, Adnan? Does it bring out my eyes?" she cooed. By this time, Kashif and Adeel Lakhani had walked back into the store and were enjoying the show – a full-figured Baby prancing around in front of the mirror.

"*I... I...um...it's nice...*" stammered Adnan, getting more and more uncomfortable and embarrassed, looking from one person to the next for help and then his jaw dropped.

Walking shyly out of the dressing room was Miriam... clad in a rose colored gown that shimmered in the light,

Miriam was a vision of loveliness. It took a while for the rest to notice. First it was Kashif, and then the old woman, then the Lakahnis and finally Baby that began following his gaze. At first it looked like one of the mannequins in the window had come to life – *just like that, it was magic.*

Miriam walked slowly towards the group. Everyone had fallen silent, their expressions blank, and their jaws hanging. Time had stopped. She was vaguely aware of the *tick…tick*…of the clock behind her.

The sales girl beamed, adjusting Miriam's hair to add a crystal choker. *It was just the right touch.*

"There, doesn't she look beautiful?"

Alas, time could not stand still forever, time had to begin again and when it did, it came down with a crash. It started with the old woman. Slowly, her blank expression became contorted with rage; her eyes became as black as midnight and her lips filled with blood.

That's when the sales girl realized she had made a *big* mistake as all three women pounced on Miriam like hyenas on a bloody carcass.

"*What is the meaning of this?*" said Humara practically jumping out her wheelchair.

"What…what is this?" she said grabbing the delicate stole off of Miriam's body looking at it with naked disgust.

"We're supposed to be finding an outfit for *Baby*," added Mrs. Lakahnis.

"Why…why wasn't I shown that outfit?" asked an outraged Baby.

"Well…well, it didn't come in your size," said Ram Virk nervously and then immediately regretted it as all three women glared down at him with undisguised fury, thus taking some of the heat off Miriam… but it would not end there.

"*For God sake Miriam, take off that blasted necklace,*" said Kashif reaching for her neck. Miriam took a step back as Kashif's fingers narrowly escaped her throat.

"*Wait!*" said the sales girl. "That's a piece of

merchandise! If you break it you will have to pay for it. It unclasps in the back," she said walking around Miriam and unfastening the choker.

"*Quickly...go back in the change room,*" she whispered. "*You need to get out of this outfit.*"

She need not have said anymore as Miriam rushed back into the change room trembling and gulping back sobs. She could hear yelling outside. Baby seemed to be in hysterics. The two women were attempting to soothe her and Adeel Lakahni was threatening the sales clerk.

Miriam came out of the room. The sales clerk whisked the clothes out of her hand, and everyone began shouting at once.

"*What were you trying to do?*"
"*We can't afford that outfit...*"
"*You're supposed to be here to help Baby...*"
"*You've always been jealous...*"

❖   ❖   ❖

Miriam's head began to spin and for the first time in her life, Miriam followed her instincts... and ran. She ran past the angry mob, past Adnan who seemed to reach out to her, and out the door - *from the heat of the store, to the cool of the pouring rain.* The faster she ran, the more she got wet.

The weather was getting much worse but it didn't matter to Miriam; she ran without thinking about where she was going. She ran until her vision blurred, her breathing became laborious and her legs gave out. A crash of thunder gave Miriam pause to think.

It had become windy and Miriam was colder than she realized. There were few shops around in this area. Up ahead she saw a light in the window and a sign that read '*Custom Tailoring*'. Miriam ran inside.

It was a tiny shop with mountains and mountains of

half-finished outfits laid out in disarray.

"Hello," Miriam called out... silence.

She walked slowly through the shop dripping on the carpet like a leaky faucet. The warm air inside made her realize just how wet she actually was.

"Hello," Miriam called out, that's when she felt something brush-up against her shoulder. "Oh," said Miriam thinking it might be a real person but when she turned around it was a common, run of the mill dressmaker's dummy made from wood and plastic.

Miriam was about to turn back when she noticed a staircase in the corner of the room. She stood at the bottom and stared up the long narrow passageway before she started her ascent. The creaking steps announced Miriam's arrival but when she got to the top, she saw no one, at first.

The second floor was as disorganized as the one below, scattered around the room was more merchandise for sale, mundane stuff: old Bollywood movies, religious items, books, scarves. This hodgepodge of items was liberally organized and, in Miriam's opinion, contained nothing useful.

She was about to go back downstairs when she heard the rustling of a curtain. At the back of the room was a dark velvet curtain that Miriam assumed led to the storage area. *Perhaps there was a salesclerk roaming around somewhere.*

Miriam lifted the heavy curtain and walked in. It took Miriam a couple of seconds to adjust to the darkness, but when she did, it became clear that the room was not used for storage. It bore the faint smell of incense, and shelves were lined with religious, almost cultish-looking items. Next to them were bottles of various shapes and sizes, all holding unidentifiable substances. Astrological charts were pinned to the walls.

Miriam picked up a bottle. The label was written in a script she could not understand.

"*That is not for sale,*" said someone from behind. "*What*

The Mother-in-Law Cure

are you doing in here?"

Startled, Miriam dropped the bottle. It fell to the ground with a *clink*. Luckily, it was not broken.

Miriam turned around. The woman before her was of indecipherable age. She wore a scarf around her hair and a loose tunic. Although her face was unlined, her complexion was dark, and her voice was hoarse, even a little raspy, like someone who had spent the better part of her life with a cigarette in her mouth.

"Let me take a look at you girl...have a seat dear," she said motioning her towards a chair in front of table.

Miriam sat down. The woman sat across from her. Miriam was about to speak, explain that she was about to leave when the woman shushed her.

"If you're here, it must be for a reason. Let me see your hand."

Miriam tentatively held out her hand. The woman grabbed it possessively. She studied the hand...she said nothing. A couple minutes passed when Miriam felt a tickle in her nose.

"*Ahh...Ahh...Ahchoo...*" Miriam sneezed grabbing her hand and bringing it up to her nose.

"You're sick!" exclaimed the woman.

Miriam held her hand out again but the woman looked at it as if it were a used Kleenex.

"That's ok," said the woman and for a moment there was an awkward silence.

"Chains," she continued. "I see chains; loops upon loops going through your lifeline, like a little bracelet... the chains of destiny."

"Happiness is for the afterlife. It's what I've always been told," said Miriam stifling another sneeze.

"Is it...? I have something for you...for your illness," she said raising an eyebrow.

She reached into her pocket and fished out a small vile held it to the light and looked at it closely.

"This will flush out all the toxins from your life."

"You mean my body, don't you?" said Miriam but the woman ignored her.

"Just follow the instructions," she said.

"Instructions . . ." said Miriam, looking closely at the label. But the wording was tiny and the cold was making her vision blurry. When she looked up the woman was gone.

Miriam was alone in an empty room. She put the vial in her pocket and hurried out, ran down the stairs and out the door. She kept looking over her shoulder as if being chased by something. She had an uneasy feeling that someone was following her. Miriam dropped the vial in a nearby garbage can. As soon as she stepped outside, her cell phone began to ring. It was Adnan.

"Where are you? We've been trying to reach you for an hour."

"Sorry, my signal has been going in and out, must be the weather."

"I'm glad I caught you. We're heading out to lunch at Lahore Tikka House. Do you know where that is, can you meet us?"

"Yeah, I'll be right there."

❖ ❖ ❖

When Miriam arrived at the restaurant, they had already been seated. They were busily looking over the menus and finalizing their selections. If she hadn't arrived when she did, they may have started without her. As it was, no one looked at her as she approached the table. She took an empty seat at the end of the table next to Kashif. *So they were giving her the cold shoulder.*

Once the order was taken, there was a stream of awkward chitchat, but Miriam need not have worried, the drab mood only lasted until the entrees began to arrive. Lahore Tikka House was not Little India's best Kebab house without reason. The aroma of seasoned beef and chicken reminded everyone of how hungry they were, temporarily lulling their tempers. The waiter lined their table with dishes of spicy beef and chicken and a truce was reached.

For the next hour the Lakahnis and the Ashrufs resembled any other family at the restaurant as they passed around entrees and the various flavors of chutneys – from spicy, to sweet and sour, to mint. Miriam's favorite was spicy beef with a tangy chutney. Everyone ate a great deal, especially Baby, who plowed through lightly seasoned lamb kebabs, absorbing herself in the meal as her mind reeled through a solution for her problems.

Upon finishing lunch, the seven adults realized they would have to run to the car. Gripping their umbrellas tightly with one hand and bags full of leftovers and shopping in the other, they advanced into the rain. The wind lashed out angrily at everything in its path, pushing and pulling at Miriam's small umbrella that now appeared as fragile as a Kleenex in a hurricane. Miriam pressed on, and the umbrella dismantled almost completely. *Well, this is great*, she thought as she let the wind claim her umbrella and carry it to the land of lost causes. She would have to fight the wind and the rain on her own. With her arms against her face, she trudged forward, afraid that a strong gust of wind would blow her away like her unfortunate umbrella, when a sturdy hand reached out and took hold of her. Miriam looked up to Adnan's smiling face. He had Miriam securely in one arm and his umbrella in the other.

"For a second, I thought you weren't going to make it. Don't let this tornado take you to Oz. It's a long way from the Midwest," he said.

Miriam smiled back gratefully, feeling warm for the first time. She and Adnan, huddled together, were the last to reach the car. Perhaps it was the fact that Adnan had his arm around her or that Miriam was smiling shyly or that the rain had abruptly started to die down, but one was left with the image of two sweethearts out for a stroll—an image that struck terror in the heart of Baby and made Humara feel nervous. Kashif sat back smugly.

Miriam could not understand the feeling of tension that awaited her in the car. Kashif was humming in a sinister way, and Humara was even more aloof than usual.

"This weather is getting quite chilly. I trust you kept warm," she said, but Miriam could not tell whether she was talking to her or Adnan.

❖ ❖ ❖

Loneliness is a withered old blanket that fails to protect you from the harsh winds outside your door. Baby felt confused, being the only daughter of well-to-do parents, she had not considered that Adnan might not feel the same way about her. So far, she had interpreted Adnan's behavior as shyness. Now, suddenly, suspicion began to take hold. *Why was he not playing the role of the enamored suitor?* She wondered. *Could there be another reason besides debilitating shyness?* There was one name that kept popping into her head over and over again – *Miriam!*

Baby's state of mind was not lost on Humara and one day she decided to intervene. The old woman crept up on the large girl like a tigress on its prey. She found Baby alone in the kitchen wondering if there were any left overs in the fridge. She invited Baby to sit down with her.

"You're such a good girl," she said stroking her hair. "Such a good girl, beautiful girl, but you do not look happy…?"

Humara had struck a nerve. All her life Baby had been in the proverbial shadow of thinner girls, slimmer girls, girls with perfect hourglass figures. Her eyes began to well up.

"I see…I see what it is now." said Humara, her voice moist with emotion.

"You want to be like Miriam. I can see it… thin and

The Mother-in-Law Cure

graceful and dainty. I have something....I've said too much. I shouldn't tempt you..."

"No Auntie... please," her lips began to tremble.

"I want Adnan to...to ...to," but Baby wasn't able to finish.

"No need to worry child. Drink some tea. It will make you feel better."

Resting before Baby was a cup of tea. She had not noticed it before. She held the cup in her hands and began to take gentle sips. Humara looked at her greedily.

Strangely enough she did feel better. Her appetite for an after dinner snack was gone. She walked out of the kitchen feeling grateful to have such an understanding mother-in-law. Maybe she could be the girl Adnan wanted after all.

❖ ❖ ❖

Humara took the cup Baby had used and carefully hid it in the folds of her Sari. No need to leave this lying around.

SIXTEEN

If I Should Die Before I Wake . . .

Miriam dreamed, not for the first time that she was running beyond the house, beyond the city, and beyond the suburbs, into a wooded area that she had never seen before. Fog was all around her. It enveloped her so that she could neither see what lay ahead nor what she had left behind. Eyes closed, she ran until she hit a clearing, and there she lay, gasping and out of breath, her eyes still closed but somehow sensing that she had passed the penetration of the mist.

Miriam tried to sit up and see where she was, but she felt an unknown weight upon her. There was a tightening around her throat, and even through her vision was blurred, she sensed small hands with a grip that was getting ever more forceful. There was something familiar about the attacker—the energy, the scent, the small stature. It was someone she knew. Summoning all her strength, she looked into the face of the unknown person, and for the first time, she saw her clearly.

The attacker—the woman is screaming, choking the

life out of her like a jealous lover, a malignant spirit, and even as the forest and the clearing fade and are replaced by her familiar mahogany furniture, the apparition lingers for a few more moments until she disappears completely and Miriam is left alone in the darkness, panting, with the familiar sound of Kashif snoring beside her. She lies breathing heavily, treasuring the large supply of air that she has always taken for granted. She checks the time. It is two a.m., and she has a headache.

She does not know where the headaches are coming from, but they're getting more and more frequent. *Better to take something now than wake up tomorrow morning with my head pounding,* she thinks. Slowly, she gets out of her warm bed and orients herself in the darkness. She hears the pattering of rain on the rooftop. *Will it ever end?* Will the rain not be happy until it's taken everything, every piece of dry land and warm sky, drowning them beneath the water like cities lost in ancient fables?

Downstairs, it is cool, making her bare arms break out in goose bumps. Miriam realizes that Humara has turned the heat down, but she doesn't mind the cold air. It feels good next to her sweat-ridden body. Miriam goes into the kitchen and grabs some aspirin and a glass of water. Not realizing how thirsty she is, she gulps the water down, enjoying its cool, smooth sensation. She should go back to sleep, but there is something about the quietness of the house that makes her want to stay awake. It's as if she is the only person there . . . as if she's the only person in the world.

Miriam thinks a bit more about the dreams she's been having; different dreams, but all ending the same way with Afsana choking the life out her and uttering garbled words that she cannot understand, as if Afsana is under water. She is angry and distressed, that much is certain, but this dream was the first time she's ever acted out. In the past, she's been content to whisper in her ear, pull a lock of Miriam's hair, and run like a playful child or a trickster.

Unable to solve much at the moment, Miriam realizes that it's almost three a.m. and decides to go to bed, hoping she can fall back asleep, but it is the rain keeping her up, each drop a warning, trickling down her spine bringing back echoes of her past. A past that was not always unhappy, sheltered in the warmth of her parent's love, Miriam never noticed their poverty. Although their meals were simple, there was enough to fill her stomach; and although her clothes were never new, her mother always managed to alter them into a shape that was becoming; and even when there was little money, there was always enough to send her to school. Miriam never considered it a life of hardship, despite the reigning belief that happiness is for the afterlife. Miriam never felt unhappy, not until she met the Ashrufs. She never felt she needed patience, to endure the struggles of this life. Yet the doctrine was always there while she was growing-up, a warning of sorts. When crops failed due drought or flood, when children were taken in their infancy, when there was not enough money for food, let alone dowries, it was this belief that kept the faithful going. *Your reward is yet to come. Endure your fate. This life is one of struggle and hardship; happiness is for the afterlife.*

It was the mantra of the faithful, of every good believer. However, it did not seem to be the mantra of the Ashrufs. It did not seem to be the mantra of Humara. The old woman was not going to wait for the afterlife for anything…

It was a notion that began as an inkling; a delicate seed, taking root and flourishing into a full-fledged wave of realization. The truth came crashing down on her like thunder. Miriam now understood what it really was… *the mantra of the poor, the weak, and the oppressed.*

This germ of truth lay dormant within her for years. Her first hint of its existence occurred to her at her own wedding when a plea to accept her destiny was whispered lovingly by her own old aunt. Now the echo she was hearing in her ear was not the desperate whisper of her aunt but the cold hiss of her mother-in-law. *Accept your fate...*

It is enough to drive away any blissful remnants of sleep, but fortunately, these are not Miriam's last thoughts before she drifts away. The last sound she hears is a voice that she thought she had forgotten a long time ago, the gentle hum of a mother lulling her child back to sleep, the sound just loud enough over the pitter patter of rain.

❖ ❖ ❖

As Kashif came downstairs, he was hit with a pang of confusion. Miriam was still in the shower, and yet there was this *aroma* coming from the kitchen. Was it his imagination, or was someone making breakfast? Humara had propped a booster on her wheelchair and was in the kitchen scrambling eggs, making toast, boiling tea. The last time Humara made breakfast, Afsana was still alive. He felt the hairs on his arm tingle with anticipation of not just the meal but of what it represented. He sat down at the dining table, and Humara put warm eggs and toast in front of him. She appeared to be in a good mood.

Miriam came down for breakfast but was not in the mood for any of it. She sat picking at her cereal. It was the only thing she could hold down. She woke up feeling tired and not looking forward to her day. In contrast, Adnan was up early and looking rather chipper, taking hearty bites out of his eggs and toast as he flipped through his new iPhone.

"Tea, Miriam?" said Humara.

"Thanks," Miriam said and wondered what the devil was going on. *What could have gotten the old woman up and off her butt so early in the morning?* Miriam didn't know, but she wasn't going to look a gift horse in the mouth, and she gratefully sipped her tea before reverting her attention back to Adnan, who was looking well. He was even better dressed than usual, if that was possible. Miriam noted the new outfit . . . *kind of nice for school*, she thought.

"You're looking good this morning," she said, wondering what he had to be so happy about.

"Is that a new watch?" she asked, noting the shiny tag on his wrist, but Adnan didn't answer, too absorbed playing with his new toy. He quickly headed out the door, barely noticing Miriam as he picked up a call on his cell.

Miriam looked over at Kashif, sipping his tea and reading his paper. "He's interning for Adeel Lakahni," said Kashif.

"What?" said Miriam. "What do you mean?"

"They made him an offer he couldn't refuse," said Kashif, doing a lousy Godfather impression.

"Seriously, Adnan is going to start interning with Adeel Lakahni, finish off the semester, and then work for him full time."

"You mean he's not going to go back? He's not going to graduate!"

"What's the use in going back? He may not graduate, anyway. We all know Adnan is not exactly an academic. Adeel Lakahni has made him an offer that's more than generous. Adnan is pretty much set."

"Well, that's just great," said Miriam, feeling too nauseous to finish her cereal and opting instead to gulp down her tea. *So that's why Humara looks so happy.*

"Isn't it wonderful?" says Humara. "Everything is finally working out, and of course there is so much planning to do," she said in that take-charge kind of voice that Miriam had come to know so well.

"We have to set a wedding date, find a hall, and get a caterer and invitations, but even before that, there's the engagement, and I'm going to need your hand in all of it, Miriam."

"Won't the engagement just be announced at the mosque?"

"Well, of course there's that. But I also think it would be nice to have a small party. There hasn't been anything festive in this house in ages."

Miriam had to agree with that. There was nothing festive about the house. She wondered whom they would invite. Who would show up to see this freak show? It was like an accident at the side of the road. Miriam started to feel guilty. She shouldn't refer to Adnan's marriage that way.

So it's finally official, thought Miriam, Adnan was actually going to marry Baby. That was why Humara was in the kitchen humming along like a *desi* Martha Stewart. But was it Adnan who was really going to be set for life, or was it Humara?

❖ ❖ ❖

Adnan enjoyed the feel of soft leather against him, the way it enveloped his body, the way it mingled with the scent of the car—*his car*. He concentrated on that even as his palms sweated against the steering wheel and the pit of his stomach felt empty, devoid of any content (even though he had had a full meal). He tried not to concentrate on the fact that the car didn't really belong to him but was a loaner from his soon-to-be father-in-law. He tried not to think of that because if he did, he'd have to think about a lifetime of Baby. The deal he had made with Adeel Lakahni was straightforward enough, and he tried to focus on that. He tried to focus on what he stood to gain. Baby was a minor obligation, and soon she wouldn't matter at all. Although people had suggested it, Adnan had never really thought of himself as a player. But with Baby tucked away in a respectable neighborhood with 2.5 kids, the world would be his playground. That was what he thought about to fill the emptiness in his gut as he drove his new Beamer to campus and parked in front of Curtis Lecture Hall.

For the first time in his student career, he was early for class, early enough to have found a parking spot. He sat for a few minutes in the driver's seat and watched students pass by. Several of them glanced in his direction—the car was definitely a nicer ride than what most students had. Adnan grinned, checked himself in the mirror, and got out of the car. He was just in time to catch Saif taking a leisurely stroll in his direction. Saif was wearing a beige blazer and sunglasses. He slowed down when he saw Adnan standing on the corner grinning.

"Nice car," said Saif. "Humara up your allowance? Or Kashif get tired of his toy?"

"I got a new job—something you might want to consider."

"Let me guess. Hugo Boss paid you *not* to appear in any more of their ads . . . or maybe this is an advance from the new father-in-law to be. I thought you said that chick was a cow?"

Adnan just smiled "Saif, Saif, you have so much to learn about the world. What are you doing tonight?"

"Why?"

"We've got to take this baby out," said Adnan as he smiled suggestively at a coed passing by. She noticed his stare and smiled back.

"I see you haven't changed your spots."

"Hey, do you want in or not? I'm having dinner today with my fiancée's family, but then I'll pick you up and we'll hit the town."

❖ ❖ ❖

While Adnan was early that day, Miriam had arrived late—not enough energy to run for the bus. The next one came ten minutes late. Not only was it not Miriam's day, but it also looked as if it was not going to be Miriam's week. Although no one had said anything directly, Miriam could tell by the curious stares and sympathetic glances that she must look pretty bad. Some offered her cough drops (though she didn't need them, she politely accepted), and many commented that she must have been working hard lately (though she wasn't working any harder than usual). Was she more stressed than usual? Maybe. There was a sense of dread that sat in her stomach like a heavy rock, unwilling to be flushed out by any amount of stillness.

During lunch, she took a look at herself in the bathroom mirror: sallow skin, dark circles under her eyes, and hair so limp it was begging to be plated and served with marinara sauce. There was definitely something wrong. Her body and perhaps Afsana, too, were trying to tell her something. When the office had quieted down, Miriam went on the Internet in search of a couple of dream dictionaries. She typed the word "choking" in the dream wizard. She didn't know if there was a category for being choked by the dead first wife of your husband. The wizard spat out a definition.

Choking:

To dream that someone is choking you indicates that you are suppressing your emotions or that you may have difficulties in expressing your fears, anger, or love. Consider the phrase "being all choked up." Alternatively, you may feel that you are being prevented or restricted from freely expressing yourself.

Choking dreams are often a fearful experience and it is not uncommon for dreamers to awaken from them.

Unsatisfied, Miriam looked up another definition, but it was no more helpful. She had been suppressing her emotions for years, but it was only recently that the ghostly apparition had started attacking her. The definitions are too generic, she thinks. It must have something to do with me, with my connection to Afsana. Next time she had the dream; Miriam would plan to work harder to make out what Afsana was saying.

SEVENTEEN

Sugar and Spice and Everything Nice that's What Little Girls are Made of...

The day was long over and his old bones were as tired as ever but Adeel Lakahni could not sleep. The time Adeel had spent with Humara had felt like an intoxicating dream, and seeing her again after what seemed like a millennium, as an old woman in a wheelchair had, had a much-needed sobering effect. He had been in love with Humara. He had been crushed when she had left with Naseer. When he saw her for the first time, he felt tears come to his eyes, the woman whose memories his heart had held onto so tightly had withered and aged and become a skeleton of her former self. Time had not been good to Humara Ashruf, and many times Adeel felt as if he was not addressing his old lover but her elderly mother. She was no longer the exotic flower he had fallen in love with, but a shrewd and calculating matriarch—*perhaps she had always been so*. Yet at times, when he heard the tone of her voice, the way she said his name...if he didn't look directly at her, he was there again...back in the desert thirty years ago.

It was for this reason that he feared for his daughter.

The Mother-in-Law Cure

Adnan was much like his mother, perhaps better looking, but they both possessed the same magnetism that drew people in, blinded them and seemed to take away their will. Every day he would see his daughter in front of the mirror eying herself in one outfit or the other, trying out one hair style after another. It was all for Adnan. Adeel thought she might even be on a diet. Last night she ate half the amount she usually did, finishing with only one dessert. Adeel hoped it was working. Although, he noticed Baby eating less during the day, the fridge was curiously empty in the morning, as if someone had ransacked it in the middle of the night. He could hear her now, grunting struggling to get into something that would unfortunately never fit.

❖ ❖ ❖

Baby took another gasp. If one did not know better, one would think she was in the throes of passion. It took one more really strong...push and then finally another gasp for Baby button up her girdle. The new purchase had fit a lot better in the store. The tight spandex of the body-shaping garment clung to her skin, making her thighs look like juicy sausages. Now, for the over garments, a soft wool dress went on top. Unfortunately, it was a bright violet instead of a sophisticated black. No matter how you sliced it, Baby could not stop being Baby. Her voluptuous bosom oozed out of the wide scooped neck and her legs seemed imprisoned in the narrow skirt, so that Baby could only take small mermaid like steps. There were a slew of outfits on Baby's bed waiting to be tried on.

She had spent all of yesterday at the mall putting together a new wardrobe, clothes that would benefit from the new shape enhancing underwear that she had bought. There had only been one store in the entire mall that had a range of plus sized clothes large enough to accommodate Baby. When Baby had first walked in, the clerk had considered turning her away, or recommending she try a specialty store but the clerk had seen the desperation in Baby's eyes. She had seen that wild and crazy look before on women and usually there was a man behind it. That's when the clerk had suggested the girdle. With the girdle, the store's largest outfits had *just* fit and they had fit fairly comfortably at the time, but now only a day later Baby felt as though she could barely breathe. It would be worth it, Baby thought to see the look on Adnan's face when she visited him that night.

But it was Miriam who answered the door when Baby arrived unexpectedly at the Ashruf residences. It was eight in the evening and dinner was over. The old woman, having eaten a particularly heavy meal, had gone upstairs for an after dinner nap. Ironically, her metabolism was exactly the opposite of Baby's; the more she ate…the less she gained.

Miriam was just about to listen to an audio book while she mopped the kitchen floor, when the sound of the doorbell punctuated her out of her thoughts. In the quiet evening it was a jarring sound. Miriam put on slippers on her bare feet and padded across the floor to the entrance. When she opened the door, she took a step back. Baby's heavyset physique framed the doorway. The porch light shone on Baby through the darkness adding to her presence. Miriam was at a loss for words. *Can I help you?* Didn't seem right. Finally, Miriam opened with, "*Baby what a nice surprise…*"

"Thank you…I thought I would…drop by," she said faltering a little.

"Yes, come in…come in," said Miriam widening the door and leading Baby into the more casual family room.

"Is Adnan home?" she asked.

"Oh, he's gone out for the night."

There was an awkward silence until Kashif poked his head in.

"Miriam, who's at the door…?"

And then he saw Baby; she was sitting at one end of the couch trying to cross her legs in her pencil skirt.

"Baby, this is...um unexpected. Your...um parents are well?"

Baby nodded.

"Good. Adnan should be in shortly. I'll let you two girls catch-up," he said scurrying off.

Miriam twiddled her fingers. She wished Kashif had given her more time."

"Baby, can I get you some tea?" But Baby declined.

"How about some cookies," said Miriam rushing into the kitchen and coming back with a box of assorted cookies. Baby grabbed a few and shoved them in her mouth.

"I'm sure Adnan will be thrilled to know that you are here. Let me just give him a call. She said punching in the number to Adnan's cell."

But Miriam only got his voice mail.

"So how are you and Adnan doing?"

"Good, we're very happy and completely in love," said Baby with a smile that looked more like a sneer. It should have been a happy statement but it sounded almost like a threat...a warning. For the next two hours Baby proceeded to go over the plans for the wedding in excruciating detail: *the colors of her outfits, the type of embroidery she wanted, her jewelry, the reception halls they were looking at, the menu and of course the bridal shower, which it turns out Miriam would be responsible for.* Her tone ranged from matter-of-fact to boastful.

"I can tell Adnan is just as excited about it as I am." Miriam gave Baby a polite smile.

"What are *you* going to be wearing," she said a little contemptuously.

Miriam wondered what she had done to make Baby hate her. She wondered when this production was going to be over but, most of all, she wondered when Adnan was going to come home and save her?

"I still haven't decided…" Miriam was starting to respond, when Adnan entered the room. *Speak of the devil,* Miriam thought.

"Hey," he said. "Let's get going," as if he had been waiting for an hour.

"Get your coat," he said looking at Miriam.

Miriam wondered where they would end up.

Adnan took them to one of those trendy dessert places in the heart of downtown, where people go to after a movie or the theater. It was open until three in the morning and most busy around midnight. When they got there, Baby took up most of the entrance, so they had to wait outside. Adnan said something to the hostess and she found a table for five that she put four chairs around. They were discreetly placed in the corner of the restaurant. It was loud. All around Miriam, there was chatter of different conversations going on and music playing in the background, people coming and going. It made Miriam's head buzz. *Night Life.*

The menu was as colorful as the restaurant. They made their own ice-cream and the menu featured many scrumptious concoctions, everything from waffles, to crepes, to sundaes, to the traditional banana split, and all with clever names like '*A Street Car Named Desire,*' or "*La Vida Mocha*'. Judging from what was on the other tables, the desserts were huge. *Probably not the right place to take Baby,* thought Miriam and then, *I can't wait to see what she orders.* Adnan also looked a little nervous as if he thought she was going to clean him out.

"Why don't we split something," Adnan said a little apprehensively.

"I'll just have a small scoop of ice-cream," Baby said closing the menu.

"Just one small…teeny weeny…scoop?" asked Adnan.

"Yup," she replied with a weak smile.

"Okay, then why don't *we* share something," he said

looking at Miriam.

Because Miriam and Adnan both liked bananas, they ordered the *Epicurean George*. It featured banana, mocha and chocolate chip ice cream with loads of bananas, wrapped up in a warm crepe and drizzled with chocolate sauce, whipped cream, brownies and of course more bananas. It was huge platter and looked mountainous beside baby's single scoop of wild raspberry ice-cream.

"Dig in," said Adnan.

The first bite was absolutely divine and Miriam let out a sigh.

"Are you sure you don't want to try some," she said to Baby.

"Maybe, just a taste," said Baby dipping her spoon and scooping up a chunk of brownie. She tried to act nonchalant, but her eyes rolled back into her head. It was the look of an addict.

"Good, isn't it?" said Miriam.

"Yes," she replied taking a deep breath.

Baby took a long drink of water her hand tightly gripping the glass. After her last gulp, she seemed satisfied, content even. Miriam was impressed by her will power and was about to say something, but she was distracted by some chatter at the next table.

The people sitting across from them were complaining about their dessert but it didn't make sense. They said that their dessert was missing…or shrinking or…something of the sort. It was hard to make out exactly, amidst the clatter of the restaurant. It started off a huge platter but it seemed to be getting smaller and smaller. Miriam was sure she could not have been hearing correctly. *Oh well*, thought Miriam getting back to her own *Epicurean George*, noticing that Adnan had already started digging in. A good quarter of it was finished.

As Miriam and Adnan chewed on mouthfuls of crepe, Baby took tiny bites of her single scoop and large gulps of water. They were saved from conversation by the fact that every other person that came into the restaurant made eye contact with Adnan, giving him either a wave or a nod, a few even stopped by their table for an extended hello that turned into a mini-conversation. Adnan, however, made no effort to introduce either Baby or Miriam. Given how much Adnan was socializing, Miriam was surprised he had time to eat at all but the dessert kept getting smaller and smaller. Miriam only had to blink and more of it was gone. When the plate was wiped clean, Adnan asked for the bill.

As they exited the busy restaurant, Baby squeezed out of the crowded doorway her large coat fitting snugly to her body, a blissful expression across her face.

EIGHTEEN

Going to the Chapel of Love

Like a chameleon, Adnan had morphed into a new version of himself. His attire, and even his demeanor, had lost those splashes of color that had made him so lovable. In the past, his vanity had always been tempered by his good sense of humor and his ability to poke fun at himself. Now, that boyish part of his personality lay buried. Instead, a more focused and more confident (if not a little arrogant) Adnan had emerged. Miriam found this new version of Adnan a little unnerving. He always seemed busy, preoccupied…plotting…plotting…plotting. Perhaps that's what working for Adeel Lakahni did.

"Hey, how are you?" asked Miriam one day when she caught Adnan alone. She was just putting away some breakfast dishes.

"You're barely around anymore," she continued.

"Yeah, well the old man keeps me busy," he said referring to Adeel Lakahni.

"I can tell. You look tired, irritable. You should take an afternoon off…play a little hooky," she said with a wink.

"I don't have time to take an afternoon off," and suddenly his tone became colder, harder. Miriam took a step back. It wasn't Adnan's voice anymore it was someone she didn't recognize.

"I don't have time to entertain *you* anymore,"

"That's…that's not what I meant."

"It doesn't matter, I'm bouncing like a ping pong ball between the old woman and the Lakahnis and you…you don't even count," said Adnan shaking his head.

He gave Miriam an insolent stare. He was about to say more but Miriam turned away. He awkwardly packed up his things and left the room.

Still, Humara seemed pleased with the new Adnan.

"Perhaps all he needed was a strong father figure," she commented one afternoon.

"He has always had me," said Kashif.

"Of course, dear, but not everyone can be a natural leader, and you've always been distracted by your personal life," she said.

Miriam smiled while Kashif silently fumed. Humara's biting remarks were usually reserved for less choice relatives such as Miriam or perhaps Adnan, but never for Kashif.

❖ ❖ ❖

If one has ever planned an event with six other people, one knows what an incredibly tricky game it is. Thus, choosing a date to announce the engagement ended up being a task considerably less straightforward than anyone had originally anticipated. Baby and the Lakahnis wanted a big and elaborate event that required more planning. Humara wanted to get the whole marriage done with right away. Kashif also favored that, as it meant keeping costs down. Mrs. Lakahni, having recently taken up astrology, wanted to pick a date where all the planets were aligned.

Her astrologer (or, as she often referred to him, her cosmic advisor) had recommended a few choice dates, some being as far off as five years in the future. No one (except for maybe Adnan) found that acceptable. In short, reconciling the expectations of two families and seven people was like putting together an elaborate puzzle that had several of its key pieces missing—there were bound to be some gaping holes.

After much deliberation, it was decided that the engagement would be announced on the third Friday of the following month after a service at the local mosque (as was the custom in the community), preceded by a small family dinner and pictures. That seemed to work for everyone (including Mrs. Lakahni's astrologer). Miriam wasn't sure whether to look upon the engagement with anticipation or dread. Baby's attitude toward Miriam had been at best erratic. She would snub Miriam one moment only to gush with syrupy friendliness the next. Miriam suspected that Baby really detested her and only put on a show in front of their families—especially Adnan.

Did Baby hate her because she feared ending up like her—the overlooked and often abandoned wife of a man who didn't love her? That could never be Baby—or could it? Was there something else that aroused her hostility? Adnan was no more hers then he was anyone else's. Yet the Lakahnis had put a wedge between. They were no longer secret friends. He never looked at her anymore. She was a ghost.

Miriam was not looking forward to a union with the Lakahnis. Already they had all but set up camp in the Ashruf residences, stopping by every other day and inviting themselves over for meals. That especially had taken its toll on Miriam, who was left to do most of the cooking and cleaning. It was not just the extra work— Miriam was also not comfortable with the way they had casually inquired about the real-estate values of the area and some of the Ashrufs' investments. It was a comment that Adeel Lakahni had made in passing—was Kashif aware of his father's assets before the family had moved to the U.S.? An idle remark, mentioned carelessly. Had Miriam not caught the look in Adeel's eyes betraying the lightness of his tone, she would have missed it—the look that said there was nothing casual or unplanned about the inquiry.

When the day of the engagement finally came, it was raining—lightly at first, but then more fiercely as the day progressed. There were many cancellations at Markham Dental. Miriam shivered. She felt cold despite the sweater and turtleneck she was wearing. The rain had left her sufficiently damp that morning, and she felt tired. She would have liked to be home resting before the big event that evening. Her cold was not getting any better but instead was turning into the flu. When she glanced at herself in the mirror, she was surprised at how haggard she looked. She had lost a lot of weight. Her skin had taken on a sallow complexion, and there were dark circles under her eyes. She smelled of cough drops and Vicks VaporRub. What a contrast she was to Sonia Rizvi, sitting in the reception area reading a *Time* magazine. She was one of the patients that had made it in despite the rain. Sonia always looked like the consummate professional in her well-tailored Italian suit and black-leather trench coat—the picture of sophistication. Not a strand out of place, her hair always looking flawlessly coiffed, even in this weather. Everything was perfect, except it wasn't.

Something nagged at the back of Miriam's mind, something that she couldn't quite put her finger on - a stiffness in Sonia's smile, a crinkle in the side of her eyes, a carefully concealed worry line. Miriam began to wonder...*was everything as it should be?*

Still, in comparison to Miriam, she still looked like a bombshell. Miriam had hastily pulled her hair back in a ponytail that morning. It had still been damp then, and now it was frizzing all over the place. Miriam self-consciously pulled back a stray lock. She did not have on a stitch of make-up—not a good idea considering the event tonight. Her eyebrows had not been plucked in so long that it looked as if two caterpillars had perched themselves on her forehead. Maybe she could leave early and fix herself up. She had brought her outfit and some basic cosmetics with her. It was going to be a pretty hopeless task. Why hadn't she thought of it sooner?

Involuntarily, Miriam let out a sigh. Sonia looked up at her and smiled. "This weather can be such a downer," she said, putting down her magazine and folding her hands in her lap. How pretty her manicure looked. Miriam's own hands were raw from scrubbing everything from the oven to the kitchen sink.

"Can't rain forever," said Miriam, staring wistfully out the window.

"What time are you getting off?" said Sonia. "Are you going to the mosque tonight?"

"Yes, they're announcing my brother-in-law's engagement. I'm leaving around six o'clock," replied Miriam.

"It's almost six now. Is someone coming to get you?"

Usually, it was Adnan and not Kashif who somehow made it to pick her up when the weather was bad, and Miriam still half expected to get a call from him asking if she was still there. But that had stopped weeks ago, and Miriam was resigned to finding her own way back.

"No, I'm taking the bus," she said.

"In this rain...?"

Miriam looked outside at the storm and hoped it might settle a bit.

"Why don't you let me call you a cab? My treat," said Sonia, pulling out her cell.

"I'd offer to take you, but I have to go back to the office. A litigator's work is never done."

Miriam started to protest.

"I won't take no for an answer," said Sonia firmly.

As Sonia got into her car, she couldn't help but feel a pang of guilt for not being able to do more for the girl. She wished she could be there today. She wished she didn't have to work – but a litigator's job was never done.

As Sonia drove off into the night, Miriam and the little dental office felt increasingly like a distant memory. Sonia's attention began to gravitate towards her own problems. A loud honk startled her out of her daydream. *Keep your eyes on the road,* she told herself, but it was not working.

Sonia's family had, had nothing short of a meltdown when she had come home from Hong Kong and announced she had married Michael. The first two weeks her father refused to speak to her. Slowly, he has started to come around, especially when Michael had agreed to convert, something that surprised even Sonia.

"*Look, I don't care what religion we are, or what God we worship, as long as we're together,*" he had said.

Her mother had even brought up the idea of having a small reception. No, it wasn't her family that Sonia was worried about now. It was the Blaines. When Sonia and Michael landed in Chicago, the Blaines had left for Europe the very next day. Veronica had rented a chateau in Italy for six weeks and Howard would work out of his London office for three weeks and join her later. It was Michael's idea to wait until they got back.

The prospect of facing Michael's family, especially his mother, nagged at the back of her mind. It was the type of dread one feels as they slowly creep up like a roller coaster. Sonia was very close to the top.

NINETEEN

Row, Row, Row Your Boat

Unfortunately, the cab never arrived. It was 6:30 p.m., and Markham Dental closed at six. All but Miriam had abandoned the office and scurried off into the night, like mice abandoning a sinking ship. Only Miriam sat looking at her silver citizen watch every fifteen minutes. It had been almost an hour since Sonia had made the call, and there was not so much as a hint of the phantom cab anywhere. *Could it have drowned?* thought Miriam. *Could it have been swept up in a tidal wave and found itself sailing toward some unknown destination?* Miriam liked to think of a lone yellow cab drifting out to sea. Eventually, she would have to stop daydreaming and figure out what to do. Why hadn't she gotten the name of the cab company Sonia had used, and why had she declined Dr. Geller's invitation for a ride?

Dr. Geller was running late, as always. That day, he was trying to make it in time for a parent-teacher interview. Still, on his way out the door, in his brown raincoat and mismatched hat, he had asked if she was waiting for someone. *Did she need a ride?*

Miriam had foolishly declined and was now giving

herself the proverbial kick in the proverbial pants. She was faced with two choices: call another cab company or take the bus. Miriam decided on the first. Quickly, she punched in the number of City Cab. It rang not once, but five times before the operator picked up.

"Hello, I need a cab to . . ." started Miriam

"Thank you for calling City Cab; please hold," said the operator.

Miriam had been on hold for the entire duration of *Candle in the Wind* by Elton John before she realized how ridiculous the call was and decided to try her hand at public transport. She looked at the outfit she had brought for the evening. It was already starting to get wrinkled. *I don't want this to be drenched on top of everything else. I'll change when I get there*, she thought. Miriam grabbed her bags, her umbrella, her cough drops, and her Vicks VaporRub. At the last minute, she took a swig of Dayquil before heading out into the unsettling night, barely holding her own against the raging of the wind and thunder.

Miriam arrived at mosque almost an hour late and made her way to the restrooms. It took her another fifteen minutes to change into the *salwar kameez* she had brought and hastily apply a little makeup. She tried to do something to style her wet droopy hair, to try and make it look less wet and lifeless. She couldn't let it down—it was hideous. She couldn't put it in a ponytail—too casual. Finally, after much frustration, she decided to put it half up.

She looked at herself in the mirror. The outfit seemed to hang loosely on her. It made her look way too thin. She looked at her makeup. The colors that she had chosen seemed like a good idea at the time but now made her look too gaudy, emphasizing her paleness. Uncertain of what to do, Miriam was faced with either looking like a clown or looking like a ghost. *Clown it is*, she thought, knowing that next to Baby's garish colors she was certain to look subtle and demure.

As Miriam stepped into the women's hall, she realized

that the engagement was a much bigger event than she had anticipated. The hall was packed. Miriam looked around for her mother-in-law (there was no point in looking for Kashif or Adnan, as they would likely be in the men's hall next door). It was a well-to-do community, and the hall reflected that. The floor was lined with plush carpet, and many ornate tapestries hung on the walls. The large windows were covered with stained glass and the marble pillars, and modern lighting bridged the gap between the old world and the new—not to mention the big-screen TVs that allowed the women to witness the sermon in the other room from a comfortable distance. In accordance with tradition, the congregation sat on the floor of the mosque. One had to walk the entire length of the hall before finding several rows of chairs that were added to accommodate the elderly, the infirm, and the pregnant. When the mosque was first built thirty years ago, there were only two or three chairs at the back, but each year, as the congregation reached maturity, a few more were added. Now one could find five solid rows of chairs at the back of the mosque. Miriam had to strain to make out her mother-in-law amongst all the other little old ladies. Humara usually sat at the end of one of the rows, positioning her wheelchair beside the last chair. Miriam knew that if she found the old woman, Baby and Mrs. Lakahni would be seated somewhere nearby.

As Miriam walked to the back of the hall, she noticed that women were dressed in their best for this happy occasion. Ironically, women that normally covered themselves from head to toe sat wearing sleeveless blouses and *langas* (skirts) and *saris* that exposed their midriffs. With perfect hair and makeup, they whispered amongst themselves or consoled their crying babies until one of the volunteers would scold them like a group of naughty children. That would keep them quiet for another ten minutes before the whispering would start up again. Miriam could hear bits of gossip as she walked by.

"I let my sister-in-law do my shopping for me in Pakistan; big mistake. The stuff she brought back was just horrid..."

"You know that woman always overcharges for threading and waxing. If I were you, I would try that other place..."

"Their engagement broke off quite suddenly, yes. I think the girl liked someone else all along..."

They looked up at Miriam as she passed by—some with idle curiosity; others looked away and whispered surreptitiously. She was used to those looks; the ones that told her that she was an endless source of pity and gossip. Feeling sick and disheveled made it harder for her to hold her head up high. As she walked, her vision became blurry. Whether it was out of disappointment, humiliation, or illness, she was not sure. Miriam may have completely missed her family altogether if it were not for Baby's glittery silver outfit that stood out like a beacon for wayward ships. Tripping on row upon row of people, Miriam went as close to her family as possible before she planted herself on an empty spot a couple rows down from Baby, Mrs. Lakahni, and Kashif's sister, Sadia. She could see them, but she knew that they could not yet see her. She would have to join them for refreshments later. Hopefully, the old woman would not be too irate.

Miriam looked around and realized that she was sitting beside two adolescent girls and a young mother, and the chatter from the two young girls was enough to distract her from the sermon. Involuntarily, Miriam began to shiver. She was soaked to the bone, and the thin fabric of her outfit did nothing to help. At least she wasn't sitting next to an exit or a window. Sometimes, when it got really packed, they would let in some air, and the last thing she needed right now was a draft. She tried to listen to the sermon, but all the words seemed to blend together, and her eyelids began to feel heavy. Her cold was getting worse, and for the next half hour, she went through the gamut of symptoms from cold and shivery to hot and sweaty. Miriam closed her eyes. There were too many people in the room. She began to feel dizzy. She could feel her wet underclothes plastered to her body. Luckily, she had caught the tail end of the sermon—it would not be much longer. When they finished the sermon, they would announce all the engagements in the community that week, and then there would be tea and appetizers.

There were a total of seven engagements being announced that day. The last was the Ashruf/Lakahni engagement. *No wonder it's so crowded*, thought Miriam.

"*. . . and we would like to announce the engagement of Maliha (Baby) Lakahni, daughter of Rosina and Adeel Lakahni, to Adnan Ashruf, son of Humara and Naseer Ashruf.*"

When the announcements ended, there was a rush of people going every which way. Some just wanted to get up and stretch; others were headed for the buffet, but most of the congregation went to congratulate the newly engaged couples and their families. This was as good a time as any for Miriam to make her way back and join the rest of the family. The Ashrufs and the Lakahnis were surrounded by so many well-wishers that it was difficult for Miriam to make herself known. Baby was thoroughly enjoying herself amidst all the attention. She stood at the center of the crowd like a majestic iceberg dressed in a sheer silver outfit with heavy crystal jewelry. It made Miriam shiver just to look at her. When the old woman finally noticed Miriam amongst the crowd of faces, her expression changed to one of contempt as she hissed inside Miriam's ear.

"Where have you been? Everyone has been asking about you."

"All the buses were running late because of the rain," explained Miriam.

"What am I going to do with you?" chided her mother-in-law. "You're a mess, and this is an important event for our family."

She looked at Miriam's outfit, now more wrinkled than ever, but before Miriam had a chance to answer, she felt herself being tousled aside in the wave of people that had come forward to congratulate the family. Miriam gasped for air amidst a sea of colorful outfits, being pushed and pulled every which way. As if by sheer accident, Miriam felt herself being tossed out of the crowd and onto the safe secluded shore of the larger hall.

The Ashrufs were well known in the community, so Miriam was not surprised that there was a rush of people to greet them after the announcement. Adnan had made somewhat of a reputation for himself as an aimless playboy, everyone was eager to see where he had landed, and when they saw Baby there would be much interest. Miriam did not want to be available for comment. It didn't matter, anyway—what Miriam didn't confirm would be filled in through speculation and conjecture.

Miriam grabbed a cup of tea from one of the volunteers and made her way to a relatively clear area. The tea was piping hot. Miriam found an empty corner. There she sat, eyes closed, sipping her golden brew. Just holding the hot Styrofoam cup made her feel better. She liked the feel of the warm liquid going down her throat. She liked the heat, the way it soothed the rawness and the pain she had been feeling all day. She coughed less now, but when she did, it was a deep, throaty cough that lasted much longer than before. *How will I get through this?* she thought, but she did not have time to think of an answer, as she was brought back to the present by the sound of a woman's voice.

She looked up to see a woman dressed in a deep navy *salwar kameez*. Her hair was wrapped in a matching scarf despite the fact that it was a ladies'-only hall. The woman's complexion was dark, but Miriam could see that the strands of hair that peeked out from underneath the cloth were not dark but coppery brown, matching the woman's

The Mother-in-Law Cure

eyes. Slim and tall, she was not unpleasant to look at. Although Miriam did not recognize her, she approached with a familiarity that made Miriam wonder if they were in fact acquainted.

"That's a terrible cold. You really should be home in bed," she said.

"Yeah...tell me about it. We should be heading out in an hour, then. I've got a small reception and some photographs. It's my brother-in-law's engagement."

"Sounds like a long night."

"It's going to be even longer. I have to stay awake long enough to do some cleaning and some prep work for tomorrow before I go to bed."

"You have your hands full. Do you have a cleaning lady? Do you get any help?"

A cleaning lady! This girl must be new, thought Miriam.

"No, sweetheart, I'm the cleaning lady, along with the cook, the gardener, and the seamstress," said Miriam, wondering why she was being so rude to the woman whom she did not even know. She wasn't generally a whiner, and the woman did not deserve her angst. Perhaps it was the cold or the stress, but she could not hang on as she normally did. She needed to let go.

"Sounds pretty messed up," said the woman.

"You're telling me," said Miriam, taking a sip of her tea, her teeth chattering. "This cold is really wiping me out."

"Poor girl, suffering away...but you have the cure."

There was something about the tone in her voice that made Miriam look at her a little more closely.

"My husband's a doctor so our medicine chest is fully stocked. In a couple more hours, I get to go home and drown myself in Nyquil."

"Yes," smiled the woman as if Miriam had let her in on a sidesplitting joke and let out a laugh – deep and throaty, her rich voice rang in Miriam's ears. Miriam was about to ask her what was so funny when she heard her mother-in-law calling her name. When she looked back the woman had already left.

Miriam picked up her purse and fished around for a Kleenex, something round and smooth found its way into Miriam's hands. It was the vial.

TWENTY

One for Sorrow,
Two for Joy

Miriam looked skeptically at the vial before she threw it in the nearest trashcan and headed out. She was grateful that the rain had stopped, but the air was still thick and threatening. The clouds loomed overhead as if waiting for the right opportunity to unleash their reserves.

Miriam was wide awake now, and as everyone chatted in the car, she remained quiet and looked out the widow several times. She felt as if something was following her. Sitting in the back seat, she strained to see what was in the shadows. Was it an old ghost, the recent memory of that strange woman, or the sinister hand of destiny that appeared to be her companion? Humara noticed her furtive glances, craning to see outside from the middle seat, and asked, "What on earth are you looking for?"

"Nothing," she said and slid back deeper into her seat. She closed her eyes, but sleep would not come. No matter how she tried to clear her head, to enjoy the warmth and security of being enclosed in a dry, warm structure, her body would not let her fall asleep.

It was less than a twenty minute ride to the restaurant.

Given the late nature of the evening, they were unwilling to take a nine p.m. reservation, and surprisingly few invitees were available on such short notice. There would be no party, so Kashif had ordered dinner to go. They parked in the lot waiting for the busboy to bring out their order. Miriam recognized the busboy as one she had seen before—a gangly teenager with a big smile and a good disposition. Kashif paid the youth and put the bags in the car. It was only then that Miriam realized how hungry she was. The medication that she was doped up on all evening was starting to wear off, and her stomach felt like an empty pit—one that needed to be filled, and soon.

It was Humara who insisted that the food be reheated and served properly in the dining room. Miriam felt almost dizzy inhaling the aroma of the chicken biryani, the lamb korma, and the chicken kebabs that she had been reheating and placing on the dining table. She felt a little irritated that no one even feigned interest in helping her. In the beginning of her marriage, either Kashif or Humara had at least made the perfunctory offerings of help, and Miriam had declined knowing full well that it was only a polite gesture—but now even that was gone.

Miriam had just finished setting the dining table and had gone back inside the kitchen to put away her oven mitts when she was startled by the first five notes of Handel's *Messiah*. It was Kashif's cell phone.

"Hello," he said as he stepped into the dining room.

It was unusual for him to get a personal call on his cell this late at night. Miriam could hear him above the chatter outside. From the way he was murmuring softly, it was clear that it was not an emergency. Miriam wondered who was on the other end of the call. Although she could not make out the exact words, she could not shrug the feeling that it was a very intimate conversation. The tenderness in Kashif's voice made her feel embarrassed. It made her think of the whispers she would hear at mosque or the

The Mother-in-Law Cure

sympathetic glances she would get from neighbors, many of whom were patients of Kashif. She had always assumed that it was because of the old woman, whom everyone knew was a tyrant. Miriam thought they must pity her because, unlike other girls her age, she had missed the chance to go to college, to have friends and a career. Now she knew that it was just the tip of the iceberg.

She waited for the call to end before going into the dining room. Kashif lingered a bit before he snapped his cell phone shut and joined the rest of the party. Miriam waited another five minutes before she went into the dining room and announced that dinner was ready. She looked at Kashif for any sign of the call that he had taken, but he failed to meet her eyes and his glances were evasive at best.

Flash . . . Flash . . . Flash!

The bright light of the camera was enough to knock the sense right out of a girl along with most of her short-term memory. *I really should not look directly into that thing*, thought Miriam, perspiring under the back lights the photographer had set up. The pictures were being taken in the lobby of their home in front of the long spiral staircase leading to the second floor. Miriam was standing beside Kashif, whose too-strong cologne was giving her a headache. For some reason, the scent was not working for him. Miriam had smelled the cologne on others—on Adnan, in fact, and it did not smell like this. On Adnan it smelled musky, sensual. On Kashif, it smelled like a middle-aged man trying too hard to recapture his youth. Funny, Kashif had never worn much cologne before. Miriam wondered who gave it to him.

"Nice . . . nice," said the photographer as he took a couple more shots. They had done the family portraits first so that Humara could go to bed. Just when Miriam thought they were done, the photographer suggested a few more combinations. *Good grief*, thought Miriam, *and it isn't even the wedding*. The photographer was starting to get on Miriam's nerves. She needed to clean the kitchen before going to bed, and this session seemed to be dragging on forever. She hoped this guy was not getting paid by the hour.

When it was finally time for the couple shots, Miriam regretted having to go back into the kitchen and even stood outside for fifteen minutes watching Baby and Adnan in their "lovey-dovey" poses. Although Adnan had put up a good show with the engagement so far, he was having trouble maintaining the same composure when it involved putting his arms around Baby and looking longingly in to her eyes. It was something the photographer had picked up on as well.

"Don't be so shy, sonny boy. There's no one here but us."

It was true. Kashif had retired to the study, and Mr. Lakahni had decided to take his wife (who was feeling quite worn out from all the excitement) home and then come back for Baby.

Miriam giggled at Adnan's awkwardness. Normally, Adnan was totally confident around the opposite sex, but today as he was asked to gaze lovingly into Baby's eyes, he could not fake his passion and looked instead like a man examining a strange creature. Adnan and Baby went through several variations of the "lovers' pose." The next pose had Adnan's arm around Baby; the one after had Baby standing behind Adnan with her arm around his neck. It almost looked like she had him in a headlock. The photographer had to intervene and adjust the pose.

"A little looser in the embrace…make it casual, loving…that's right. That's good."

Baby adjusted her grip in line with the photographer's instructions, but even this casual embrace resembled a noose. Baby wasted no time slobbering over Adnan, positioning herself closer to his body, squeezing his knee. Her lips trembling, she looked into his eyes as if she was going to wet herself right there and then. Adnan looked a little more pale and aghast, as if looking into the eyes of a salivating dragon.

To Miriam, this scene was utterly delightful. It made the day almost worth it. Inside, she felt giddy as she considered a lifetime of Baby and Adnan together. She walked back to the kitchen, smiling for the first time in weeks. Even the mess waiting for her did not bother her. She cheerfully scrubbed pots and pans, loaded the dishwasher, and wiped down the counters. When she finished, her eyes had become blurry from weariness, and she realized that she was too tired to do anything about the floors.

The last thing she did that evening was pour herself a glass of warm milk that she sipped slowly at the kitchen table. She could hear the photographer packing up and the sounds of Mr. Lakahni, who had come to collect Baby. They talked softly amongst themselves, and Mr. Lakahni paid the photographer. Miriam was still smiling, thinking that finally someone had a fate worse than hers, and for once, Miriam was not ashamed of her feelings.

When everyone left, her smile vanished and she felt empty and alone. *Well, that takes care of Adnan's miserable life. Now what about mine?* She thought. It was something that had been hidden in the back of her mind for many days. Up until then, she had felt as if this life was enough. She may have been overworked and underappreciated and she may have even have had her dreams crushed, but she had at least always felt safe and secure, as if she was under everyone's radar, and that feeling had given her a sense of freedom. Since the upheaval of the Lakahnis and the bad dreams, that feeling had trickled away, and now she was left with a feeling of danger and disposability.

When Miriam reached her bedroom, she could hear Kashif's rhythmic snoring in the darkness. Over the last couple of years, she had learned to recognize her husband's odor. She recognized it in his towels, his dirty laundry, and his comb. Miriam took the shirt Kashif had just taken off, held it to her face, and took a deep breath. There was a subtle difference in the smell that was not there before, something that lingered softly in the background, perhaps a new soap? It scared her even more than the old woman, though her mind was too tired to comprehend why. As she undressed and got ready for bed, she felt something in the pocket of her jacket . . . smooth and sleek. It was the vial! She thought she had thrown it out. With a big yawn, she dumped it into the wastepaper basket along with a handful of used Kleenexes and got into bed. The last image that she saw before her minded descended into sleep was that of Afsana.

TWENTY ONE

Life is but a Dream

Miriam moaned as she slept. She could no longer feel her body as it transported her through a fog that was so thick she could barely see where she was going. She was not running this time, not panicked. She knew this place. She had been here before. This time, she was being led. Someone was gently holding her hand, urging her forward. The gray of the fog was such that she could not see the guide in front of her. She tried to listen for what lay beyond the fog, but whether the sounds belonged to man or animal, she could not tell. Sensing Miriam's apprehension, her guide gripped her hand a little tighter. It felt soft and reassuring, and Miriam felt something stir inside of her. As long as she held on, she would be OK.

When they reached the clearing, the fog seemed to dissipate, not going beyond the patch of trees that encircled them like a protective field. It was only then that Miriam could see the figure before her—of course it was Afsana, not as Afsana looked before she died, with weary eyes and a nervous smile, nor as Miriam had witnessed in discarded family albums. This was a pure, untouched

Afsana, unscarred by the trials of life. Her face was clear and free of worry, her dark hair flowing onto the bare shoulders of her summer dress. She looked at Miriam directly and intimately, and for the first time, there was nothing standing between them. Miriam was paralyzed.

She came closer as if to say something privately, secretly in her ear, but as Afsana was standing inches away, she raised her hand toward Miriam's cheek and drew her into a kiss--deep and penetrating, as if Afsana was filling her with all that she knew. Miriam could feel her body responding to Afsana's touch, her caresses, the sweet taste of her mouth, and all around her was the sweet smell of gardenias. When Miriam looked up again, Afsana had morphed into a mirror image of herself. Like an evil twin, she saw her image reflected back at her. Although Miriam was scared, this version of herself seemed to have no fear. Miriam wanted to pull away, but even as she attempted to retreat, her twin pressed into her deeper and deeper, oblivious to Miriam's struggles. Miriam began to panic, to suffocate. She was drowning, and all around her, all she could feel was this entity who was as familiar as her every breath and as foreign as her darkest desires. With one last breath, she broke through the surface of the invisible ocean and sat up in bed gasping for air, her hands around her throat.

Miriam looked around. It was still dark in their bedroom, as it had been every morning since it had begun raining several weeks ago. Kashif's flannel pajamas and gray t-shirt lay crumpled on the floor. He was gone. Miriam glanced at the clock on the nightstand. It was four p.m.—not early at all. She stayed inside the covers a little longer, taking her time to get out of bed. She did not hear anything, and she hoped that the house was empty. As Miriam strolled into the hallway, she peeped downstairs and heard voices. It was Humara, talking to Mrs. Lakahni. *Shit! They are all here. Don't they ever go home?* Miriam thought.

She went to the bathroom and quickly brushed her teeth, slapping some water on her face. She thought about the dream, now a distant shadow that was already fading from her memory and leaving her with a feeling of serenity. For the first time, she did not feel as if she was waking up alone.

When Miriam went downstairs, everyone was sitting around the living room, an unopened box of chocolates lying on the coffee table. Adnan and Baby were sitting on the loveseat, with Baby taking up most of the space. In her lap, she had several copies of *Asian Bride*. Kashif, dressed in khakis and a sweater, sat going over the financial pages with Mr. Lakahni, who was wearing a blazer on top of a casual shirt. Looking at Kashif's chocolate-colored sweater, Miriam could not help but recall that it was Afsana's least favorite color on him because it made his complexion look sallow and washed out...funny how that should pop into her head, as if Afsana was standing next to her whispering in her ear.

Humara, Miriam noticed, was seated at the far end of the room. As small as she was, her presence conveyed a stronger stature, perhaps even commanding. She observed that even Baby and the Lakahnis noticed this and always dealt with the old woman with the utmost precaution, for she would be family soon.

Humara was the first to notice Miriam standing by the doorway.

"Ahhh... you're up, Miriam," she said, giving Miriam a curious look. "We tried to wake you this morning, but it was like trying raising the dead," she said, sounding almost disappointed.

"Yes, the Lakahnis were nice enough to bring over brunch," added Kashif.

"There's still some food left over in the kitchen. Why don't you grab a bite?" said Adnan, surprising Miriam with his attention.

"So what's the agenda for today?" asked Miriam

cheerfully.

"Oh, Adnan and Baby are just going to go ring shopping, and then I'm taking *Ammah* and Auntie and Uncle to see a new Indian movie that has come out at the cinema. Care to join us?"

"Thanks, but I think I'll pass. I haven't had breakfast yet, and there is a ton of stuff to do here," said Miriam, starting to get up and make her way to the kitchen.

"Miriam, *Berta*, while you are in the kitchen, can you get me a cup of tea?" asked the old woman. "Does anyone else want anything?" asked Humara, looking around the room.

As it turned out, everyone did want another cup of tea. As Miriam entered the kitchen, she wondered if the cleaning she had done the night before had just been a dream, so quickly had it been wiped out. Dirty dishes lay stacked in the sink when they should have been in the dishwasher. Trays of food that Miriam presumed were from brunch had been left on the countertop and the kitchen table when they should have been packed and put into the fridge, and the microwave looked more than a little splattered from warming up uncovered food. The floors were sticky and begged for a wet mop.

Miriam ignored everything. She carefully took out the tea bags and put the kettle on the stove. Her stomach was growling, and she looked over to the leftovers. It looked as if they had been dining on *halwa*, (a sweet, sugary dessert, kind of like a dry pudding, often containing nuts or raisins) usually eaten with *puris*, a thin, pancake-like bread. It was a popular breakfast dish in the old country but not easy to find in suburbia. Miriam grabbed a plate and filled it with food. She loved *halwa*. It reminded her of her childhood, when her mother would make *halwa puri* for special occasions and Miriam would eat it all week long. When she was finished, the kettle on the stove had just started to whistle. She was about to get up, when she saw Kashif come in.

The Mother-in-Law Cure

"Just wanted to let you know that Mr. and Mrs. Lakahni will take two teaspoons of sugar in their tea with milk, Baby will take five teaspoons of sugar, and *Ammah* and I will take the usual. You don't need to bother bringing tea for Adnan; he already had a cup earlier. Is that the kettle? Better get a move on. You might want to put on a little makeup, too, if you intend to go out. You look terrible."

"I've been sick," said Miriam. "I've barely had a chance to rest."

"Oh. Well, you can rest all you want after you serve the tea and clean the kitchen. I also have some shirts that need to be ironed. We'll be out for the afternoon, so there won't be any interruptions. Really, Miriam, you need to be a little flexible and not just focus on you. The Lakahnis are family now . . ."

Miriam, turning red, got up to make the tea. The feeling of serenity she had felt only twenty minutes ago had certainly vanished. *I must be PMSing,* she thought. *I really feel as if I'm going to scream.* Miriam put her hands in her pocket to avoid clenching them, and that's when she felt it—*the little vial she had thrown out the night before.* She felt its smooth, cylindrical shape in her palm and she felt strangely calm. Her fingers would run the length of the tiny bottle over and over again, and when she was finished caressing it, she took it out and really looked at it. The vial contained a tiny inscription on it that she had to squint to see. The style and the language eluded her but reminded her of religious scripture. Miriam read the directions and as Miriam looked at Humara's teacup, everything became very clear. She had thought the remedy was something *she* was supposed to take. She was wrong.

"Miriam . . . almost done?" asked Kashif, poking his head through the door. "*Ammah* wants you to take out a couple of the *mehtai* we have in the fridge."

"OK," said Miriam, stopping to take a couple of deep breaths so that she would not go ballistic. She closed her eyes; one, two, three deep breaths. Miriam became very calm. She could see her twin's face. She could smell the sweet fragrance that had enveloped her, see the shadow of invisible hands, identical on top of her own, urging her, guiding her to break the chains of destiny. . . and then she went into the fridge to find the sweets Kashif had requested.

When she went outside, she served the tea and placed a plate of sweets on the coffee table. Everyone nibbled on the *mehtai* as they gulped down the steamy brew Miriam had placed before them. They were in a hurry to get out. Miriam cleared the empty plates and poured the remainder of the tea down the sink and waved goodbye to everyone as they headed out the door. The empty vial remained in her pocket.

When everyone finally left, Miriam let out a long sigh. She felt strangely tired, as if she had spent the last two hours running a marathon. Her muscles felt sore, and in a cloud of fatigue, she went upstairs, climbed back into bed, and slept soundlessly, dreamlessly, and without interruptions. When she awoke ten hours later, the house was quiet and Kashif lay snoring beside her. She had not even heard the Ashrufs come in. Miriam rolled over, grabbed a bigger share of the blanket that she tucked under her cheek, and went back to sleep until Kashif's alarm went off at six a.m. Kashif turned it off and went back to sleep, for it was Sunday and he did not need to get up again for another two hours. When he did finally get up and go to the bathroom at eight, Miriam laid in bed feeling the first pangs of anxiety. What had she done? She lay motionless, cowering for another hour, not knowing what to expect when she went downstairs.

Surprisingly, everyone made it down for breakfast by nine, including Adnan, who had a reputation for sleeping until noon. As it had been a strenuous weekend, everyone sat quietly drinking their teas, buttering their toasts, and reading their papers. Miriam was more than a little nervous, half expecting the old woman to drop dead in front of her cereal...or start crying in pain, or to at least mention an upset stomach or indigestion, but nothing. Miriam brought out more eggs and refilled cups of tea... still nothing. Finally, when breakfast came to a close, Miriam collected the dishes, cleared the table, and went back to the kitchen and waited. Nothing happened. Feeling relieved and maybe even a little irritated, she concluded that it had all been a big hoax, and she would not be responsible for bringing misfortune and plague on to her family after all—no, that was her mother-in-law's job.

Miriam let out a long breath and shook her head from side to side, shaking out all the cobwebs. She was about to include a couple of stretches when she heard the chiming of the doorbell. She looked around but, as usual, she was left standing closest to the door.

A gust of wind blew into her face as she opened the front door and a delivery guy dropped a package into her hand. The parcel was addressed to the old woman and judging from the return address had come from the photographer. Miriam placed it in front of her mother-in-law. She couldn't help but notice how deftly the old woman unwrapped the package with her long spidery fingers – *witch's fingers*. It was as if each part of the old woman's anatomy embodied the spirit of a different monster...the skin of a reptile, the tongue of a vulture and the heart of a snake. With her hawk eyes, the old woman looked over the proofs of Adnan and Baby's engagement shots. She looked them over without smiling. No doubt one would be chosen to blow-up and display during the wedding reception, one that did not make a mockery out of this union. The trick would be to find one that didn't look like Adnan was being eaten by a whale. At last there was a closely cropped headshot that looked like it might do the trick, with their heads tilted together with Adnan's big grin and Baby's shy smile they almost looked like a normal couple.

There were even a couple group shots of the family. Miriam couldn't help but eyeing herself next to Kashif. She was in very few family pictures and rarely beside Kashif; usually she was tacked on at the end. This time the photographer had made certain to position them together. Surprisingly, she looked much better than she felt that day she even had what some might call a Mona Lisa smile – *as if she possessed a secret*. It was a smile that belonged to someone else altogether. Miriam had seen it before in an old family album kept in a forgotten room full of mementos and junk. She knew where to find it but before she could make her way to the attic, the old woman abruptly shoved the proofs into her hand and told her to put them away in her bedroom drawer upstairs.

TWENTY TWO

*Little Drops of Water, Little Drops of Sand
Make the Mighty Ocean, and the Pleasant Land*

This wasn't the picture she had in mind when she made her way upstairs, but it had found her nonetheless, slipped into her hands. In truth, it could have been any wedding picture, carelessly taken by an amateur hand, the shy bride, the uncomfortable looking groom. At some point, a drop of water (perhaps a tear drop, or a trickle from a glass) had fallen onto the photo smudging the colors. It was fitting for a photo taken many years ago, for the past is itself a stream that flows endlessly towards an unknown sea. It is where the web of our intentions trickles through their sometime convoluted paths. It is also why we cannot see the future. *Any spider will tell you that.*

But Humara Ashruf was no spider. She was what spider's feared the most, from her scales, to her hiss, to the way she could slither seamlessly in and out of any situation, and by now there was no mistaking the potency of her venom. Still it was a curious decision. Many wondered what the old serpentine was thinking. Surely, there were many young eligible women willing to marry a prominent doctor - *no matter what his past*.

In truth, Miriam was not her first choice, though she would never care to admit it. She knew that the family had begun to stagnate in prominence and social status. Kashif had been single for too many years. It was starting to look odd. No, the energy of the household required the presence of another female, someone younger. Humara could not argue with what she felt in her bones. If he did not marry soon, he may be labeled *an old bachelor* and never come off the shelf. As it was, he was getting a little stodgy, a little set in his ways. It was just a matter of finding a suitable match.

Humara had learned from her experience. This time she was not inclined towards a puffed-up, over educated, hoidy toidy girl that was too good to get her hands dirty, wasting money on cleaning ladies, gardeners and dry cleaners and who knows what else…a couture wardrobe? *Her last daughter-in-law had shown her where that could lead.*

This time she was looking for a sturdy girl with strong limbs that could manage a workload, someone that wasn't afraid of putting her back into the scrubbing and cleaning, and perhaps fill in as substitute sitter for Sadia's children (who themselves were little demons). A girl from the old country might do. Humara preferred a girl with a profession in the trades, someone that could follow instruction but wasn't encumbered with too much thinking. A pleasant face would be nice as well, but not too beautiful.

It was only by chance that Humara had come across Miriam, only by chance that the old aunt recognized her. Miriam's aunt was a woman who knew her from the days when she no longer cared to be remembered, from the days when Humara Ashruf was not Humara Ashruf, but a friendless orphan relying on the kindness of relatives (the irony was not lost on her). Yes, the aunt remembered her…. *and a certain girl of genteel birth whose path was unlucky enough to cross that of an aspiring orphan.*

These were days that Humara had thought were long gone, but an old crow had followed her, even as she crossed the seven seas. Humara had always taken care of such loose ends but society had camouflaged the woman and silence had concealed her until the most opportune moment. Humara had to admit the woman was remarkably crafty for someone whose situation was so dire. When they met, she spoke slowly, languishing her words as if she were royalty (*instead of an old widow*), taking the scenic route towards her true intention (*she could have been a politician's wife*), and all the while pretending they were not nearly as meager as they actually were.

There are very few things that Humara's hawk eyes did not see coming, but age has a way of changing appearances and although this woman had never been a beauty, her once smooth face was now a leathery facade, a caricature of what it used to be, her lush hair now a hornet's nest and her once bright eyes now cloudy with cataracts - *but the way she drank tea was still the same.*

Once upon a time, as young girls, they had spent many hours at tea houses discussing the latest fashions and dreaming about the future. So, it was fitting that over tea perchance they should become reacquainted: sitting in the living room of a shabby little bungalow sipping Kashmiri chai - *even her best china left much to be desired.* Humara had, had many such afternoons with mothers, aunts, and elder sisters trying to nudge their candidates in her direction, when the old aunt made a seemingly innocent comment about the brew they were drinking.

They were sipping Kashmiri chai, which is known for its delicate pink color, a delicacy in the old country and not at all common in the Mid-West. Humara had never come across a brew of this quality. The flavor was just enchanting. It was the most noteworthy aspect of the entire afternoon. When Humara asked where they found it, her host paused briefly and then explained she always had it brought back from a little teashop back home, one that was near the local college and the shopping district. The flavor of the tea always took her back to her youth.

The way she played her trump card and the smug little smile she gave her was enough to transport Humara in time. It was the same smug little smile her girlfriend had given her when her late husband, Naseer, had walked into that teahouse so many years ago. She had said, *"now there goes a prince in pauper's clothes."*

It was true as well. The way he was dressed in those shabby pants and wrinkled shirt with his sleeves rolled-up he could have been any commoner off the street. But there was something in his stance and the way he held his head that made you take him seriously and when he spoke, there was no questioning that he was educated abroad. He was routinely seen with an English language newspaper. Humara was surprised by her friend's perceptiveness and when he had approached them outside the teahouse she had given her a knowing glance.

It was the same knowing glance before her now, over the unremarkable china and the third rate scones, the one that said *heed my message*. Humara was no fool.

The girl was sufficiently unremarkable but that was not the problem. Miriam was too delicate...too wispy...to fragile...too empty-headed. She was also very young. Miriam's level of comprehension was not apparent and Humara wondered if she were somehow slow. Humara was not looking for a genius but she was hoping for someone with at least average intelligence. She couldn't tell from Miriam's expressionless face if she knew what was going on. Her eyes, which were normally a tell tale feature on most people, seemed glazed and impenetrable. Had she not seemed so innocuous, these traits would have given Humara a sense of foreboding. She reminded Humara of someone she knew (perhaps a muted version of an angelic little girl that had almost stolen her future right from under her). They both had a similar air about them. It grated on her nerves to no end – *that self- righteous innocence.*

And so over tea, the die had been cast…the date had been set. Miriam joining the Ashruf household was as uneventful as any second marriage could be, with no honeymoon to speak of and Kashif departing for a conference shortly thereafter. *"I never promised you a rose garden,"* was Humara's response to the aunt's inquiries and questioning glances.

As the months went by, Miriam physically inhabited the Ashruf residence but her mind seemed to be somewhere else. She seemed to float through her life, her work, and her chores as if she was merely biding time…*but for what?*

There was nothing else out there for her and Humara did what she could to quench whatever ambitions she may have had early on. What use was college, didn't she have a husband to provide for her? Friends, why did she need friends when she had a family? She expected her disappointment to be more apparent. There was something about the girl that was not quite humility and not quite defeat, in the way that she succumbed to every blow that grated on her nerves more than any kind of pride or defiance.

Humara believed that people such as these deserved their fate; people that never fought but always yielded and so Humara strove to find the extent of the girl's limits. The old aunt's sudden timely demise had paved the way for Humara's free reign.

Most people's characters were more than apparent. Humara had learned to read people early on. Yet there was something impenetrable about the girl, not quite stone and not quite water but opaque nonetheless. It only added to the quality that made her otherworldly, as if she did not belong here and was just visiting. Soon, like air and water, her presence seemed to be forgotten. Humara always had more pressing matters on her mind and Miriam seemed to blend seamlessly into the background, a dangerous quality - *a blind spot.*

As the years passed, Miriam became her right hand. There was something very familiar about her. It was the type of familiarity one has with one's shadow; always a stone's throw away, always patient and always diligent. It was familiar... too familiar. It should have reminded Humara of someone else, another orphan who had been forced to rely on the kindness of relatives, but the old woman had disowned the past a long time ago. It wasn't until Humara had invited the Lakahnis that she had opened the door to her history but once Pandora's box has been opened, it is not so easy to close.

Carefully, Humara put Kashif and Miriam's wedding picture back in the drawer. Over the years, it had become creased and folded and the corners had started to chip, aging it beyond its years, becoming so fragile that it threatened to crumble at her very touch. It had fallen out when she was looking for something else entirely. Perhaps she would ponder this picture while soaking in steamy water; her bones were beginning to ache. Humara decided to ask Miriam to run her a bath and then bring her a nice cup of tea but before she could recall summoning her, Miriam was at her side, waiting patiently ...*but for what?*

❖ ❖ ❖

It was many hours later that Miriam finally made it to the attic upstairs. The old woman was snoring softly after her bath not having finished the tea she had requested. Most people would have hesitated venturing into a creepy attic at night but there was nothing about this house that scared her anymore. Just about everybody had forgotten that this room existed.

The feeble light bulb did little to illuminate the room and Miriam found herself fumbling around with her penlight. The attic was a place of forgotten furniture and clothes from a different time period, as well as books that no one read anymore and were too out of date for the Ashruf's countless book shelves.

She knew the album she was looking for. She could recall the worn out leather of the album and the binding that was becoming loose, it was old, it was forgotten, it was tattered – the perfect place for a secret. It was not with the other books. It was in an old wardrobe, at the very back.

The album contained a hodgepodge of pictures, *like a quilt*, in no particular order and with no particular subject matter. Miriam started at the beginning of the book and flipped to the very end but it was not there. There were pictures of Afsana where she was grinning, others where she was distracted or stony faced. Miriam flipped through its pages once more and then she saw it, *that secretive little smile*. She understood now why she had missed it, but there it was now laughing back at her. It was in a family picture taken outside. Afsana stood seriously beside Kashif. On Kashif's other side was a much younger Humara with just a hint of a smile. Afsana had never possessed such a smile – *it had always belonged to Humara*.

TWENTY THREE

All the World's a Stage;
And All the Men and Women Merely Players.

Humara's bones ached. She had started to lose her taste for food (nothing seemed to satisfy her palette these days) yet Humara was smiling, not her regular polite societal smile (which was scary in itself) but her true smile (the smile of a reptile), the smile that is hidden beneath her scaly exterior. She had much to smile about. The stage had been set, the actors had their lines and she, *the old director*, sat in a corner watching her production...like eyes in the mist she was always there quietly observing, her clever mind behind a benign exterior matriculating every detail. For all intents and purposes, it was a reenactment of the photo shoot.

Baby and Adnan holding hands, looking longingly into each other's eyes, head tilted as if someone had frozen time right before a passionate kiss...frozen in time.

The romantic photo session with the photographer had done well in preparing them for the next few weeks. Soon after the engagement, a flurry of social activity began as the new couple made their debut into society. Until now, the Ashruf's had been as intriguing as the 'Adam's Family'. The Lakahnis had given the Ashrufs a new status, doing much to repair their old tarnished image. The Lakahni seemed to drag them into the realm of normalcy, even glamour, with anecdotes of Adeel Lakahni's travels, business contacts, and luxurious lifestyle.

The sale of his properties abroad had brought in a hefty profit and he was positioned to invest in a development scheme that was said to be ten times more lucrative than any that he had so far. They were exactly the type of family any up and coming social climber would want to attach their son or daughter with.

After a while, there was a rote to the social engagements, the women had their lines, the men had theirs. It bore a faint resemblance *(and perhaps caricature is a better word)* to the Ashruf's glory days in the Middle East. This incarnation, however, was a cruel joke. One just had to look, *really look* at Adnan who ranged from having a blank expression to a plastic smile. The plastic smile was reserved for chitchat and the blank expression appeared when Baby was slobbering all over him – *which was often.*

Baby always made her appearance at social events, bejeweled and bedazzled from head-to-toe, wearing shimmery and gauzy fabrics. Miriam wasn't sure if Baby was going for modest or mysterious, femme fatale or Heffalumps *(the honey-eating elephants in Winnie the Pooh).*

In contrast, Adnan's armor was his toothy smile (the one that made him look like a game show host) and confidant gait. It was a persona that had politician written all over it. He even had Miriam believing that this engagement was all his idea – *maybe he did have a career in TV*. Miriam wondered if she ever knew him. Adnan had become someone with a chiseled exterior, rock hard *(not unlike his abs)*. It was like watching a character in a soap opera.

The truth however can never be erased, only concealed. It was only a matter of digging deep enough through the dense façade, the thick polish, the buff exterior. One just had to look with the right eyes, shine the right light...the cracks were there like veins beneath the skin's surface. Adnan's pain had a voice and it screamed out at Miriam in unison with all the voices both alive and dead that had crossed the old woman's path.

❖ ❖ ❖

Miriam was sitting within a circle of women; Adnan was at the other end of the room standing in front of a bookcase. She could hear his voice. He was speaking to Sadia's husband. They were discussing everything from food to property values, when Miriam felt her spine tingle, *the weight of his gaze made her turn around and look in his direction.* When their eyes locked, there was so much anguish that Miriam felt the whimper of a wolf caught in a bear trap. It was only when the evening was over and his performance was over did Miriam notice Adnan's face begin to soften. It was this softness that nagged at the back of Miriam's head and in one instant Miriam felt dread so dark, so black it could only have come from another world, from a soul long forgotten. *We are all just marionettes being pulled by her hand*, she thought.

If Adnan was full of despair, Baby was full of desperation. It oozed out of her the way jelly oozes out of a powdered donut. The harder she tried to play the role of the loving fiancé, the more grotesque, more distorted she became. *Baby was hiding*...the only way someone like her could hide. Baby had always had a pretty face but now her make-up was so thick that it was almost theatrical. Her flamboyant appearance was merely a way to take attention away from her size. In Miriam's mind, there was no doubt about it. Baby had begun to balloon. Baby was mountainous, now when Baby gave someone a hug, she seemed to envelop him or her entirely.

As Baby's size increased, so did her antagonism towards Miriam. It seemed to radiate from her; in the way she tried to crowd Miriam out...to pretend Miriam wasn't there. Miriam wished that she could look the other way, but Baby could not be ignored. There was a weight to Baby's presence that went beyond size, and an intensity to her rage that went beyond fury. *A woman scorned!*

Miriam was a bug that Baby wished she could squash. However, this connection between Baby and Miriam seemed lost on everyone else. *Everyone, accept the old woman.* The old woman seemed to relish in the indignations that Miriam received. Miriam could not speak two sentences without Baby interrupting her and hijacking the conversation. As if she were a gofer or a personal servant Baby would send Miriam on little tasks.

"Miriam, be a dear and put away these dirty dishes...Miriam do grab some sugar for the tea...Miriam see if any of the men want more dessert..."

Baby always made certain that Miriam was never seated in a place of visibility, even if Miriam started out sitting in the middle of the room, she would somehow end up secluded in a corner. If Miriam were to ever leave her seat, she would come back to find it occupied by someone else and Miriam would be left scrambling looking for a place to sit. *Miriam knew that Baby was behind it.*

Miriam also had to watch herself physically. If she happened to be in Baby's path, Baby would brush Miriam aside with so much force and agility it was like she was sweeping a fly out of her face. Miriam felt like she was a twig that Baby could snap at any time. The old woman never missed any of it. She said nothing...but there was a smugness, perhaps even amusement in her eyes.

If Miriam was a gentle twig hanging precariously from a branch, then Baby was as thick as the trunk of an ancient tree. Adeel and Rosina Lakhani helplessly watched Baby grow and expand. Their attitude spanned from anxious, to optimistic, to defensive. In their denial they often made excuses for Baby.

"She's always been a big girl..."

"She's trying to lose weight..."

Through it all, the old woman was as serene and impassive as if she were merely an observer but Miriam knew, *in a place in her heart that she dare not visit*, that it was the calm of a cobra before it strikes and the depth of quicksand as it waits for an unwitting victim.

In contrast to how the old woman treated Miriam, she would dote on Baby. She would caress her hair and whisper in her ear often handing her a cup of tea, and then indulgently she would say.

"Baby, you're not eating enough. Take more."

Curiously, she was right. Miriam never saw Baby eating anything; no more than a nibble here and there, no matter what was served. *Yet Baby never got smaller...*

Miriam wondered if the old woman's feelings for Baby came from love or revulsion. Everyone knew that Baby was a rich heiress. Everyone knew she was Adeel Lakahni's daughter. Few, not even Miriam, would ever guess that she was the progeny of Humara's old lover; the man that had occupied her bed and perhaps at one time her heart. This detail was lost the way a pearl becomes lost in the all-encompassing ocean. Ignorant of this connection and moved by the momentous event about to take place in her daughter's life Rosina Lakahni began reminiscing about her own wedding.

It was towards the end of a dinner party. The hosts (both doctors) were colleagues of Kashif. They had been part of the community for many years and their children had grown-up if not with Adnan, then around him. Dinner was long over and the last morsels of dessert were trying to find space in an already crowded stomach. Everyone was on his or her second cup of tea. Rosina Lakahni had broken a lull in the conversation that had occurred just a few minutes ago.

"It seemed like only yesterday," she sighed and looked

overhead as if looking back into time, her beaky nose acting as an arrow into the distant past.

"If I close my eyes, I can still smell the henna that decorated my hands," she added.

"I'm sure you must have made a beautiful bride," said the host's daughter, a young girl not much older than Miriam.

"I don't know. In those days we were not so confident or so advanced when it comes to make-up and clothes and…I was such…such a small wiry thing."

The girl was about to say more when Adeel interrupted.

"Don't believe her. She was a beautiful bride," said Adeel Lahkani grinning. "I was taken with her from the first instant I saw her."

Rosina Lakahni's blush carried so much charm that Miriam felt her heart melt.

"Was she the most beautiful bride you ever saw," now the girl was starry-eyed.

"Yes," he said.

Everyone was taken by the warmth of his response and for the first time at a dinner party Miriam's heart felt toasty. Miriam was still basking in the tenderness of the moment when she inadvertently looked over at Humara. Her lips were curled in what should have been a smile but looked more like a sneer and the only thing in her eyes was contempt.

As Miriam looked at the old woman her mouth felt dry and metallic. Miriam went into the bathroom and hurled.

TWENTY FOUR

Ashes, Ashes; We All Fall Down

The taste of bile still lingered in Humara's mouth. It had been bothering her for days...ever since the engagement. She felt like a snake bringing up its own venom. It colored the flavor of everything she ate and made it just a little bit metallic. Her bones felt heavy today. She was tempted to ask Miriam to bring up breakfast to her bedroom, but it was not like Humara to give in to fatigue. Instead, she would take a long bath that night and perhaps a nap after lunch. Work always made her so weary, she thought looking down at the smooth photograph in her hand – *scraps of the past*. The figures stood side by side holding hands. Humara fingered the contours of their profiles as if she could feel their smooth skin beneath her fingers. The colors in the snapshot had become muted over time but still a good likeness. It almost made her feel nostalgic, for a second...only for a second. Humara had not come as far as she had in life by being indecisive.

There was a time when Humara had not been so sure of herself. When she had stumbled fleetingly through a forgotten cemetery and the ground beneath her feet seemed to crumble at every turn. Day-by-day and year-by-year, the appetite that had been awakened that night only became stronger. What had seemed foreign to Humara as a girl had now become second nature and it craved more and more – *it had always been so hungry.* It was a hunger that resulted in remarkable things even as it consumed her flesh, and drew the strength from her bones, as it drank the color and luster of her hair and the smoothness of her skin. Now she realized that the youth it taken had only been a down payment. It would take more. It was still hungry. No matter, it would live after she was gone, but Humara was not done yet. She needed strength. She needed food. Perhaps, she would summon Miriam and let her know she would not be taking her usual breakfast this morning. She was feeling her appetite coming back. She would have eggs and paratas (bread) and tea, maybe even some mehtai (sweets). *Now where was that girl?*

❖ ❖ ❖

Miriam hated being in such a small space with Humara. She hated the feeling of intimacy it gave her, standing in her private chambers, smelling her musky perfumes and the underlying odor of mold that always seemed to follow her. Miriam stood inside as the old woman looked up at her from her cushioned seat by the vanity. It was like the room was watching…the heavy curtains…the mahogany furniture…the thick carpet and the beautiful crystal jars and the talisman. It made Miriam want to run out but, Miriam always stood firmly rooted in her spot as if held by invisible chains; it was a feeling like paralysis. No one could leave the old woman's confidence without being dismissed. It often filled Miriam with dread as if even when she was looking away, it felt like she was concentrating on her every word, every expression and every thought.

The old woman was giving Miriam the details of her

meal plan, what she wanted for breakfast and what she might want for tea later on. It was like any other day, but today she eyed Miriam curiously, *as she never had before*. A wave of guilt, shame and dread overcame her. She wondered if Humara had read something in her face, in her gesture, found some little act of treachery. Miriam did what she always did, she retreated within herself to the place she knew an unseen force watched her back and put on a mask that she hopped was impenetrable.

Miriam helped the old woman dress and make her way downstairs. Humara felt her bones creak with each step, even though Miriam was supporting most of her weight. Still, Humara could not help being vexed. The girl with her dour appearance and subservient nature etched annoyance on her last nerve. Humara enjoyed toying with the weak, as she had with Miriam, but the girl's humility had provided a shield that did not let anything Humara did touch her. This infuriated the old woman beyond measure and she barked at Miriam with unintended gruffness.

It was a small thing. Miriam had left Humara's shawl upstairs. It was always drafty with this terrible weather. Humara was never complete without her favorite shawl.

"For God sake, go back and get it," she snarled.

The coldness in her voice made Miriam jump and she ran upstairs. She only hesitated for a moment before entering the old woman's room (*and who could blame her*). The door creaked as she opened it. A vague uneasiness filled Miriam as she entered the room as if at any moment she could get caught, as if she were somewhere she shouldn't be…Miriam looked around, the shawl was right there, draped over the chair the old woman had occupied only a few moments earlier. Miriam grabbed it and was about to run out when she saw something fall out of its folds…a picture. She recognized these people, had seen them before and now she realized she had even met them. It was an old picture of Adeel and Rosina Lakahni on what looked to be their wedding day. It was a lifetime ago and they looked as young and as innocent as children taking their first shaky steps. *How had Humara come across this?*

Not knowing why, Miriam left the picture on the floor underneath the chair and hurried down. When Miriam returned with the shawl the old woman decided she didn't want it anymore. Miriam was about to put it back.

"No leave it…leave it, I'll use it later," she snapped when Miriam handed her the shawl.

"It's not raining after all and I may use it to go outside."

"Is there anything else I can get for you *Ammah*?"

But there was nothing the old woman wanted and she sent Miriam on her way. Humara set about organizing her kitchen and knitting sweaters for her grandchildren, (the only ones she would likely have if things did not work out with Adnan) and if the weather held, she may sputter around in the garden. Her herbs needed tending to. Towards the middle of the day, Humara opened the living room window and let in a breeze. It had become a stuffy afternoon but it was still gray outside. It was apparent that the dark clouds still had not rescinded on their threats and the pretty suburban lawns had not been punished enough. Humara could not help but notice an odor that had followed the wind into their house. It was not the moist, muggy smell of too much rain or the earthy scent of soil as it turns to mud. It was not the moldy smell of leaves after they turn brown and before they disintegrate to the earth. Today the wind smelled of acidity. No matter where she went, how many windows she opened, or how many candles she lit, the faint smell lay just below the surface until it sat like a rock in the pit of her stomach. She could feel it, a lump just below her breastbone, a gaseous little knot that would not leave her alone. It was there when she was having breakfast in the morning. It was there as she sat knitting mittens for her grandchildren. It was there as she planned Adnan and Baby's wedding and while she planned Adnan's career and Miriam's demise. Humara was not sure why it bothered her and why she could not ignore it until she realized that it was the type of acidity that implied decay.

When that thought came to her, it came with the certainty of thunder and the knowledge of lightning before it strikes. It came with an urgency her old bones had not felt in several lifetimes. Humara began going through the bedroom like a bat sniffing out its prey. Drawer after drawer, she searched for the smell of the odor—an empty packet, a misplaced charm, a piece of jewelry that should not be there carefully hidden inside the folds of a sweater or a scarf. She emptied her drawers and her closet until there was nothing left but the yellow stench of acidity, even stronger than before.

Next, Humara went to the garden and began to dig. She began with the patch where she would normally plant her vegetables, and then the herb garden that she tended to every year, and finally she moved to the flowers that grew around the perimeter like a long garland. It all had to come out, for she could feel the stench stronger than ever.

When Humara's fingers were raw and cold and muddy, when her sari had long been ruined, her hair disheveled, and her face streaked with the unrelenting trickle of rain, the stench still lingered inside her, and she began to understand that it was time to go inside.

❖ ❖ ❖

Miriam had watched Humara sniff at her breakfast that morning, as if she was trying a foreign dish. The old woman, who normally had a good appetite, spent more time dissecting her over-easy eggs and letting the yolk spill out of them than she spent actually eating them. Miriam wondered if the old woman had something on her mind. Was she really not hungry, or was this a jab at Miriam's cooking? Miriam looked at the old woman's face, but the deep creases and loose skin made it hard to detect emotion—such was the mask of old age. It was only her eyes and the tone of her voice that ever revealed or betrayed her true feelings. Miriam never tried to understand the old woman. It was like trying to understand a chameleon. Miriam was simply glad that she was spending the day at the office instead of at home with Humara's erratic moods.

In fact, she was feeling lucky today. No harm had come from that precious little vial, and she spent her day smiling as if a big weight had been lifted off her shoulders, even joking around with Dr. Geller and some of the patients. Usually, she just greeted her patients and let them have a seat. Today she asked about their weekends, their work, their children, and their grandchildren. Her pleasantness was contagious, and many of them felt more relaxed than usual going into the dentist's chair. Several patients commented on how well she looked, and it was true. The flu that had turned Miriam into a walking zombie the week before was long gone, flushed out of her system, and Miriam had gotten some of the color back into her face.

Miriam finished her day in good spirits. Even the clouds that had been threatening rain all morning let Miriam pass through them warm and dry, though they did offer a slight gurgle now and then. It is possibly for that reason that Miriam did not notice the quietness of the house as she entered. At first Miriam mistook the emptiness for peacefulness, but it was not so.

Instead, it was the type of silence that waits surreptitiously and lurks in the corner of rooms and abandoned hallways. It was the type of silence that creeps up and then pounces just as one reaches the end of a long corridor. That is what Miriam would discover when she came home that afternoon.

She did not think anything of the quietness or the

echo of her voice as she announced her presence. She did not notice much until she went looking for the old woman and found the house in disarray. As she went through the different rooms, she found cushions overturned, magazines spilled, and cabinets emptied. If she did not know any better, she would have thought that the old woman had had a party—but no, the rooms were the not the result of any party. Miriam went into the kitchen and noticed that the back door had not been completely shut, allowing a cool gust of wind to bring in specks of rain—just enough to shrug off, but also enough to know that it was really going to come down later.

When Miriam went outside, the Ashrufs' pretty backyard looked no better than the living room, with tools on the lawn and plants uprooted and Humara nowhere to be found. Miriam finally found the old woman in her bedroom, curled up in a chair, shivering with a vacant expression on her face and staring at nothing in particular. Miriam asked her if she needed anything and if she was looking for something in the house, but Humara simply said that she was doing some spring cleaning and working in the garden. Not knowing what else she could do, Miriam helped the old woman into bed, for she felt warm and cold at the same time and Miriam was concerned she might be coming down with something. Miriam left the curiously disheveled room and spent the next hour straightening up the house, the overturned pillows, and the emptied drawers. All had to go back before she went ahead and started dinner. Miriam thought that Humara would come down at any minute and attempt to supervise dinner or point out some area of the house that had not been straightened up, cleaned, or properly organized, but the old woman did not appear. Miriam finished dinner went into the living room and watched an hour of TV. Adnan came home and quietly joined her in front of the tube, and then Kashif. It was almost like old times.

The three of them had a quiet dinner without the

Lakahnis. An outsider could have mistaken them for a real family, with Adnan inquiring about everyone's day, Kashif complaining about the weather, and Miriam filling everyone's plate. Without Baby around, Adnan had acquired a softer disposition, even joking around with her a bit (his demeanor tinged with remorse). It seemed to Miriam that there was something he wanted to say. Something that should have been said a long time ago, but Kashif who was normally sullen, kept yammering on and the air was still thick with the old woman's absence.

Soon they ran out of small talk. Kashif thought ahead to some journals he wanted to read, Adnan contemplated calling some of the guys he had not seen since the Lakahnis had come into his life, and Miriam pondered what was going on with the old woman and how she was going to get that ringing out of her ear, the soft lilting ring that sounded like a woman's laughter. Even those plans seemed not to fill the empty space of the large dining room. The house was silent except for the pitter-patter of rain on the rooftop. Everyone chewed their food soberly, savoring the flavor and helping themselves to seconds.

Since the old woman had not come down for the dinner, Kashif wondered if she was feeling all right. Miriam fixed a plate and took it upstairs to the old woman's room, but she was sleeping soundly. Miriam put the leftovers into the fridge, helped herself to some ice cream, and curled up with a book she had borrowed from the library. It was ten weeks overdue, and Miriam still had not started it. *Well, there's no time like the present,* she thought and began with chapter one.

In the morning, Miriam was the first to rise. It had stopped raining the night before and the dark clouds had lightened, some letting rays of sunlight peek through. Miriam had decided, for the first time in ages, to go for a jog before breakfast. When she arrived back at home thirty minutes later, she was sweating and panting—*Gosh, I am so out of shape*, she thought. Miriam poured herself some orange juice and began cracking eggs and putting on coffee, but curiously, only Kashif and Adnan came down for breakfast. Miriam in all her years as part of the Ashruf household, could not ever recall the old woman sleeping in. She was usually up at dawn, puttering around in the kitchen or the garden; although what exactly she was doing Miriam had yet to figure out. She wasn't helping with breakfast, that's for sure. Both Kashif and Adnan noticed her absence.

"Has *Ammah* gone out this morning?" he asked.

"No, she is still in bed," said Miriam.

The brothers exchanged worried glances that made Miriam feel she should go upstairs and check on the old woman.

❖ ❖ ❖

Miriam stood silently outside the old woman's door, but she could hear no movement on the other side. She tapped lightly, feeling a little uncomfortable, but there was no sound and no acknowledgement from the old woman. Miriam rapped a little louder.

"*Ammah*! *Ammah*, it's Miriam," she called out, but when she still got no response, she slowly opened the door.

The curtains were drawn, and it took Miriam a minute to adjust to the darkness. The air inside the room felt thin, as if she had entered a tomb. Miriam started to feel cold despite her rigorous workout. She took a couple of anxious steps toward the bed.

The old woman lay almost lost in the massive comforter. Her eyes were closed, and her skin looked chalky—she was clearly out. Miriam put a hand on her forehead and nearly jumped back. So cold was the touch that Miriam thought she had passed on, but no—there was a faint breath . . . she was alive. Miriam began to shake the old woman.

"*Ammahh! Ammahh . . . AMMAHH!*"

Then she began to yell for Kashif to come quickly.

TWENTY FIVE

I'll Huff and I'll Puff...
And I'll Blow Your House Down

The room had an ominous odor that made Miriam reluctant to stay inside. She lingered back behind the door while Kashif went to check on the old woman. The curtains were drawn, and when Kashif lit the little lamp on the night table, it populated the room with shadows that leapt from the walls to the ceilings, seeming to watch them from above. From that angle, she looked quite frail, sinking deeper and deeper into the plush bed and soft pillows, getting lost in the willowy folds.

Kashif sat at the edge of her bed. He took one look at her and turned pale. He felt her pulse; it was weak.

"Miriam, call an ambulance."

Since the rain had started, children had stopped playing basketball or soccer on the street. Mothers stopped taking their babies to the park, and grandparents rarely went out for long walks in the afternoon, putting an end to the circulation of news in the quiet little burrow. The salivating tongues of the gossipmongers had finally run dry. It was a drought that had left the residents bored and a little bit anxious, making the neighborhood as humdrum as the monotonous rain, whose thirst for land never seemed to run dry.

So when they heard the piercing of the ambulance and saw the flash of red as it zoomed by, they raised their eyebrows, quickly tore themselves away from their newspapers, and let their breakfasts sit cold for a few minutes while they shamelessly looked out their windows. Outside, the cars slowed a little more than was necessary. Windows rolled down despite the rain, and necks craned back a little more than was comfortable—all this in the hopes of catching a glimpse of where that bright flash was headed. When the ambulance was out of earshot and when the bright lights had become a fading star, they sighed a little, knowing that this flash in the middle of their morning was an omen, an omen that news would follow that afternoon. For of all the houses on all the streets that the ambulance could have gone to, it turned onto the quiet road at the end of the block where the Ashrufs' large house laid waiting. And for reasons unknown, a nervous energy—not quite excitement, not quite dread—trickled through the neighborhood. It was that and that alone that would bring life back into the community. For the next several weeks, the Ashrufs' household would resume its old position as the center of gossip, and for the first time in many weeks, phones would begin to ring as residents began their slow emergence from hibernation. Shaking out their umbrellas and braving the unpredictable weather, they began to drop by for a warm cup of coffee—for now, more than ever; there was news to tell.

At eight in the morning, it was quickly decided that Kashif would ride in the ambulance with Humara, answering the paramedics' questions and providing details regarding her condition and medical history while Miriam and Adnan would follow behind.

Like a boisterous prophet, the ambulance led the way, clearing a path for them amongst the rush-hour traffic, and Miriam and Adnan passed through like favored disciples all the way to the emergency room, where Adnan dropped Miriam off and proceeded to park the car. The morning shift in the ER had been on duty for a couple of hours already. The distant sound of the ambulance resonated somewhere in the collective sixth sense that always seem to know when a trauma case was coming, but when the ambulance arrived and the patient was rolled into the E.R. (along with a haughty middle aged man) it was only an old woman—an old woman who was barely breathing.

If the staff did not recognize his name or his face right away, they were certainly familiar with the authoritative manner in which Kashif described her symptoms and the details of her medical history. It was the calm, reassuring *"I-know-what-I'm-talking-about"* manner that his patients and staff had learned to trust. It was that manner that had implied his status even before they ever learned his name. Many of Kashif's colleagues practiced there, and several of his patients had passed through its doors and so it was not long before someone who knew Dr. Kashif Ashruf either personally or professionally turned up. This provided Miriam and Adnan some relief as they filled out the paperwork. It wouldn't be until much later that Kashif's strong demeanor would begin to crumble and Miriam would see his faith disintegrate into nothing.

In the end, there was nothing for Miriam to do but sit and wait and watch the ticking of the clock, make the appropriate phone calls, and flip through outdated magazines with the pictures and recipes cut out by overzealous readers. No, there was nothing to do but watch the expressions on the faces of the other visitors or turn her gaze toward Adnan, who sat silently flipping through his iPhone and who had not said a word to her all morning.

It was still early the old woman would be fine, thought Miriam and so the silence of the quiet waiting room did not bother her, it did not pluck at her conscience, it did not make her reconsider her actions, but this would soon change.

Miriam feeling sufficiently useless and not wanting to talk to Adnan or interrupt Kashif, did the only thing one can do in these situations—she went to the cafeteria to grab a couple of coffees. That provided enough distraction to keep Miriam's mind off the old woman, for the hospital was like a labyrinth unto itself. A large self-sustaining community opened up to Miriam as she passed the various departments and waiting areas to the cafeteria that resembled a modern food court more than any cafeteria she had ever seen. Instead of women in hair nets and mystery meat, there were contemporary serving stations that included pizza and pasta, a deli, Chinese food, and sushi, plus a bakery with an assortment of sliced pies, tarts, and brownies. When Miriam got to the coffee station, it was akin to stepping into a Starbucks—there was Irish Cream, Hazelnut, French Vanilla, Amaretto, and several blends she did not recognize. Miriam stood for a couple of seconds contemplating her decision. Randomly, she chose French Vanilla and carried the three coffees back to the waiting area along with cream and sugar.

Kashif was still talking to the doctors. Adnan sat by himself hunched over a textbook. Normally, Adnan had a reputation for turning coffee into a dessert, but today, either not noticing or not caring about the cream and sugar, Adnan took a cup and drank it black. Miriam took the other coffee, added two creams and two sugars, and gave it to Kashif.

Kashif was in the middle of a conversation with one of the residents about Humara's blood work. The young resident, who had been quiet for the last five minutes, began to look annoyed. It became apparent to Miriam that Kashif may have been overstepping his bounds. Not wanting to interrupt, Miriam held the coffee out to him. Kashif took it without as much as a glance in Miriam's direction.

"Please sir, we're trying to do our jobs."

With that, Kashif was relegated to the waiting room with the rest of the family.

By the second day, the Lakahnis had arrived. Baby walked into the hospital, turning several heads with a presence that was as commanding as her girth. Mr. and Mrs. Lakahni followed behind, looking around distastefully as if they had stepped into a hotel that wasn't quite up to par. The Lakahnis offered their regards to Kashif and inquired about the old woman's condition. There was little information available to them, and only family members were allowed to visit. Still, the Lakahnis sat down in the waiting room, a little shaken, for their daughter's future was at stake. They were worried about what would happen to the wedding plans if the old woman did not make it. Even then, everything had to be put on hold until Humara was reasonably recovered.

With little else to do, Mrs. Lakahni selected *Good Housekeeping* from the magazine rack while Mr. Lakahni flipped quickly through an old issue of *Newsweek* and then began responding to emails on his Blackberry. Both glanced at each other with worried expressions.

Only Baby seemed to be in her element, turning from shy bride to pushy housemother overnight. She stroked and coddled Adnan as if he were an injured animal. She ordered Miriam around, making her bring tea, get lunch, make phone calls, and arrange for Mrs. Lakahni to be picked up and dropped off at the hospital, all at the Ashrufs' expense. Since it was a crisis situation Baby decided to temporarily forgo her 'diet'. It was making her weak anyway and she would need her energy now more than ever. Whenever Miriam saw her, Baby was chewing on a muffin, bagel, doughnut, or slice of pizza, with the food giving her the gall to exert herself.

❖ ❖ ❖

Time moved slowly for Adeel Lakahni. He was not used to sitting with his legs crossed all day. Twice, he had been shushed for speaking too loudly on his cell phone. Eventually, after an hour and half in the waiting room, he decided to see if the cafeteria offered any tea. When he got to the cafeteria, it was in between meals and the large seating area remained mainly unoccupied. It was quiet enough that he could prop open his laptop, look over some documents, and make a couple of calls. He had only planned to be in the cafeteria for thirty minutes or so, but before he knew it, three hours had passed, and Mrs. Lakahni, tired and hungry, was standing in front of him and asking him to drop her off at home.

"Alright," he mumbled, as he saw an urgent message pop up in his e-mail. His developer was having some finance trouble. He needed to take care of it right away, and so they packed up and headed out. The two gave their sympathies to the family and proceeded back. Baby decided to stay at the hospital with Adnan.

By the second week, no clear diagnosis of Humara's illness had been made. At first the doctor's thought that it might be the result of complications of the flu or pneumonia, but that was not the case. Day by day, her symptoms seem to worsen, and become increasingly unconventional. The doctors scratched their heads and took more and more tests. Eventually, a strange rash began to appear, and slowly, Humara's body stopped functioning on its own.

When the long days turned into even longer weeks, Kashif was the only one who chose not to go home, preferring instead to sleep on a cot or in a spare room. Until then, Miriam had not realized how attached Kashif had been to the old woman. He had gotten Claudia to pass his appointments off to his partners and cancel all his meetings and conferences. After several days of absence when Claudia asked him to come over and let her fix dinner he answered coldly, "I can't be bothered with this right now."

The routine eventually began to take its toll. Kashif began to look old and haggard. People began mistaking him for Miriam's father with his gray beard, wrinkled clothes, loose skin, and dark circles under his eyes. Finally, Adnan convinced him to go home for a night and get some rest. He promised to stay at the hospital in Kashif's place.

Although Kashif agreed to leave the hospital, he did not want to go home. He spent an hour driving around the city. The road had led him back to his practice, where he sat in the parking lot staring blankly at the dashboard. As the car idled, the windows fogged up, giving him the distinct impression of being in a coffin. He had been there for an hour thinking not of the old woman, but of Afsana. For the first time he truly hated her.

Finally, he called Claudia. He was expecting Claudia's soft, sultry voice to make him forget the way she always had in the past, but a strange man answered the phone. Claudia was in the shower. Could he take a message? When Kashif asked who the man was, he simply hung up the phone. Astonished, he didn't know what to do. It was undoubtedly the end.

TWENTY SIX

The Old Man is Snoring

Perhaps it was the dull thudding of raindrops or the tedium of the hospital or Baby's incessant chirping, but it was enough to lull Adeel Lakahni into a false sense of security. So when the first message popped up on his Blackberry, Adeel, overcome with monotony, ignored it. Delays in construction happened all the time. *These things generally work themselves out;* he thought and so he left it unanswered for several days.

The old Lakahni, *sharp-as-a blade Lakahni* would have seen through the tepid words. The old Lakahni could sense a run around the way a shark sensed blood. It was this damned weather; it was dulling his senses. And so instead, Adeel Lakahni merely gave the message a cursory glance before he moved on to other matters, confident to leave the problem in other people's hands. After all, the developer had come highly recommended and had a solid reputation. Normally, he may have asked Adnan to look into the temporary halt in construction and report back with more details, but since Humara's illness, Adnan had rarely shown up for work, leaving Adeel to pick up the slack and run his own errands; all this on top of showing up at the hospital every day for a couple of hours . . . it was family duty after all.

Adeel looked over at his wife. They had been there for three hours, and Rosina was looking tired. He had noticed her looking more and more fatigued lately. The town did not seem to be agreeing with her. He decided he would take her home. Baby could stay if she wanted, but he needed to get back and do some proper work—and besides, he was running out of things to say to Kashif and Miriam. It was strange, he thought. Since the ordeal, Kashif's mental health seemed to be deteriorating. He looked depressed, even morose, but Miriam seemed to be increasingly serene, even well rested. There was an evasiveness about her, as if she knew exactly what was going on. It unnerved him if he thought about it too much.

Miriam wished that she could stop Baby's constant yammering, although most of it was directed toward Adnan. Baby barely acknowledged Miriam's presence if she wasn't making a request or barking an order. Still Baby's presence was hard to ignore. She seemed to fill the whole room, both literally and figuratively. As hard as Miriam tried, she could not concentrate on the *Reader's Digest* she was flipping through. She had been doing her best to try to ignore what had happened in the last couple of days and was, instead, daydreaming about what it would be like to go on one of those exotic expeditions. She could see herself traipsing through the desert on a camel like an ancient nomad, feeding berries to a friendly llama, but every time it would open its large mouth to accept Miriam's gift, out would come Baby's voice, saying she preferred fruit only in the mornings, covered with sugar and with fresh yogurt—that was the best way to stay regular, and when Humara Auntie was well again, she was going to take complete control of her diet, ensuring that

Humara Auntie would be as happy and healthy as she was...

"She doesn't eat enough; that's what the problem is," said Baby as she nibbled on a meatball sub from the cafeteria.

Miriam noticed that Mr. Lakahni had grabbed his briefcase and jacket. He looked distracted. He was standing beside Mrs. Lakahni, who was looking rather green. Miriam watched him walk over to the couple. She could hear him tell Baby and Adnan that they were going home. Baby barely looked up. She had a sandwich in her mouth and her eyes on Adnan.

"You'll see that she gets home safe," said Mr. Lakahni.

Adnan nodded and looked up from the conversation with an expression that seemed to say, "Are you sure you don't want to take her with you?"

❖ ❖ ❖

It was near the end of the day. Rosina Lakahni had just finished making a pot of tea when she felt it starting again. It had become more frequent now—the fatigue, the nausea, and the dizzy spells. *It must be the flu*, she thought. Going to the hospital every day, full of germs, she must have picked up something; and the hectic schedule did not help—that's what the rational voice inside her head told her. It was the voice she had chosen to listen to, because the alternative was something her mind could not comprehend; and so she would not give it credence, but she knew—she knew deep in her heart, as darkness washed over her eyes, that this was no ordinary flu. The nausea she felt was consuming her like a living, breathing entity. She could feel it living in the pit of her stomach, warm and slippery, waiting to come out. Rosina struggled to remember what she was about to do when a loud noise punctured her thoughts. It took a few moments for Rosina to recall that she was about to ask her husband if he wanted a cup of tea.

The bang echoed that much louder as Adeel Lakahni slammed the phone onto its cradle and sat back down on his chair, waiting for the ringing to dissipate. Further research into the delays revealed something more disastrous than he had ever imagined. Local residents were petitioning to declare the site of the construction project historic marshland. As it turned out, the developer had overlooked the fact that the area contained some rather rare flora and fauna, and construction would disrupt the ecosystem. *Those lawyers better do their jobs*, thought Adeel. If the petition was granted, the land would belong to the state and the project would go down the tubes, taking with it the funds of some rather large investors, including Adeel, who was one of the major backers of the development.

Adeel could feel prickles of apprehension going down the back of his neck. He did not like feeling uneasy. Tomorrow he was going to get another status report from his lawyers, and then he was going to talk to the developers. He was about to get his file from his briefcase when he looked up to see Rosina standing at the door, bleary-eyed, trying to steady herself.

"Rosina, are you all right?" asked Adeel, looking up. "Perhaps you should go lie down . . ."

Rosina was about to answer and say that was a good idea when the warm, slippery feeling that had been creeping up her body reached her throat. Despite her dizziness, she found that her feet had successfully guided her to the bathroom across the hall, where Rosina heaved the contents of a soup and sandwich that she had eaten for lunch. It was that first time she had thrown up that day, but it would not be the last.

It was only when Rosina finished vomiting that she realized her husband was kneeling on the floor beside her. He brought her a cup of mouthwash to rinse her mouth and carefully guided her into the bedroom and tucked her back into bed. He thought she might have a fever. He could feel the heat emanating from her body. He wanted to take her temperature, but she was already drifting off, and although her hands were cold, he could see beads of sweat glistening on her forehead. Who should he call—Kashif? No, he would not be much help. He would see how she was feeling when she woke up; maybe get her a nice cup of soup.

It was after sunset when Miriam and Adnan put Baby in the taxi and headed home for the day. Baby had wanted to come back to the house with them and stay with them while Humara was in the hospital, but to Miriam's relief Adnan had insisted she go home. They stood outside waiting for the cab. Baby had a large Frappuccino in one hand and leftover dessert in the other. Miriam looked at Baby and rubbed her eyes. Was it just her, or was Baby getting bigger? She had not noticed until they had gotten into the elevator and it had seemed obscenely small. Wedged in between Baby and the wall, Miriam felt she was going to be smothered by Baby's large breasts. The scent of Baby's perfume was strong enough to make Miriam think she might pass out. It was with much relief that she stepped out into the lobby of the ground floor gasping for air. She looked over to Adnan; perspiration had plastered his locks to his forehead.

During dinner, Baby was the only one who had finished her plate and had dessert. Normally Miriam would not think this was strange, but Baby was eating all the time now without the customary hour or two to come up for air, and it was really starting to show. When the cab came, Miriam almost missed it because Baby was standing a few feet in front of her. Miriam watched as Baby struggled to squeeze inside while the cabby held the door open for her. First she had to get one half of her body in and then the other, and when Baby was fully inside, the cabby shut the door, gave Adnan the thumbs-up sign, and proceeded to drive Baby home. Adnan wiped his forehead and gave Miriam a relieved smile. They could finally go home, but when they got home they were both too wired to sleep. Adnan flipped the channels on the tube. There was an old monster movie marathon going on featuring classic Godzilla films. It was another thing that Miriam and Adnan had in common. Miriam nuked a large bowl of popcorn. It took the edge off the events of the last couple months. They watched most of the night letting the horrific, incredible, fantastic and sometimes even hilarious monsters on the screen crowd out the monsters in their own lives.

❖ ❖ ❖

Baby arrived home from the hospital. She unlocked the door and maneuvered herself through the frame. She could hear her parents sleeping. Her father was snoring softly. It had taken Baby ten minutes to climb out of the narrow door of the cab; in the end, the driver had to come out and give her a hand. Baby softly thudded into the lobby of the building, finding that she had to go in through the automatic handicap doors rather than the revolving doors that were meant for the rest of the public, and then she took the small elevator up to the twenty-fourth floor. All day, she felt jittery, with Adnan being distant and remote and Miriam laughing at her with those wide, innocent eyes that did not fool anybody. The only thing that seemed to calm her for at least a couple moments was the warm feeling in the pit of her stomach after she had finished a meal. Generally, this urgent desire came only a couple of times a day, but lately it was becoming more and more frequent; every time she passed by the cafeteria or a snack bar or even a vending machine, she could feel it calling out to her. She could feel her stomach responding—the urgent need for satisfaction. She saw herself growing out of her clothes more quickly than she could buy them; she had trouble fitting through doors. Still, she could not resist. It was calling her. She needed it. She needed it badly . . .

Instead of going to bed like she had originally intended, Baby went shamelessly into the kitchen. It was dark, but she did not need to turn on the light; she knew where everything was. She opened the fridge; the bright light shone out, nearly blinding her. When Baby looked directly into the light, she felt at peace. She felt at home, and she was about to shut the door when the light whispered to her. It was alive, and it beckoning her like a sly lover. Baby knew she shouldn't give in, but the light could be so tempting. She wanted to lose herself in it, to feel it envelop her, and to let go of all that she had been hanging on to for so long. And Baby did.

TWENTY SEVEN

When the Bough Breaks

The rain had curiously stopped. The pavement remained dry as dark clouds loomed overhead. Residents, in turn, walked nervously outside with umbrellas and rain gear in hand, looking furtively up at the sky, suspicious that the clouds threatening overhead were merely assembling their forces before they made another attack.

This collective paranoia was not lost on Miriam as she watched the old woman get weaker day by day and her husband, a strong, domineering man, disintegrate before her eyes. It was as if they were still joined by an invisible umbilical cord, Kashif's psychological disintegration paralleled by Humara's physical one. Miriam finally began to feel the first pangs of guilt seep through the carefully constructed wall that protected her conscience. No more could Miriam attribute the events to mere coincidence, as something was about to happen that would leave no room for doubt.

It seemed like such a small thing in the beginning, nothing that would raise an eyebrow. The Lakahnis always came and left the hospital at odd hours, showing up one day in the morning and the next in the evening, so when a whole day passed and none of the Ashrufs had seen a single Lakahni, no one thought it was unusual. Miriam figured that she had either just missed them or that they had other obligations to attend and were getting on with life. Frankly, the old woman was not even cognizant as to who was there and who wasn't, while Kashif could barely speak without turning into a blubbering idiot. Gradually, one day of absence turned into two, and two into three, and the nagging feeling at the back of Miriam's mind progressively got worse until finally she decided to approach Kashif.

Miriam caught Kashif pacing in the hallway, muttering to himself. He looked agitated and extremely tense. His head was facing downward and slightly to the left, as if addressing someone beside him. He had the angry tone of someone defending himself in an argument.

"You are a liar. How dare you accuse me! Yes . . . yes, it's terrible, but there was nothing I could do. Don't you dare take that tone with me! Now listen here . . ."

Several visitors walked by, keeping their distance and doing their best to avoid eye contact, and on more than one occasion, the hospital staff had looked at him with a raised eyebrow. It was only Dr. Ashruf's history with the hospital that kept him from being mistaken for a psychiatric patient.

Miriam had to repeat the question several times before Kashif appeared to understand what she was saying. Finally, he confirmed what Miriam suspected—that no, he had not heard from Adeel Lakahni.

Do you think you should call them?" she asked.
"Call them—whatever for?" he answered.

Next, Miriam decided to approach Adnan. Miriam found him studying in the cafeteria. Adnan's schedule had become routine, so she knew exactly where he was. As a third-year grad student, Adnan was only able to miss so many classes before it became impossible to catch up. Adnan now scheduled his lectures for the morning, after which he would drop by the hospital, visit the old woman, and speak with the nurse in charge. He would do his readings before he grabbed something to eat (usually with Miriam) and went back home. It was a nice routine and one that Miriam was starting to enjoy. Gradually, over several weeks, his grades and his study habits had become almost respectable, and it looked as if the old boy might graduate after all.

When Miriam found him, he was sitting with his economics textbook splayed open to a chapter on Rational Expectations, his head bopping ever so lightly to the tunes on his iPod.

"Sorry, I didn't see you," said Adnan, looking up in her direction and seeming more relaxed than he had in a long time. Miriam asked him if he had heard from the Lakahnis. He hadn't. Miriam asked if he didn't think it was strange that he had not heard from Baby, but he merely shrugged his shoulders, "*Why look a gift horse in the mouth?*"

It would have been easy to turn a blind eye, to leave well enough alone, but the instrument that had been using Miriam for the last couple of weeks wanted her to go forward. It kept whispering in her ear. It would not stop, and by then, Miriam knew better than to ignore it. It was for that reason and against her better judgment that Miriam borrowed Kashif's car and drove from the hospital to the Lakahni residence.

❖ ❖ ❖

It was the middle of the afternoon, and the sky had turned an eerie black, making it feel like dusk. Miriam, like everyone else, had learned to fear the weather's temperament too much to risk getting caught in the rain. She had left several messages for Mr. Lakahni the day before without receiving an answer back. Her last message said she would pop by for a visit. She hoped that they would be home. The Lakahnis were staying uptown in an elegant condominium complex where they were renting a furnished suite.

When she got to the building, the concierge in the stiff black suit reluctantly let her up. No one was answering the phone upstairs, and it was against building policy to let visitors up without authorization. Miriam was able to convince him that she was family and that it was urgent, and that was enough reason to get him to ring the Lakahnis a couple more times before someone appeared to answer on the other end, thus permitting Miriam to ride up to the twenty-fourth floor. The journey to the penthouse took a full minute, and as the lift increased in altitude, Miriam's stomach began to drop, her courage began to waver, and she began to worry if this visit was indeed the right thing to do. When the elevator door opened, she was left with no other choice than to move forward. The air felt thick, and every step felt heavy, as if Miriam was facing a monster at the end of the hall. Still, she walked down the corridor and rapped on the door.

When Mr. Lakahni opened it, she literally took a step back, thinking she had the wrong apartment. Adeel Lakahni stood in front of her, looking like a mad scientist rather than a sophisticated tycoon. His pajama shirt was tucked halfway into his pants, as if he had started getting dressed but then forgot what he was doing. His hair was disheveled and standing on end, Don King-style, looking like the victim of an electrical shock. The expression on his face was most agitated.

"Come in . . . come in," he said, scratching his head.

Miriam reluctantly entered the apartment, more certain now than ever that something was amiss.

"Sorry I have not returned your messages," he said, his voice wavering slightly. "It's these damned developers. They're trying to pull a fast one on me, but I see through them, and I'm going to make sure they get what's coming to them. Yes, they will rue the day they decided to mess with Adeel Lakahni. I will not accept defeat."

"Um…OK," said Miriam, not quite understanding. "We were just worried about you. We had not seen you for a couple days at the hospital."

"Oh, yes. How is Humara?"

"She's still the same . . . no change."

"That's terrible," said Mr. Lakahni, eyes watering, appearing to choke up a bit.

"Um . . . how is Rosina Auntie?" asked Miriam, not having seen her around.

At the mention of his wife, Adeel started blubbering.

"Poor Rosina. I've been checking on her constantly, but it only seems to be getting worse."

"What do you mean? What's getting worse?" asked Miriam. But all she could decipher amidst his tears was, "I left her in the bedroom."

Miriam followed Mr. Lakahni into the bedroom. She could hear Rosina's soft moans even before she approached the bed. Miriam looked at Rosina, who lay feverish and semi-conscious. Miriam laid a hand on her forehead. It felt hot enough to fry an egg, sunny-side up.

"Have you taken her temperature?" she asked.

"Her temperature." Adeel Lakahni looked at her, a bit confused.

"Yes, I think we should take her temperature," she said.

When Miriam took Mrs. Lakahni's temperature, she saw that it was 110 degrees.

"Oh, my God," she said. "I think we better call an ambulance."

The paramedics confirmed what Miriam already thought—that Mrs. Lakahni was very sick and may need to be admitted. It was thought to be a rare mutation of the flu that had somehow migrated to the Midwest from the tropics. The doctors would have to confirm the diagnosis. It had been on the news for some time now. As long as it was diagnosed early, it could be treated with antibiotics, but in advanced stages it was quite severe, even known to be fatal.

Mr. Lakahni left with the ambulance and Mrs. Lakahni, while Miriam stayed behind to lock up. Miriam took a quick look around the apartment. It looked haphazard and cluttered and was in dire need of a dusting. *I guess the help hasn't been coming in.* Miriam was about to leave the when she noticed that she had not seen Baby around. Usually, Baby was too big to miss. Miriam decided to ring Baby on her cell phone to make her aware of her mother's circumstances. She had gotten Baby's cell number just in case. Probably Baby was at the hospital with Adnan. Where else could she be?

Baby's cell phone rang several times, but there was no answer. Miriam was about to hang up when she heard a faint sound—a ringing. Miriam disconnected the line; the ringing stopped. She tried dialing Baby's number once more; there was that faint sound again. Was it possible that Baby's cell was somewhere in the house? Miriam followed the sound as it gradually became louder. She began to walk through the Lakahnis' apartment, from the foyer to the living room to the den and finally down the hall to the bedrooms, certain that the cell phone was somewhere in the house. The master bedroom was open but unoccupied. Miriam looked around. The bed was unmade. There was a walk-in closet with a neatly maintained wardrobe and vanity, and a powder room. That left one room that could possibly be Baby's. As she approached the bedroom, the sound heightened. Miriam put her ear to the door. She could hear a crunching sound, almost like the cackling of paper. She opened the door without knocking and took a bigger gasp than she had when she had seen Mr. Lakahni.

Inside sat not Baby but a caricature of Baby. Ballooned to a monstrous size, Baby now truly resembled the monster at the end of the hallway.

Baby said nothing as Miriam entered the room. There were bags of potato chips, pizza cartons, and cake trays everywhere. Baby sat focusing her attention on a chicken pot pie with the zeal of a starving lion. Miriam called out to her, but when Baby looked up, she had tears in her eyes...

"I can't make it stop," she said.

A chill went down Miriam's spine, as if she had looked upon the face of vengeance for the very first time.

"We're going to get you some help," she said and proceeded to call an ambulance for the second time that day. When the paramedics got there, they quickly ascertained that they would not be able to get her through the door without help from the fire department. So the fire department came, unhinged the door, and knocked out part of the wall to make it easier to get Baby out. Six strong fireman carried Baby down the staircase in a stretcher and into the ambulance.

When the doctors examined Baby, they found her to be a medical anomaly. Even when they stopped feeding her and only allowed her controlled substances, she continued to gain weight. At first, it was thought that someone must be sneaking in food. Miriam, Kashif, Adnan, and Mr. Lakahni were questioned. Her room was closely monitored, but the doctors could not find any evidence of unsanctioned meals.

The extra weight was starting to take a toll on her health; her heartbeat was slowing down, and her blood pressure was going up. She was a heart attack waiting to happen. Specialists were called for a second opinion. All the while, Baby had become foul-mouthed and cranky. The more they decreased her food intake, the bigger and the crankier she got, hurling obscenities at visitors and staff. Mr. Lakahni cried big watery teardrops when he saw what had happened to his little girl. Now almost bankrupt, he had little to manage but his time. His only consolation was that his wife was too sick to see this day.

TWENTY EIGHT

Who's the Fairest of Them All?

The drumming of raindrops provided a constant beat to the gentle hum of the machines that act as one's breath, one's heartbeat, one's pulse, and, in one old woman's case, one's consciousness. Yet it would not make a difference, for the woman in the hospital ward was dead already—she had died a long time ago, despite the fancy machines that kept her body alive. Still, she struggled for every breath, for every heartbeat—there was so much still to do. Relatives came and went. She looked at them as if they were strangers, ghosts. They were not real to her anymore. The veil between the living and the dead had become thin, and it was the spirits of the past who seemed more real than any flesh and blood. She had waited a long time to meet them. She could tell by the drone of the machines and the drip of the IV that the time was close at hand. She saw them all now; she heard their voices; she remembered their names. She could smell the scent of her husband's cologne once more.

    The currents that were crucial to keeping her alive made their way up the wires that had become as much a part of her body as the veins, blood vessels, and capillaries that lay beneath her skin. Her lips twitched a little, just for an instant, in what might be construed as either a smile or a grimace. As she was taking stock of her body—the old bones, the wrinkled skin, the failing organs—it occurred to her that, this was not the first time she had been an old woman. No—she was born an old woman in the height of her youth on one parched Lahore day.

One saw deep within the breast of a young woman that a notion as simple as curiosity could turn into desire and that desire, nursed properly, could blossom into ambition, and ambition was not innocent in the very least—for when ambition was threatened, it unleashed that which was the opposite of innocence. First, a day had passed when she had not seen the object of her ambition, and then a week, and two more. On the fourth night of the fourth week, she lay awake listening to the chirping of the crickets that punctuated the silence of the drought that always put her right to sleep. At first, she thought it was just the noise that was keeping her awake, but when she listened a little more closely, she could tell that their song brought bad tidings. When she awoke the next morning, she knew her love was gone, his heart plucked out of her hands like a stray breadcrumb. Despite the squawking of fate, she was not one to let her life crumble so easily. It was then that she made the decision to sacrifice her youth, dirty her hands, and turn herself into the young old woman she was destined to become. It was with a chuckle that she revisited her past, looking back on her days with full knowledge that it was not the first time in her life that she had, had to walk with a stooped back, musty breath, and bleary eyesight. It was not the first time that the stench of death had followed her like a shadow.

Even in the crowded marketplace, filled with the aroma of people and animals and food cooked outdoors, the vague sense of rot followed her. The animals were the first to sense it and move out of her way. Next the sea of people, asleep with their everyday agendas, experienced a prick of consciousness as their pulse quickened, the hair at the back of their necks stood up, and they experienced the feeling of lightness one gets just before falling asleep or waking up. That was enough to distract them from their paths ever so slightly, so that it appeared as though the crowd had parted to let her through—a raggedy old beggar.

Her appearance, though disturbing, was no accident—her skin old and wrinkled, her clothes dirty and tattered. A scarf covered her hair, and she stooped forward as she walked, bearing the weight of a large protruding back. Yet she was invisible in the crowd—no small feat indeed. The old woman walked slowly and intentionally, for the girl was not too far ahead, her loose hair flying behind her like a kite in the wind. She watched as the girl carelessly went in and out of shops. She knew too well that, given her appearance, she was not likely to be welcome in many of the shops that sold wares too precious for the likes of her, so she waited quietly.

Finally the opportunity that the she was waiting for presented itself. The girl stopped to examine some fresh fruit from a street vendor. The old woman appeared beside her so quietly that the girl did not notice. She was lost in her thoughts, in her appraisal of the fruit. The old woman silently assessed the girl, who was like a ripe piece of fruit herself—her complexion as smooth as cream, her eyes large and expressive, her rich brown hair trickling down to her hips with ribbons of unending locks.

While the old woman was at the brink of death, the girl was the never-ending fountain of life. She hated the girl. She looked at her with such venom that it was surprising that the girl did not feel the sting of her glare, but it was only for an instant, and within moments, a kindly expression crossed the old woman's face. It was only when the old woman spoke that the girl became aware of her presence. The girl turned around to see the ancient-looking grandmother lovingly caressing her hair.

"*Berta*, what lovely locks you have," she said, stroking a curl between her fingers. It was a little odd for one of her station to be so bold, but the girl, given her polite manners and good breeding, did not object. Instead, she looked up at her with a smile that was so fresh and so sweet that a shadow passed over the old woman's face, for if there was ever any doubt about what she was about to do, it had vanished like an icicle in the desert.

"*Berta*, will you reach to the back of the stand and grab a fresh piece of fruit for an old woman?"

"Of course, Auntie," she replied sweetly.

The girl reached over and selected a fruit that was not too ripe, for the scorching weather had shortened the life of many of the fruits and vegetables. As the girl was engrossed in her task, the old woman snipped a piece of hair put it into her pocket. When the girl turned around to show the old woman what she had selected, she found herself standing alone in front of the street vendor.

Later that day, the old woman took off the rags and burned them. She wiped the dirt from her still-young face and let her long, dark hair out of the scarf that had held it back, but it did not make a difference, for she could not change the eyes that would forever belong to an ancient creature—and the lock, the lovely curl that she stole from the young girl, she had given it a funeral she could not give its owner. She had taken it, dressed it, and buried it with the dead—an early grave, so that the owner's youth and vitality might wither away like a brittle piece of dead hair.

From that day forth, no matter what her outward appearance may have suggested, she remained an old woman. For when innocence dies in such a fashion, it can never again be recovered. Even after crossing oceans and deserts, leaving entire continents behind, the old woman found that there was one face that had never left her side. It was the smiling face of a young girl on the brink of womanhood that waited for her on the other side. She felt regret as her body began to disintegrate before her. She had been careless. Before she went, she would have liked to smoke out the source of the enchantment, but she felt her strength ebbing away from her second by second. She knew that she would be gone before the day was done.

No matter—there is still time.

TWENTY NINE

Twinkle, Twinkle Little Star

It was late. Too late be out alone at night, driving in the rain but Sonia was plagued with problems—her own problems, as well as the ghastly business with the Ashrufs (the town was talking about nothing else). She had even gone to see the old woman, for Miriam's sake. She had never realized how small and wispy she would look in that large hospital beds, barely conscious—only her eyes refused to die.

It was funny; she had always felt sorry for Miriam, that is until she had met the Blaines (until she met Veronica). Sonia had never had a migraine before but the Blaines seemed to be synonymous with it. The pitter-patter of rain felt like ammunition against her windshield and the roof of her car, intensifying her pain.

The driving conditions were hazardous, and several times Sonia felt her car skid a little when turning a sharp corner. She needed to slow down before she hit someone, but there was no one around. She felt safer and more secure in her car out in the middle of the night than she had all evening—driving aimlessly around town, circling the suburbs several times before she let her car guide her to a parking spot. Even before she turned off the ignition, she knew where she was. She sat inside until the stuffiness of the car got the better of her.

It was partly nostalgia, and partly the loneliness of the empty swing, blowing in the wind like a forgotten child that made Sonia park her car, turn off the ignition, and walk toward purgatory. There she sat and watched the puddles get bigger and bigger. It was only here that she felt safe enough to go back to the night's events.

Sonia had never met Michael's parents long enough for them and especially for Veronica to give her anything more than a passing glance. They were rich, staunch, and Republican, and their demeanor reflected all the clichés one would expect; so did their neighborhood. It was the type of neighborhood where things were either black or white. The residents were white, the "help" was black, and anything in between didn't count. Any one of the former or the latter knew where they stood. They were on the map—but there was no room for any other shades of brown or gray. People from Pakistan or the Middle East were barely even considered American. Knowing that, Sonia should not have been surprised at the way the evening had unfolded.

Dinner with the Blaines had seemed a feat no less daunting than asking a Klan member for directions to the mosque. They had known something was wrong from the very beginning, with Veronica's stiff smile and Howard's furtive glances. Veronica was no-nonsense, from her mahogany hair color down to her Jimmy Choo stilettos, always immaculately dressed. Her brown hair was cut into a short bob and tucked beneath her chin. On that day, she was wearing a black cashmere sweater and gray slacks.

The Mother-in-Law Cure

There was an antique pendant around her throat and a matching bracelet on her wrist. Her voice carried a hint of a British accent, which Sonia always assumed was fake.

"How nice to see you again, Sonia," said Veronica, giving her a hug and a peck on the cheek that felt as cold as marble.

"We so rarely have Michael's friends over for dinner—what a treat!"

Sonia could hear the steel under Veronica's cheery voice. She had heard it before, in Michael's voice when he was in a tough negotiation. It was the only time Sonia ever saw Michael's resemblance to his mother.

Often, Sonia had wondered how easygoing Michael could come from such an uptight woman, but then she only had to look at Howard, whose class and integrity always shone through. It was a pity he had ended up with someone like Veronica. Although Veronica had claimed to be highbrow and had alluded to old money, Sonia had heard a rumor that Veronica had started out as a cocktail waitress at a country club—although officially, Veronica had always claimed to be the club's social director.

Sonia doubted she would be able to get into the country club where Michael's family had belonged for over a generation, even after they were married. Although it was not known as a private club, its guidelines were dubious, and despite the fact that everyone was encouraged to apply (should a spot open up), many well to do African Americans, Latinos, and Arabs found themselves waitlisted. Sonia knew that Michael hated the club, never attended, and rarely went into detail about why he did not feel comfortable there, but from Veronica's banter about her friends and the club's socials, Sonia could not blame him.

No matter how many times it occurred, Sonia could not get over the way Veronica spoke to the help - slowly and an octave louder, as if speaking to a child that was a little underdeveloped. She did it with Sonia as well, always commenting on how well Sonia spoke English (even though Sonia was born in Chicago). She would often say things like "and how do they do things *in your country*?" or "what are the economic ramifications of this in *your country*?" to which Michael would always reply, "She's American, Mom. This *is* her country."

"Of course," Veronica would correct herself, looking at Sonia with open suspicion. Sonia was not sure whether Veronica was more afraid of her being a gold digger or a terrorist.

It was obvious from Michael's glow and Sonia's nervous energy that something was up. Michael always liked to pace things out and stick to the plan, but today he could not wait. Sonia could see where he was going as he opened the conversation and was relieved they were going to get it out of the way as soon as possible. She could not deal with any more of Veronica's polite conversation.

The Blaines artfully concealed their curiosity. Perhaps they suspected that Michael was going to announce that they were moving in together—or worse, that Sonia was pregnant (to which Sonia was sure Veronica would have suggested a discreet termination). When Michael told them that they were married and had eloped in Hong Kong, Veronica gasped. Sonia could hear her sucking in her breath—was it possible to choke on air alone? The appearances of civility that Veronica had been putting on over the last couple months evaporated like a popsicle in the Sahara. Words began to fly out of Veronica's mouth like poison arrows. Had this not been Sonia's life, she might have thought it was funny, like a skit on late-night television.

"Michael Jeremiah Blaine, you're not serious, are you? Marrying the chauffeur's daughter—who ever heard of such a thing?"

"He's not a chauffeur, Mom. He's a taxi driver."

"That's not any better. She's also... you know... foreign."

"She's not foreign, Mom. She's American, and she's biracial. Her father's a Pakistani immigrant and her mother is American."

"Pakistanis...how can you be sure they're not terrorists?"

"Mom, you sound like a bigot."

"I am no such thing. Howard, explain to him what I mean."

Michael's father just looked at them and smiled.

"I think Sonia's a lovely girl."

"But what do they really know about each other?" said Veronica. "They've only been seeing each other for a couple months."

"Honey, they're old enough to make their own decisions," said Michael's father.

"Sweetie, if there's a problem, if she's pregnant"— (Sonia had wondered when that was going to come up)— "we can do something about this. You don't need to ruin your life."

"Mom, no one's pregnant."

Veronica began to respond, but by that time Sonia had had enough of her bizarre accusations. She grabbed her things and began to leave.

"Sonia, wait! Where are you going?" said Michael, following her out of the living room.

"Michael!" Veronica cried, chasing after her son. Even in stilettos she was able to catch up with him, and before Michael could stop her, Sonia was out the door. Her car was waiting for her like a welcome friend. Sonia started the ignition and began driving around, turning on the radio and turning off her cell phone.

THIRTY

Out Came the Sun

Miriam had been walking beneath angry clouds for so long that their presence no longer intimidated her. She understood the rain now, knew its purpose and she knew what lay beyond those dreary skies.

Miriam put her hands in her pocket to guard them against the chill. The wind was nipping at her flesh but this did not bother her as much as the chill going down her spine. There was only one thing that could warm her now. In her hand, she carried a lighter. *Sometimes, the end is the beginning and the beginning is the end.* This had to be the end.

The shiny marble tablet was there just as she knew it would be, tall and erect and foreboding. In one hand Miriam held the lighter and in the other the picture she had stolen from the attic. She couldn't get it out her head, that Mona Lisa smile…so deceivingly innocent. Miriam watched the flame from the lighter flicker in the rain for a couple seconds before she held it to the picture. She watched the picture turn to ash and become consumed within the grave beneath her feet.

For an instant, a disturbing feeling came over her, as

if she expected a hand to spring out of the muddy lawn and grab hold of her ankle—and why not? She would deserve it. She knew it, and the old woman knew it. She may not have pulled the trigger, but she had certainly loaded the gun. The old woman was gone; she was not sorry. Her husband was a broken man; she was not sorry. She had left Kashif shortly after Humara's funeral. The Lakahnis were gone, too. The only one that was left was Adnan.

Adeel Lakahni had taken his daughter to see a specialist in Europe who had done a lot of research on rare metabolic disorders. After his wife passed away, Baby was all he had left.

Kashif, once a formidable opponent, had barely said a word when Miriam had presented him with the divorce papers, but merely shook his head silently. Adnan had become the big brother, the caregiver, making sure Kashif took his antidepressants on time, taking over the maintenance of the estate, and renting out the unused portions of the house. The last few months had been a riddle set inside a puzzle and cloaked in a cloud of enigma. Perhaps, it was for that reason that it had felt a little too easy, like throwing water on the wicked witch—but there was no denying it, it had happened.

It was thoughts of Adnan that pushed her forward. There was only one more thing standing in her way. Miriam looked at the gravestone one last time, paying homage to her old life. For Miriam, the yellow brick road had finally come to an end. She got back into the sleek Mercedes with heated seats and soft leather interior (a car that had once belonged to Kashif, but Miriam was now getting more and more used to) and wrapped her scarf around her a little tighter. She loved the feel of cashmere next to her skin. If the old woman could only see her now…

She drove to a place she had passed by many times. On that day, there would be someone waiting. Miriam parked the car. The drizzle of the rain had all but turned the nicely manicured lawn to mud—not that anyone could tell at this time of night. Miriam did not mind getting wet—not that day. She welcomed the rain like an old friend, letting it wash away her guilt. Miriam felt the smooth vial in her pocket. When an unsettling feeling came over Miriam about what she was about to do, it was the rain that urged her forward; it was the rain that whispered in her ear. Miriam got out of the car. As if on cue, the rain petered down. It became very quiet, and the moon began to peek out amidst the heavy clouds. From the streetlight, Miriam could see a small figure hunched over, rocking back and forth on a swing. From a distance, it looked like the petite frame of a young girl. Oblivious to everything around her, the girl did not look up until Miriam was only steps away.

"Hello," said Miriam.

Sonia looked up, realizing for the first time that there was someone there, her nose was running and she began to sneeze. It was the onset of a terrible cold. Miriam looked to her like an angel standing in the moonlight, so serene was the expression on her face.

"Are you all right? You don't look so good," said Miriam, gripping the vial in her pocket. The rain had quietly stopped.

"But don't worry. I have a cure . . ."

The Mother-in-Law Cure

ABOUT THE AUTHOR

Farha Hasan is a librarian at Boston University. She has been writing and publishing short stories for ten years. The Mother-in-Law Cure is her first novel. To read more by Farha visit her blog at
www.bostonchronicles.wordpress.com

Made in the USA
Charleston, SC
16 January 2014

Katrin Daum

Civilisation, marriage and tenderness in D.H. Lav

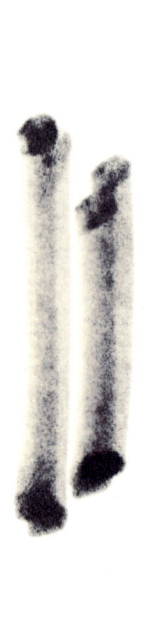

GRIN - Verlag für akademische Texte

Der GRIN Verlag mit Sitz in München hat sich seit der Gründung im Jahr 1998 auf die Veröffentlichung akademischer Texte spezialisiert.

Die Verlagswebseite www.grin.com ist für Studenten, Hochschullehrer und andere Akademiker die ideale Plattform, ihre Fachtexte, Studienarbeiten, Abschlussarbeiten oder Dissertationen einem breiten Publikum zu präsentieren.

Dokument Nr. V117115 aus dem GRIN Verlagsprogramm

Katrin Daum

Civilisation, marriage and tenderness in D.H. Lawrence's novel "Lady Chatterley's Lover"

GRIN Verlag

Bibliografische Information der Deutschen Nationalbibliothek: Die Deutsche Bibliothek verzeichnet diese Publikation in der Deutschen Nationalbibliografie; detaillierte bibliografische Daten sind im Internet über http://dnb.d-nb.de/ abrufbar.

1. Auflage 2008
Copyright © 2008 GRIN Verlag
http://www.grin.com/
Druck und Bindung: Books on Demand GmbH, Norderstedt Germany
ISBN 978-3-640-19517-6

Universität Würzburg
Neuphilologisches Institut / Anglistik
Wintersemester 2007 / 2008

Proseminararbeit:

Civilisation, marriage and tenderness in D.H. Lawrence's novel *Lady Chatterley's Lover*

Proseminar: Pastoral Novels

10.04.2008

von

Katrin Daum

Englisch / Französisch
2. Semester

Contents

1 Introduction 3
2 Civilisation 3
   2.1 The First World War 3
   2.2 The Class System 4
   2.3 Industrialisation 6
3 Marriage 8
4 Tenderness 10
   4.1 Connie and her Lover in Germany, Michaelis and Clifford 10
   4.2 Connie and Mellors 11
5 Conclusion 13
6 Bibliography 14

1 Introduction

When the first version of Lady Chatterley's Lover was published in 1926, the readers had been shocked, because it was about sex. Since then there have been various speculations, books and articles about if there was more to this book than sex – and there certainly is.

The term paper concentrates on three main aspects: civilisation, marriage and tenderness. I chose three points of criticism of society, namely the war, the class system and industrialisation. In the chapter 'marriage', I decided to focus mainly on the Chatterley's marriage and the relation between Connie and Mellors, though also the couples Ted and Ivy Bolton and Mellors and Bertha Coutts come up shortly. For the last point in this term paper, I grouped the aspects of Connie's relations before she had met Mellors and her relation with him. In this last chapter, I tried not to give too many examples to show in which way the two lovers behave tenderly, but I rather attempted to give an overview over their relationship and the ramifications of tenderness for them.

2 Civilisation

2.1 The First World War

The consequences of the First World War for Constance Chatterley were not only a husband, Clifford, who was physically paralysed from the waist downwards and impotent, but whose soul was also damaged. At first glance, everything appeared 'normal': Clifford was a famous author, liked receiving friends at Wragby Hall, the family seat, enjoyed having conversations with them and his wife, and was fond of going out for a walk in his motor-chair in the nearby wood. But in one of their discussions, Connie noticed

> [...] one of the great laws of the human soul: that when the emotional soul receives a wounding shock, which does not kill the body, the soul seems to recover as the body recovers. But this is only appearance. It is, really, only the mechanism of reassumed habit. Slowly, slowly the wound to the soul begins to make itself felt, like a bruise which only slowly deepens its terrible ache, till it fills all the psyche. And when we think we have recovered and forgotten, it is then that the terrible after-effects have to be encountered at their worst. (49)[1]

For her, at the age of 23, it was not easy to handle this situation as she had to face it everyday and there was nothing to distract her at Wragby Hall – except the conversations with Clifford's friends which soon started to bore her, too.

---

[1] All the numbers given in brackets after quotations refer to the number of the page in the primary text: Lawrence, D. H.: *Lady Chatterley's Lover*. London: Penguin Classics, 2006.

It seemed to her that "[a]ll the great words […] were cancelled for her generation: love, joy, happiness, home, […]." (62) She suffered, because she failed to live happily with her husband, inwardly searching for the meaning of her life without yet knowing it. Lawrence gives the explication for her sentiments himself: "It is the day after."[2] Connie's generation was the one who survived the First World War and who had to deal with the after-effects of it. Even the very beginning of the novel tells us that "[o]urs is essentially a tragic age […]." (5)

Nevertheless, Connie will find her true love Mellors, whereas Clifford is going to be abandoned by his wife. So when the novel develops, it becomes clear that he is – regarding interpersonal relations – actually the tragic figure.

On the one hand, one could lay all the blame for Clifford's destiny in the hands of the war, but this would be too easy. He's certainly not the poor figure that doesn't know how to live on, as becomes clear when his person developed with Mrs Bolton's help. But who knows how the Chatterley's marriage would have evolved without the war? Perhaps they would have lived happily together until the end of their days. But for Lawrence there would have been no necessity to write about a happy couple. He wanted to criticize the war and its consequences for human lives. In Doris Lessing's eyes, *Lady Chatterley's Lover* is even "one of the most powerful anti-war novels ever written."[3]

2.2 The Class System

Clifford, as the owner of the collieries in Tevershall, was responsible for the workers. His idea was, that the aristocracy "has given the colliers all they have that's worth having: all their political liberty, and their education, such as it is, their sanitation, their health-conditions, their books, their music, everything." (181)

On the one hand, he felt superior to them, as he was a member of the upper class. He had "power" (108) over them. In his eyes, "they are not men. They are animals […]" (182) and "he saw them as objects rather than men" (15). "The masses have been ruled since time began, and till time ends, rules they will have to be." (183) His duty was to rule them and to give them work. Apart from that he didn't care for them.

On the other hand, "he was just a bit frightened of the vast hordes of middle and lower-class humanity, and of foreigners not of his own class." (10) This could be explained by the fact that he was crippled and the workers were physically in better condition than he was. Perhaps it had even something to do with him not being able to go wherever he would

---

[2] Lawrence, David Herbert. "A Propos of 'Lady Chatterley's Lover'." In: Lawrence, David Herbert. *Lady Chatterley's Lover*. London: Penguin Classics, 2006.
[3] Lessing, Doris: "Introduction." In: Lawrence, David Herbert. *Lady Chatterley's Lover*. London: Penguin Classics, 2006. P. XXI.

have liked to go and to run away in case of a rebellion. Probably one could even argue that his "supercilious and contemptuous" (15) behaviour towards members of the other classes was only jealousy.

At the same time, he was aware of the fact that the class system had been made up and was only a "romantic illusion" (183). He told Connie:

> Place any child among the ruling classes, and he will grow up, to his own extent, a ruler. Put kings' and dukes' children among the masses, and they'll be little plebeians, mass products. It is the overwhelming pressure of environment. (183)

Having a look at her attitudes towards the different classes in English society, Mrs Bolton is a very conflicting person. When she at first felt "a resentment against the owning class" (81) and "was [at the same time] thrilled by her contact with this man of the upper class" (100), she soon realized, that Clifford, "a real gentleman" (99), "wasn't so very different from the colliers after all" (83). Finally, she accepted his superiority over her and liked working for him. She would even stay awake a good portion of the night to gamble with him. When Connie was furious about them playing cards for money, Clifford just raised Mrs Bolton's wage (215). So much for how to solve problems in the upper class – namely with money.

For Connie, the ruling of the aristocracy "was all cold nonsense" (72). She didn't care about her ladyship and even hated it. (cf. 124) When her sister Hilda predicted that she would feel ashamed of having had an affair with a gamekeeper, she ignored the warning. Yet Hilda's reason why one should not get mixed with working class people seems a little bit far-fetched: "because the whole rhythm is different." (241) None the less, at a moment, Connie thought of her affair as "humiliating" (264), but quickly changed her mind.

For the reader, it is surprising, that Clifford's godfather, Leslie Winter – as an example for people from the upper class – "would detest and despise her [Connie]" for having an affair with a working class member. "A man of her own class he would not mind." (128) One should think, that infidelity is bad, irrespective of the class to which the man with whom one has an affair belongs to. But potentially, he would only accept it because of Clifford's impotence.

These statements (of Hilda and Leslie Winter) show very well how really different people of lower classes were seen in the upper class. One was not allowed to have any sort of relation with them except the master-servant-relationship and apart from that: no talking at all. Because if one did – or if one had even an affair with a worker - like Connie –, society would sooner or later find out and the reputation and respect would be gone.

Curiously, there were however people who decided against climbing the social ladder. (Probably there were only few who had had the chance.) Mellors "had come back to his own class" (142) after having been a soldier in the army in India and having become a lieutenant. His reason was that

> [t]here was a toughness, a curious rubber-necked toughness and unlivingness about the middle and upper classes, as he had known them, which just left him feeling cold and different from them. (142f)

Lawrence criticizes in his novel "[c]lass hate and class-consciousness"[4] and he shows, that real love, like in the case of Connie and Mellors, doesn't know class restrictions.

2.3 Industrialisation

But Lawrence criticises not only war and the class system, but also industrialisation. First of all, the story takes place in a "ghastly world of smoke and iron" (212), in a "terrifying, new and gruesome England" (156) in which the "civilisation is going to collapse" (75). In this world, "the industry comes before the individual" (180). This isn't a too positive starting point of the story.

The present situation being bad, the future is predicted to be even worse: "It seems soon there'll be no use for men on the face of the earth, it'll be all machines" (106). Lawrence foresees the further development of the industrialisation and with it, the different working conditions that will emerge. Of course, he concentrates mainly on the coal mining industry. The work that was in former times done by men will in the future be done by machines. This will cause unemployment.

The fear of redundancy and the already bad working conditions had bad influence on the workers. They are described as "grey-black, distorted, one shoulder higher than the other, slurring their heavy ironshod boots." (159) "Their lives are industrialised and hopeless […]." (182)

Clifford, as the owner of the collieries, didn't "give one heart-beat of real sympathy" (182) to the workers. At the beginning of the novel, he wasn't interested in the pits at all, because they didn't concern his own income. He had enough money to live a happy life and a probable close-down of the pits wouldn't regard him. When after the arrival of Mrs Bolton his interest in the collieries arose, "[h]e felt a new sense of power flowing through him: power over all these men, over the hundreds and hundreds of colliers." (108) This sort of superiority was a new feeling for him and it made him feel mighty. But this doesn't change anything of

---

[4] Lawrence. P. 332.

the fact, that the most important thing for him was to make the pits more profitable and that the workers were only a means to an end.

Nevertheless, the biggest problem in society was its awareness of money. In Connie's eyes, society was "over-conscious in the money and social and political side, on the spontaneous side dead, but dead." (153) People were "worshipping the mechanical thing" (217) and forgetting at the same time the important points of life.

They on their part are represented by Mellors. If he had a chance to speak to the workers and influence their ideas, he would say to them:

> Let's live for summat else. Let's not live ter make money, neither for us-selves nor for anybody else. Now we're forced to. We're forced to make a bit for us-selves, an' a fair lot for th' bosses. Let's stop it! Bit by bit, let's stop it. We needn't rant an' rave. Bit by bit, let's drop the whole industrial life, an' go back. The least little bit o' money 'll do. For everybody, me an' you, bosses an' masters, even th' king. The least little bit o' money 'll really do: Just make up your mind to it, an' you've got out o' th' mess. (219)

He would like to show them the difference between "living and spending" (299) and thus make their lives happier. He himself was satisfied with his simple life before he had met Connie: he worked as a gamekeeper for the Chatterleys, earned enough to survive and lived in the woods, shielded from society. "But he knew that the seclusion in the wood was illusory. The industrial noises broke the solitude, the sharp lights, though unseen, mocked it. A man could no longer be private and withdrawn. The world allows no hermits." (119)

The wood, into which Mellors retreated, was also loved by Clifford. But he on his part, wanted to protect it because of different reasons: for him, "the old oak trees [...] were his through generations." (42) He wished to keep the heritage of his ancestors who were representing aristocracy and the wealth of his family.

Coming back to Mellors, he furthermore was pessimistic concerning the future: "There's a bad time coming. There's a bad time coming, boys, there's a bad time coming!" (300) Doris Lessing interprets this as Lawrence's prevision of the Second World War[5] but I wouldn't go as far as that. I think that industrialisation itself was enough to preview a bad future – in Mellor's eyes - even if I have to admit, that Mellor's statements, that he doesn't "believe [...] in the future of our civilisation" (277) and that "nowhere's far enough away to get away" "when I feel the human world is doomed" (220) contain somewhat a mood of war.

---

[5] Cf. Lessing. P. XXf.

3 Marriage

"Never has there been a more persuasive propagandist novel for marriage [...]"[6], says Doris Lessing in her *Introduction* to *Lady Chatterley's Lover*. Lawrence himself wrote in his *A Propos of "Lady Chatterley's Lover"* his definition of marriage: "Man and wife, a king and queen with one or two subjects, and a few square yards of territory of their own: this, really, is marriage."[7] He praises Christianity for having established marriage as something basic in human life. "This is Christianity's great contribution to the life of man"[8], he says. Furthermore, he thinks, that marriage gives inward peace to a couple, because it is supposed to last forever.

Nevertheless, he opposes "counterfeit marriage"[9], which is only based on the "affinity of mind and personality"[10], like in the case of the Chatterleys. "Connie and he [Clifford] were attached to one another, in the rather aloof modern way." (15) "Their marriage [...] [was] based on a habit of intimacy [...]." (50) But physically, they were not intimate at all, and couldn't be. After the arrival of Mrs Bolton, even this little intimacy was cleared away. "There was nothing between them. She never even touched him nowadays, and he never touched her. He never even took her hand and held it kindly." (112)

But even before Connie's affair, they couldn't talk openly to each other. Clifford couldn't put himself in Connie's position. He suggested her to have "a child by another man" (43). In his eyes, "the casual sex thing is nothing, compared to a long life lived together" (45) and Connie's infidelity in order to get a child wouldn't make a difference for their love for one another (cf. 111). Connie shared at the beginning of the novel his opinion about sex ("Love, sex, all that sort of stuff [...]", 64), but was after a while quite happy about Clifford not minding her having an affair, because this meant some tolerance to her.

When Mrs Bolton undertook the support of Clifford, he "inside himself never quite forgave Connie for giving up her personal care of him to a strange hired woman." (83) At this point, one can see that Clifford lived in a sort of dream world. He didn't recognize that he and his wife had drifted apart and he regarded their living together as completely positive. Therefore, it came as a shock to him, when Connie announced that she was going to leave him. She was so important to him, that "he didn't feel safe in her absence. Her presence, for some reason, made him feel safe, and free to do the things he was occupied with. (214) Without her, "he would be lost like an idiot on a moor." (110) Connie felt restricted, because

---

[6] Lessing. P XX.
[7] Lawrence. P. 321.
[8] Lawrence. P. 322.
[9] Lawrence. P. 325.
[10] Lawrence. P. 325.

she had to abandon her own private life to help him whenever he needed her. When she reflected about why she had married him at all, "she felt she had always really disliked him. [...] Almost it seemed to her she had married him because she disliked him. But of course, she had married him really because in a mental way he attracted her and excited her." (97) This was not the best fundament for a harmonious marriage. After the episode in the woods, when Mellors had to push Clifford's motor chair up the arduous hill (cf. 192), Connie even hated him, which was the beginning of the end of their common life.

Another example for an unsuccessful marriage is the couple Mellors and Bertha. After their separation, he hated her and "hoped never to see her again while he lived." (141) Connie made him aware of the fact that without a legal separation, his wife could come back to him one day. He consented to get a divorce, for which he had "to live an exemplary life for the next six or eight months." (226) Through this information the reader gets to know that in these days it wasn't as easy as that to get a divorce. Moreover, there was the chitchat of society which Mellors feared.

A rather good sample for a perfect couple are definitely the Boltons. Certainly, one has to admit that their marriage was reported by Mrs Bolton 22 years after the death of her husband, which might have had an influence on the accuracy of her narration. When she learnt of his death after three years of marriage, she couldn't believe it. "And it took me a thousand shocks before I knew he wouldn't come back – it took me years." (163) For her, "[h]e was one in a thousand" (82).

The reader doesn't learn a lot about their daily life, but probably only one more important fact. Mrs Bolton tells Connie: "[...] But usually he gave in to me. No, he was never lord and master. But neither was I. I knew when I could go no further with him, and then I gave in [...]" (236). And she gave her the warning: "if you really set your will against a man, that finishes it." (236) This sounds as if she had had a very balanced partnership.

. Even when Connie and Mellors weren't married as long as the novel narrates their story, one could analyse their behaviour in some ways as that of a couple. First of all, Connie felt at ease with him. He was "the only home she had ever known." (278) She wanted "the other ghastly world of smoke and iron" (212) disappear and to live always together with him "in a world of their own" (213). Furthermore, she admitted to her sister Hilda that she would love to be "Mrs Oliver Mellors, instead of Lady Chatterley" (240). When she discussed this with her lover, he pointed to the fact that he had nothing to offer to her. She refused to compare marriage with a bargain and said that it's enough "that we love one another" (276).

Secondly, Connie was pregnant by Mellors. Even when it seemed to him "a wrong and bitter thing to do, to bring a child into this world" (218), she could persuade him that having a child would be wonderful.

Last but not least, "she [Connie] was fiercely on the side of the man, she would stand by him through thick and thin." (241) Although she had the chance to have an affair in Italy, she refused it and stayed faithful to Mellors without being obliged to it by a promise of marriage. This is called by Doris Lessing "the deep fidelity that comes not from public morality, or from making 'resolutions' or from religion, but from that oneness between a man and a woman that makes casual sex, or any infidelity at all, impossible."[11]

Lawrence leaves the end of the story open to give the reader the opportunity to imagine an ideal marriage of the two at some time in the future.

4 Tenderness

4.1 Connie and her Lover in Germany, Michaelis and Clifford

"Life is only bearable when the mind and the body are in harmony, and there is a natural balance between the two, and each has a natural respect for the other"[12], wrote Lawrence. Tommy Dukes, a friend of Clifford, had a different opinion: "A woman wants you to like her, and talk to her – and at the same time love her, and desire her – and it seems to me the two things are mutually exclusive." (56)

This was the problem in Connie's relationships. Her lover in Germany, Michaelis and the other friends of Clifford and her husband himself preferred the mind to the body. "Connie quite liked the life of the mind, and got a great thrill out of it. But she did think it overdid itself a little." (36) Sex was even seen by her as an "anti-climax" (7) and as "ridiculous" (171).

For the students in Germany that Connie had met, "[i]t was the talk that mattered supremely" (7). Connie accepted to have sex with one of them, but only because it seemed to be ordinary. She let it pass and learned by it, that "[t]he beautiful pure freedom of a woman was infinitely more wonderful than any sexual love." (7) Yet, ten years after this chapter of her life, she thought back to the "fresh, clumsy sensuality" (71) of her lover.

Michaelis, an Irish author, got into closer contact with Connie after having talked to her. He "buried his face in her lap [...] [and] she could not help putting her hand with tenderness and compassion on the defenceless nape of his neck [...]." (25f) Nevertheless, the

---

[11] Lessing. P. XX.
[12] Lawrence. P. 310.

tenderness found its end when sex started. "Because after all, like so many modern men, he was finished almost before he had begun." (54) Connie liked and "wanted the physical, sexual thrill she could get with him, by her own activity, his little orgasm being over." (29)

With Clifford, she had apart from their honeymoon no sex. Their relationship based only on a mental harmony and was without tenderness. "Their interests had never ceased to flow together, over his work." (18) "She and Clifford lived in their ideas and his books." (19) Clifford's problem was that he lacked "warmth" (72). He was no exception of all the other men of his generation. "They were all so tight, so scared of life!" (69)

Before Mrs Bolton's arrival, Connie had at least touched him when "[s]he had to help him in all the intimate things [...]" (71), but this ceased. Towards the end of the novel, they lived together, spoke to each other, but passed most of the time separated from each other.

4.2 Connie and Mellors

Tenderness was firstly planned to be the title of Lawrence's novel.[13] He put his ideas about it mainly in his figure Mellors. The gamekeeper "was a passionate man" (121) "who was not afraid and not ashamed" (248). Connie told her sister that "he really understands tenderness" (238) and she told him, that it was "the courage of your own tenderness" (277) that makes him different from other men of his generation. He said about himself:

> I believe in being warm-hearted. I believe especially in being warm-hearted in love, in fucking with a warm heart. I believe if men could fuck with warm hearts, and the women take it warm-heartedly, everything would come all right. It's all this cold-hearted fucking that is death and idiocy. (206)

"Connie's 'crying need', like that of her generation, is for tender love."[14] And Mellors could give it to her. They had their first physical contact at the hut in the wood: "[...] and he put out his hand and laid his fingers on her knee. 'You shouldn't cry!' he said softly." (115) Later in the hut, his hand "stroked her face softly, softly, with infinite soothing and assurance, and at last there was the soft touch of a kiss on her cheek." (116)

Mellors is different from Connie's past lovers: She hadn't really known him and had slept with him without having had a real conversation with him before. The body is in this relationship – at least at the beginning – more important than the mind.

But it wasn't until their third sexual contact, that they "came-off together" (134). From this moment onwards, their relationship became closer and closer. Lawrence "always believed

---

[13] Cf. Spilka, Mark: "Lawrence's Quarrel with Tenderness." *The Critical Response to D.H. Lawrence.* Ed. Jan Pilditch. Westport: Greenwood Press, 2001. P. 171.
[14] Spilka. P. 181.

that nothing would do in lovemaking but the mutual orgasm."[15] At another time, "she felt him like a flame of desire, yet tender, and she felt herself melting in the flame. She let herself go." (173) She became "shameless" (247). Both got to know each other so well, that they were no longer embarrassed to talk openly about sex, their genitals – to which they refered to as "Sir John" and "Lady Jane" (228) – but also about their ideas of life.

Through this relationship, Connie changed. The importance of the mind over the body decreased in her eyes and she started liking her own body. When Clifford asked her after the scene where she ran naked outside in the rain, if she liked her physique, she answered: "I love it! […] I believe the life of the body is a greater reality than the life of the mind: when the body is really wakened to life." (234), whereas she had thought before having had the affair with Mellors: "what a frail, easily-hurt, rather pathetic thing a naked human body is: somehow a little unfinished, incomplete!" (70)

Furthermore, she was happy about her pregnancy. Specifically, because it would be Mellor's child: "I should be fearfully proud if I had a child by him." (238)

And the affair and with it the changes of Connie's ideas and feelings were only possible, because she had taken refuge in the wood.

> Connie withdraws largely from ugly industrialization and sterility and, to some extent, from the sexuality of men like Michaelis. Mellors, on the other hand, withdraws largely from women with overpowering wills and, to a lesser extent, from an industrialized and economic society.[16]

He wanted to be left alone and to avoid human contact as far as possible. Their common sanctuary changes through their affair to their "locus amoenus"[17]. "[T]hey were together in a world of their own." (213)

---

[15] Lessing. P. XIII.
[16] Squires, Michael. *The Pastoral Novel*. Charlottesville: University Press of Virginia, 1974. P. 205.
[17] Squires. P. 201.

5 Conclusion

"And this is the real point of this book. I want men and women to be able to think sex, fully, completely, honestly, and cleanly. Even if we can't act sexually to our complete satisfaction, let us at least think sexually, complete and clean."[18]

Even when Lawrence's statement here seems to tell us, that the book is about sex only, the reader should know that he refers to a special kind of sex, namely "tender-hearted sex"[19].

Furthermore, he also criticises in his novel social circumstances and praises marriage as an important institution in his times.

Therefore, one can't argue that the novel is about sex only and should be censored, as it makes the reader think about his own sexual behaviour and the importance of sexuality in our society generally.

---

[18] Lawrence. P. 308.
[19] Lessing. P. XVII.

6 Bibliography

Primary Literature

Lawrence, David Herbert. *Lady Chatterley's Lover*. London: Penguin Classics, 2006.

Secondary Literature

Lawrence, David Herbert. "A Propos of 'Lady Chatterley's Lover'." In: Lawrence, David Herbert. *Lady Chatterley's Lover*. London: Penguin Classics, 2006. 305-35.

Lessing, Doris. "Introduction." In: Lawrence, David Herbert. *Lady Chatterley's Lover*. London: Penguin Classics, 2006. XI-XXX.

Shiach, Morag. "Work and Selfhood in 'Lady Chatterley's Lover'." *The Camebridge Companion to D.H. Lawrence*. Ed. Anne Fernihough. Cambridge: Cambridge University Press, 2001. 87-102.

Spilka, Mark. "Lawrence's Quarrel with Tenderness." *The Critical Response to D.H. Lawrence*. Ed. Jan Pilditch. Westport: Greenwood Press, 2001. 170-83.

Squires, Michael. *The Pastoral Novel*. Charlottesville: University Press of Virginia, 1974.

CPSIA information can be obtained
at www.ICGtesting.com
Printed in the USA
254589LV00001B